DEFIANCE FROM FOXFIELD

Two System satellites had vanished from orbit around Foxfield. Now the One Organism—central will and intelligence of the Commensals—claimed that their disappearance had been "practice" for Her coming destruction of the United Nations Interplanetary station.

A hoax? UNI Adjustor Maio didn't think so. "But the alternative explanation is worse yet," she said. "That these creatures appear to threaten UNI with *no* technology at all. And we cannot meet the One's demands. To be perceived as backing down before some nonhuman power—the Board cannot accept that."

"Well, what *can* you accept?" Clifford asked ironically. "Thermolyse the planet—wipe out the whole biosphere?"

A pause lengthened in the room.

"We hope to avoid that..."

Other Avon Books by
Joan Slonczewski

A DOOR INTO OCEAN

STILL FORMS ON FOXFIELD

JOAN SLONCZEWSKI

AVON BOOKS ◆ NEW YORK

AVON BOOKS
A division of
The Hearst Corporation
105 Madison Avenue
New York, New York 10016

First Avon Books Printing: December 1988

AVON TRADEMARK REG. U.S. PAT. OFF. AND IN OTHER COUNTRIES, MARCA
REGISTRADA, HECHO EN U.S.A.

Printed in the U.S.A.

K-R   10 9 8 7 6 5 4 3 2 1

Acknowledgments and Dedication

This book owes its existence to my educational and spiritual growth in the Bryn Mawr–Haverford College community and in the New Haven Friends Meeting. For invaluable criticism I thank members of the New Haven Science Fiction Writers' Workshop, especially Kevin O'Donnell, Jr., who also helped me survive the initiation rites of publication.

Finally I dedicate this book to Stacy Jackson, whose example inspired me to write, and to my husband Michael for his infinite patience and faith.

Contents

I. Foxfield

The wind thrust against her back and whipped out her shirttails as she grappled with the radio telescope on the narrow platform.

Allison Thorne clung to the rail and paused for breath. Above her the immense silver dish reflected the brilliance of Wheelwright's Sun as it tilted skyward like a hand cupped behind a lost ear. At her left, the roof slanted below in sheets of glassy solar panels. The opposite side dropped directly down the face of the Technical Services Center to the factory modules which clustered on the hilltop.

Beyond the hill lay the houses of Georgeville, the First Settlement, surrounded by farmlands carved from the moss fields. When Allison squinted, she could just make out the form of a human farmer driving a tractor across the Crain land. Farmers would get little rest throughout the sowing season, even on Sunday. Their "commensal" companions, on the other hand, did not know such concepts as "work" or "rest."

Allison inhaled the fresh air with its scents of growth. Her blunt hand shoved aside wisps of hair which had strayed from the tie in back, and she faced the radio telescope once more.

Something had gone wrong with it, somewhere. It had happened last week, actually, during the hailstorm, but she had not had time to fix it until Sunday after Meeting when the workload was minimal and Dave could be left to tend the communications array. The radio telescope simply refused to send data downstairs in its usual punctual manner. It was nothing mind-shaking, she told herself; just another reminder of entropy's inexorable march through this universe.

She strained to loosen a weatherbeaten amplifier

connection. A screw shot forth, glanced off the rail and struck out on its own in the world below.

The programmer's face darkened. "Why the hell did I ever dream up this project?" she demanded of the wind.

A clang came from the hatch door. Allison turned to see a sturdy youth braced against the rail. "Look out you don't fall, Dave," she warned, her words half lost in the rush of air.

The boy looked downward and grinned. "At least you haven't blown away yet."

"Thanks a lot. What gives in the pits?"

"Aw—" He shrugged. "Most radio bands are back in."

"Good; ion storm's subsiding." The planet's magnetic field was a hundredfold stronger than that of Earth, and frequent ionospheric disturbances played havoc with communications.

"Think you'll get that up by antinight?" Dave asked.

Allison wrinkled her nose. "Chances now infinitesimal-to-zero. In other words," she added, joining the wind's scream, "prognosis sucks!"

Dave nodded sagely. "Yeah, that thing's a fossil." True enough, the instrument was vintage Earth hardware, salvaged from the *UNS Plowshare* before a meteor had knocked the colony ship out of commission.

"I'll fix the godforsaken thing yet," she vowed, returning to her task.

"Fifth Query, Mother," Dave replied sweetly as he watched.

"So," she muttered, "you've learned something in Sunday school after all."

"By the way," he said with deliberate nonchalance, "there's a message for you."

"What's that?" she grimaced as a blast of air scraped her face.

"Message," he hand-signaled in Transac.

"Who from?"

The wind abated.

"Don't know for sure." The boy dug his free hand in a pocket of his overalls. "It's someone that *I* never heard of. Except in the Records, maybe."

2

"Frequency?"

"Band Yod."

"Can't be right, that's the space monitor."

He shrugged. "Suit yourself. It says something about 'United Nations.' "

"What?"

"I told you, Mom; it's like history class."

Allison looked her son over; his hair tossed, and his features seemed innocent. Dear Dave, she thought, just turned twelve, on the brink of "that age," and showing signs of impatience with this life. A father might have helped . . . She brushed aside the thought.

"David, is this a joke of some kind?"

"What do you mean?"

"A sick joke. You know the United Nations ended in holocaust a century ago."

"It is *not* a joke, Mom." Dave pouted and turned away. The hatch door banged after him.

Allison sighed. She raised herself with care and stretched her limbs, which were short yet thick-boned from the planet's strong gravity. She followed him downstairs, absently leaving the open tool kit to fend for itself on the roof top.

Allison's spirits lifted as she entered the computer room with its familiar hum of machines. She had worked here for over a decade now, ever since the Sixth Settlement disaster. The flood had taken her folks, and Joshua, too, but she had brought her young son back to Georgeville and her programming skills to the Tech Center. Within a year she had found herself running the operation.

It was not a bad job, really—keeping the modules going, maintaining the switchboard, refining weather forecasts. On occasion the Meeting even granted one of her requests to fix up odd bits of equipment like the radio telescope and the long-range reflector. Some had grumbled, for what use was it to waste precious time on astronomy when nobody was out there? She recalled convincing them that it might be a good idea to watch regularly for impending meteors. That they could understand in light of the derelict *Plowshare*, still in lonely orbit about Foxfield.

3

"Okay, Dave, let's see what you've got." She passed by her desk top, an organized chaos of papers and Bloch units, and approached the cheerfully blue-paneled Deltron videoscan. Delphis Electronics, with the arched dolphin trademark, was a remnant of the turn-of-the-millennium "small technologies" movement. She knew what dolphins were and what an ocean was; but she had never even traveled to a Foxfield ocean.

Dave pointed to the screen.

TO ALLISON AND ALL FRIENDS OF FOXFIELD: GREETINGS FROM ADJUSTOR SILVA MAIO OF THE SHIP UNIS-11. WE CITIZENS OF UNITED NATIONS INTERPLANETARY REJOICE IN THE SUCCESSFUL SETTLEMENT OF YOUR PEOPLE. WE HOPE TO RE-SUME CONTACT ACCORDING TO UN CHARTER 61A. WE AWAIT YOUR REPLY.

For a moment Allison's scalp prickled, then she laughed. "That's not half bad, Dave. It's a shame we can't yet afford real artists."

"But Mom, I *didn't*, I tell you."

He certainly looked serious and perhaps a bit scared.

"Well, I wonder who did, then," she said. "Darn good job, I must admit. Imagine them from Earth, congratulating *our* survival. They would, too."

She tapped a command and letters spewed out across the screen. "What the devil? Sender coordinates . . . a new 'meteor.' Someone went to a lot of trouble here. Noreen could have set it up, though only Seth knows about my—"

"Naw," Dave rejoined, "Seth's too straight. Besides, he knows less about Deltron than Ghareshl does."

"Dave, that's not true. And you shouldn't say that about Ghareshl—she's the best nonhuman friend we have."

"So what good is a commensal Fraction for a friend? She'll conjoin this year anyhow, and muddle up so she forgets."

"How do you know?" said Allison. "All five of them

4

remembered us one year." She stared abstractedly past the purring console. "All right," she said, "it should be bright enough to show up in daytime."

"On the telescope? Oh, wow!" He dashed out of the room.

Minutes later they stood under the small observatory dome and took turns peering at the undeniable image of some sort of space vehicle.

"It looks like a squashed doughnut," said Dave.

"Toroid."

"Yeah, like a doughnut. What are all those funny black crisscrosses, do you think? China letters?"

Through Allison's mind swept memories of Earth Records like a video reel. Earth, the planet her ancestors had left four generations before, in the year of the Lord 2022. What was Earth? Giant cities and empty deserts. Exotic jungles and poisoned oceans. Monuments modern and ancient, beautiful and grotesque.

"What's wrong, Mom?" Dave's voice was muffled by the eyepiece. "It's just what you dreamed of, remember? Earth people . . . Maybe they broke the light-speed barrier. Hey, then we can all go back to Earth again!"

What had happened, then? Why had the home contact signals failed to resume by the time the *Plowshare* had decelerated from relativistic velocity? Had there been no holocaust?

Earth people. Light-boned strangers who spoke the tongues of Babel . . . who worshiped many Gods or none. What were they like now, she wondered—and what would they want with the community of Friends on Foxfield?

The Friends were Quakers, descended from the Philadelphian branch of the Religious Society of Friends. They conducted all manner of affairs by communal Meetings—the spiritual, in Meeting for Worship, and the temporal, in Monthly Meeting held every four "weeks" of the fifteen "month" year. The matter at hand, Allison reasoned, included components of both. And, by chance or by design, the visitors had called just in time for Georgeville's Monthly

Meeting Nine, set today as usual for seventeen hours east.

There was little time for supper, so Allison telephoned the clerk from the kitchen of her cottage just down the hill. A warm soup aroma filled the room. Dave was cracking eggs into the sizzling pan.

"I know, Lowell, but how else do you explain it?" She held the receiver in a tense grip. "Sure, I double-checked and triple-checked. Twenty years in the business, you know." The connection was bad today, and she made a mental note to look into it as she tried to block out the kitchen noises.

"Coo, c-coo, coo," called the pet wurraburra sprawled over the radio as it languidly stretched an eyefoot. Dave had christened the beast Rufus Jones out of vengeance against a particularly dry history lesson.

"No," Allison replied, "I sent no response; I think that's up to the Meeting . . . What do you mean, 'discourteous'? Whatever would I say?"

Rufus's tone rose insistently. "Coo, c-c-*coo, oo.*"

Dave tossed a bit of bean cheese toward the radio. It promptly disappeared.

"All right, Low . . . I'll be there." The receiver slammed. Allison sniffed. "Do I chemisense oxidized albumin?"

"Fried eggs, Mom. You'd make a good commensal." He flipped them expertly onto two dishes.

"Real hen eggs? What's wrong with soup?"

"Aw, Mom, I'm sick of all that commensal stuff."

"Now, David, where would we be today without the Fractions helping us all to grow things?"

"But this is a special occasion. Just think, Mom, some day you'll be telling your great-grandchildren, 'Oh, young Friends, I was just a spring chicken of thirty-six years the day the Earth folks came back!'"

Allison frowned at this wicked imitation of Celia Blyden, sole surviving member of the *Plowshare* crew and grandmother to half the community. "Speaking of chickens, don't forget to bring them in before antinight." She sat down at the table and gulped her soup. "Also keep a good eye on the board until Noreen gets in. Never know when Lanesbridge will have another power shortage or run out of drill bits."

"On Sunday evening?"

"Smart aleck." She crumpled her napkin, briefly pressed Dave's shoulder and headed for the door.

"Mom, you'll never reach a hundred that way. Ulcers will get you before the Earth folks do."

Her fingers shot back a Transac syllable.

"Fifth Query, Mother," Dave warbled after her.

The wurraburra waved all five eyefeet in excitement as Dave set the leftover soup down before it on the tiled floor.

II. The Meeting

Allison walked briskly down the road. Georgeville proper was less than a kilometer distant from the Tech Center hill, so she reserved the electrojeep for inter-settlement trips unless heavy equipment was involved. She took care as she walked to avoid stumbling into pavement cracks caused by extreme swings in temperature.

Rustling sounds and odors of awakening emanated from the fields of ground moss. The air already steamed from approaching rainclouds. At least they would afford some protection from the sun in its anti-night glory.

The star, Tau Ceti, was commonly named after the astronomer Wheelwright, who first observed its planets from Earth and proposed their colonization. Allison had once asked Doctor Poyser why their forbears had not chosen one of Wheelwright's thirty-odd planets with a twenty-hour day instead of a roughly Earth-sized year. The detailed explanation she had given her boiled down, essentially, to—that's the best the Lord gave us, so be thankful. Not that a forty-two-hour period was unlivable; the commensals seemed to love it. Humans simply divided it, alternated east-days and west-days, and slept through the sun's hottest hours.

Commensals were active at this time of day and she came upon three of them now, pale green forms like cucumbers half her height, who swayed and fluttered leafy appendages. By their size she judged them to be four or five years old, perhaps ready for first conjoining. One she knew by name.

"*Yshrin. Enjoy warm sun.*" Allison signaled in Transac, but they failed to respond. Scent or chemisense was their own natural idiom, and Allison could tell that they were using it. She approached with care as the spurts of odor intensified, one more pungent than the last, as though in contest.

Burning, sulphurous fumes abruptly hit her face. She coughed and her eyes streamed.

The creatures straightened, and one turned her eye toward Allison. "*You smell distressed, Plant-spike,*" signaled Yshrin with her inner corollar tendrils.

"*Hurts. Please stop,*" Allison signaled.

The substance dissipated. As soon as Allison had caught her breath, she hurried on to Georgeville.

The weathered gray Meeting House was the largest structure built by humans on Foxfield. Other towns had their own Meeting Houses, but everyone still gathered at the First Settlement at year's end.

"Allison!"

Her brother Clifford hailed her from the doorstep.

"I'm so glad to see you," she said with relief. The Fullers were practically "elders" now, she figured.

Clifford beamed and the creases deepened in his bald scalp. Like most Foxfielders, he stood less than one and a half meters tall. Martha Fuller's gray eyes fixed Allison keenly, yet with warmth, and Allison guessed that she had heard from Lowell.

"Are the Meeting accounts in order yet?" Allison asked, to head off questions. "I hope that grain shipment finally made it to Lanesbridge."

"To be sure," Clifford said. "Nothing escapes her, you know; she's got the eye of a commensal."

A trace of a smile crossed Martha's broad face,

which looked careworn beneath her streaked hair. "Supplies are in balance," she said, "no shortages, but we've few surpluses, either."

Allison winced. She herself favored larger stockpiles of grain and minerals. "How's the school?" she asked her brother. "That takes a sharp eye, too, eh?"

"Oh, we keep them in line. The young folks are really going strong this year; I just wish we had wider horizons for them. Your boy, now, he really keeps us hopping!"

He grinned broadly, and Allison laughed to hide her confusion.

Martha smiled. "Allison," she said, "you're the one with news for us, so I hear. Perhaps, Lord willing, new vistas will open soon. Yet I'm glad I'm not in Lowell's shoes this evening, for all that."

"Why not?" Clifford asked. "You managed Meeting pretty well two years back."

"The *Meeting* managed well."

They stepped aside as Anne and Edward Crain guided their lively brood through the doorway. Allison followed after their youngest daughter, who already toddled stoutly in her gold-checked smock.

Commotion filled the main Hall. Adults conversed, and children raced among the bench rows until the appointed overseer bundled them away . . . The community was growing, all right. It had to, to insure survival. This hall would hold about a thousand; soon, that would be too small for Yearly Meeting.

A palm touched her shoulder—not really a palm, but a fold of photosynthetic flesh.

"Ghareshl!" Allison exclaimed as she turned, and she hand-signaled, though this Fraction had a limited ability to read human speech.

"One enjoys full sunshine." The fronds of Ghareshl's half-open corona waved gracefully. Beneath the radial fronds her fist-sized compound eye peered iridescently from between vertical folds. The fissure closed below like a seam which reached down to the base of the body stalk, where pseudopods extended for locomotion and scavenging.

"New sky-object observed," Allison signaled.

"Star nova?"

9

"Much more interesting. Do you conjoin soon?" Allison asked, noting her swelling folds. It was the season, after all.

"Soon," Ghareshl replied. *"One seeks mates now. Seth has returned here,"* she added, *"from Coral Vale."*

"Seth? Where?" Allison scanned the hall. Seth Connaught usually came to her as soon as he was in town, but he could be moody at times.

There he was, across the bench rows, staring at her.

"Seth! How long have you been up here?" She dodged the chatting Friends and embraced him.

"Not long. I've come to report," he said.

Allison searched his square features, framed by thick dark waves. She pressed his dimpled chin. "I look forward to hearing it. How are things in Coral Vale?"

"Well. And my niece?"

Noreen Connaught, Allison's right-hand assistant at the Tech Center, was Seth's niece. "She's on swing shift tonight, so stop by later. How's your father?"

"He'll outlive us all."

"Even the Dwelling?"

Seth smiled faintly. "No. The One is active, as always," he said, using the most accurate rendition of the commensals' concept of their own kind. "Transmissions have run very smoothly this year," he added. "We appreciate it."

Allison laughed. "I'm glad to hear about something that works right, for a change. Usually the only feedback I get is complaints, until Yearly Meeting when the Service Committee tells me how indispensable I am and begs me to stay on another year." She contemplated his fierce eyes. "I'm so glad you made it back in time for . . ."

"I'm always glad to see you, Sonnie."

Most people were quietly seated by now, closed sunshades resting against the hard benches. The bench rows were arranged in four trapezoidal domains which all faced inward to a central space. Lowell Braithwaite sat near the center, with the Fullers and the Crains, and the venerable Celia Crain

10

Blyden. Grandma Celia's spare build made her appear deceptively frail; vitality shone through her eyes. Her skin was an intricate lattice of wrinkles which sparkled, almost, Allison imagined, like the compound eye of a commensal.

Lowell half rose from the seat. "Friends . . ." His eyebrows bobbed questioningly.

Murmurs died for a customary moment of silence to await the Light within.

The clerk rose again. "We are gathered for the Ninth Monthly Meeting for Business of the Georgeville Friends. Our usual agenda stands, but an urgent item has just appeared which, with the leave of Meeting, I propose we take up first."

Heads nodded in acquiescence.

"We'll hear from Allison Thorne, Technical Services Coordinator."

The programmer's pulse quickened as she stood, brushing back her hair. "Ninety Foxfield years ago our people arrived here from Earth to settle this planet. We have always assumed that Earth was destroyed by then, or even if not, that the light-speed factor and the projected odds against our survival would discourage any future visitation from Earth. Today, however, at fourteen twenty east, the Tech Center picked up a signal from someone in a ship orbiting Foxfield—someone who claims authority of the United Nations."

People gasped. "Louder please?" a voice called several rows to the left.

"I said, we've got a message from Earth people, or so they claim. Whoever they are, they've got a ship in orbit right now," she added flatly.

Martha rose to speak. "Allison, are you certain it's genuine?"

"Well, the ship's up there; I have a close-up video-cap for anyone who cares to look. The design is unfamiliar to me, as you'd expect from folks who—hopefully—have advanced a bit since our latest records."

"Well what did they have to say, for heaven's sake?" called someone else.

Allison read from the bland printout slip. " 'To

11

Allison Thorne and all Friends of Foxfield: Greetings from Adjustor Silva Maio of the ship *UNIS-11*. We citizens of United Nations Interplanetary rejoice in the successful settlement of your people. We hope to resume contact according to UN Charter 61A. We await your reply.' That's it," she finished.

"You didn't reply?" asked Clifford.

"No; I await the sense of the Meeting."

"Then surely we must get back to them to find out on what basis they invoke that statute."

The clerk leaned back to catch a whisper. "Query just raised, Cliff," he called, "as to content of Charter 61A."

"Dear me, back to the classroom." The schoolmaster shook his head. "In the year of our Lord 2000, the UN agency UNESCO released a study which predicted a ninety percent chance of global nuclear war, on Earth, that is, within the following two decades. Nations responded to the report by forging ahead on colonization of Sol's less desirable planets in order to insure that somebody would survive. Of course they also sent missiles along to protect the colonists, so some nations then developed the Ramscoop relativistic drive to send settlers to planet-bearing stars—Barnard's, Centauri, others.

"But the year 2020 came and went with nothing more than conventional carnage here and there, and so folks began to think they were 'safe' again. Many would-be star voyagers lost interest and one UN-sponsored mission disbanded altogether.

"Then a group of Pennsylvanian Friends offered to take over the project, and the ship, and set off for Wheelwright's Star. They got the ship, which they renamed the *Plowshare,* on one condition—that they accept the political charter originally drafted by the UN. Charter 61A says in effect that the *Plowshare* crew and their descendants acknowledge full sovereignty of the UN or of any succeeding panterrestrial government."

"Thanks, Clifford." Lowell motioned to an impatient woman in back.

"But they broke off," she objected. "What kind of sovereignty is that? We all know the H-bombs plowed

12

them under—that 'message' still sounds like a hoax to me. And suppose they *have* come back. Do we really want them? I mean, rules and regulations are one thing; Quakers learned well enough over the centuries how to deal with *that*. But suppose it's missiles they want to throw at us; what'll we do then?"

Several people stood at once.

"Patience, please," said the clerk. "Frances?"

Frances Poyser was the best trained "doctor" on the planet. Her bone structure was unusually fine, for a Foxfielder, but her voice carried a sense of conviction which gave weight to her presence. Now she rose across from Allison and addressed the Meeting. "It would seem to me," she began, "highly unlikely that anyone, even from our incorrigibly godless ancestral planet, would go to the trouble of sending us such a communication were it their intent to incinerate us. As for other dire intentions—we're hardly likely to prevail by ignoring them, are we?" She glared challengingly about the room and adjusted her glasses. "Their technology is advanced, as Allison pointed out. And who knows, they may have learned some other things as well, since they did survive.

"May I suggest we give them the benefit of the doubt for now? I confess I'm curious about them, and about what they know of us already. They know who Allison is, for one thing." She sat down.

"They were thoughtful enough," Clifford muttered dryly, "to chose a Monthly Meeting date to say hello."

"Allison," Martha asked, "have you any idea why the visitors would single you out?"

Allison suddenly wished she were somewhere else. "Well, I think—" She struggled to her feet. "It's obvious that they are familiar with our communication system. They know which band to use for telex, and they would recognize my name from its frequent appearances." But that wasn't all, quite.

"Just how do they know all this?" Lowell asked.

"Well, any settlement acts like a giant radiotransmitter. Our broadcasts aren't strong, but they do leak out into space . . ." She paused. Seth was sitting right there, and he knew; she would have to say it.

"There is another thing. Occasionally I used to fool around with deep-space signals—just for fun, you know—sending out something like, 'Hello, I'm Allison Thorne; is anybody there?' "

This revelation drew mixed reactions. Clifford slapped his thighs, saying, "So *that's* how you spend your extraplanetary budget, eh, sister?" Others were distinctly not amused.

But Allison saw mainly Anne and Edward Crain, who gazed back at her, not in reproof, though perhaps with a touch of concern. Why, she imagined them asking, why have you not called thus in worship, rather than in the void of space? When did the Meeting for Worship last hear your ministry?

"When did you last send such a signal?" Lowell asked.

Allison started, then collected her thoughts. "About six months ago," she said in a small voice.

The clerk's eyebrow lifted. "Ed, what do you make of all this?"

Edward Crain stroked his beard. "Indeed, I share the apprehensions voiced by some. Nonetheless, I ask, if our heart opens not to the stranger, how shall it open to the Spirit?"

Anne nodded. "It's the Lord's will; fear not the truth, but seek it out, wherever it may be."

The Agricultural Resource Coordinator rose and crossed his arms. "I understand all that, but—I still can't help feeling we ought to be ready to defend ourselves, somehow. Think of all that we've built up here over the years: the farms, with tremendous help from the commensals; five growing townships, God willing; and freedom to live by the Light, above all.

"Yet all of this could dissolve tomorrow—in more ways than one . . . I wish that I knew some positive way to address that fear, but—" He shrugged and sat down.

A few heads nodded in sympathy. Then ancient Celia Blyden lifted herself with care, supporting her arm on granddaughter Anne's shoulder. "Friends," Celia began in a hoarse voice. "I was only seven . . . when my family, all six of us, entered the portal of the *Plowshare* for the last time. The youngest of us was

14

then eight months old." She paused for breath, "I was only seven, but I was old enough to know that it was not *fear* which made Friends journey to the stars, but the calling of God. Had it been *fear*, the voyage would have been fruitless. For though all weapons may be left behind, the instinct to create them can never be wholly shed from human hearts.

"What defense do we have ever? 'The Lord is my shepherd'; that is our defense. If we but fear the Lord, then we need never fear evil."

Silence reigned for some time after Celia had sat down.

"I'd like to get a sense of the Meeting," said Lowell at last. "Do we respond to the overture of these visitors?"

"It is our duty and privilege," said Martha, "to welcome the message and to reply to it in the same spirit in which it appears to have been sent."

Most of the Friends seemed to agree. A machinist from the Tech Center rose to say, "I think it's marvelous that these folks have come and all. I mean, think of everything we've been missing out here—a fantastic world, with billions of people in it. And there must be lots of ways they could help us out, too. So let's welcome them to come on down and see us. Like Celia says, we don't need to be scared of anybody."

Allison winced. She had shared that dream, once—when it had been just a dream.

Then Seth rose beside her. "It is on my mind," he stated, "that the view of the One should be noted before we proceed."

The clerk considered this. "We'll send word to the Dwelling, of course. Also we are glad to hear from any Fractions now present." His fingers sent a stream of Transac symbols to a commensal who stood in the left aisle. Allison recognized her as Rashernu, a frequent attender.

The commensal unfolded pale filaments. *"One welcomes more blood-sharers on this world."*

A sense of unease tinged the silence.

Lowell stroked his chin, then signaled again. *"Visitors from sky, though human, may differ from us."*

The concept of "difference"—Allison doubted

15

whether this simple idea could convey to the One the tangled concerns at issue here.

Rashernu responded, *"All blood-sharing wave-forms, though distinguishable, contain the same substance."*

There seemed to be nothing left to say. At last Clifford spoke up. "Just what kind of reply did you have in mind, Low? Something like, 'Hi, there; do join us for our next potluck supper,' maybe?"

Laughter rippled through the Hall. It was a welcome release of tension.

"The other towns'll want a say, too, you know," someone pointed out.

"Exactly," said Frances, with an impatient wave of the hand. "Let Allison immediately send a signal to the effect that, 'The Monthly Meeting of Georgeville has received your message and welcomes further contact with you.' In the meantime we'll get in touch with the other Meetings. Remember, we still have a long agenda tonight."

This suggestion struck a responsive chord. "Approved," murmured voices.

With consensus achieved, Allison slipped out by a side door to find the phone next to the schoolroom. The Deltron program was preset for the same band she had received, but she took care to avoid any chance of error.

The resource report was in progress when Allison returned to the Hall. She heard talk of the latest crops of NuSoy and Wheat-31, strains which the commensals had helped to develop for Foxfield viability. There was also an unusual mineral request.

"I'm not entirely clear on why the One needs cobalt," the Resource Coordinator said. "The request comes from the Dwelling, though; Friend Seth may tell us more."

Why cobalt, wondered Allison as she took a back seat to avoid disturbance. Commensals usually needed more iron than anything else.

"Unfortunately," said Lowell, "our own cobalt supply is minimal this year; am I right, Martha?"

Seth rose again. "The mineral is needed for growth

16

in new directions. The Meeting knows that the One puts our resources to good use."

Allison's curiosity sharpened. She would be sure to worm the truth out of him later.

A rugged Lanesbridge woman stood up several rows over to the right. "Friends, I know we've got a fair cobaltite reserve at Lanesbridge Mine, and I believe Meeting will approve a transfer. We should have kept you up to date but—at times it's hard enough to keep body and soul together, and the records straight, too."

When the agricultural report was done, Anne Crain spoke for Ministry and Counsel. Nell Daniels' baby boy was recorded; a nephew and a second cousin of Allison's received marriage sanction; a farm border misunderstanding was discussed at length ...

A distant telephone rang. Someone hurried out to catch it and returned to hand the clerk a slip of paper.

Lowell rose quickly. "Noreen Connaught sends word that the Tech Center has just picked up another signal from the spaceship. It reads, 'From Adjustor Silva Maio of United Nations Interplanetary to the Friends of Foxfield: Your response is received, and we look forward to meeting you. Please stand by for representatives to arrive on the Georgeville landing strip at local time ten hours, day two, month Nine. For your information, UNI is an egalitarian government founded in 2051, Westerran, to encompass all human beings in the galaxy ...' "

There were gasps and sharp whispers. Lowell's eyebrows went wild as he made a rarely needed appeal for attention.

"But that's tomorrow, Low," someone called out.

"Precisely. May I suggest, therefore, that we appoint a reception committee ..."

It would make little difference, Allison thought. Every Friend whose work could be set aside would be there on the landing strip tomorrow.

III. Those Who Survived

Rhythmic tapping sounded from the far end of the computer room, where Noreen observed the stuttering decwriter. The west-morning sun sent rays through cracks in the window shades to stream across Allison's desk. Allison paced back and forth by the desk, phone in hand.

"For sure, Martha. Everyone has a right to . . . What? How much space the landing craft needs? Well how the devil am I—excuse me, how am I supposed to figure that?"

Seth entered the room. His enigmatic gaze swept her work area, encrusted with printouts, pencils and nondescript metallic artifacts. The shelf above contained reference volumes held in place by an old "Thinker" statuette which her grandmother had left her.

"Half-past eight, now." Allison's finger-watch dial was a standard product of the manufacturing modules located behind the computer complex. "We're still tracking the craft, but it hasn't changed course yet."

She watched Seth pick up a curious stony object from where it sat on a stack of compiler test runs. It was porous and looked like a tangle of pale orange ropes suddenly rigidified.

"Sure, I'll let you know. Bye, now." The receiver fell into place.

"Well, Seth, what's up?" She planted a brief kiss on his cheekbone.

"I need to see you," he said. "We're both so busy, always."

"I know, I know. I needed *this* like a hole in the head. Oh, well." She shrugged. "Say, what's all this about the One needing cobalt? Commensals don't use

18

cobalt, as far as I know; it's too scarce here. Humans need it, though, for vitamin B-12."

Seth nodded slowly. "We don't want to raise false hopes yet."

"But there *has* been progress, hasn't there?"

"A native life form has been modified, at the Dwelling, to produce human amino-acid and hexose requirements, plus some of our vitamins."

"That's amazing." Allison was not expert in biochemistry, but Seth had to be to deal with the One. "What sort of life form is it?" she asked. "Plantlike, I suppose."

"More like a slug or a snail, I'd say."

Allison laughed. " 'Escargots a la Foxfield,' as they'd say in those old books! We'll wait and see. Could be a fair breakthrough; not for nothing do we call the Fractions commensal . . ." For the first time she noticed a troubled look in his eye. "Something wrong, Seth?"

"No, only—" He glanced away. "It's on my mind that I want to spend more time here with you. It's not good the way it's been."

She smiled wryly. "It could be better, that's true. But then, connections are just hard to work out. I'm always glad when we're together, whether for two days or two months." She lowered her voice. "We know what we mean to each other, Seth. What else can I say?"

"Yes, but . . . I want to stay here, Sonnie."

She paused. "You can't leave the Dwelling, Seth. It's important what you're doing; you belong there, at Coral Vale." Immediately she wished the words unsaid.

Seth's knuckles whitened on the desk edge. "You think I'm not serious, don't you? That it's just my state of mind, because the Fractions are conjoining now? Is that what your Deltron tells you?" He turned and strode briskly from the room. Allison heard the outer door open and slam shut.

Noreen approached with a sheaf of printouts, half of which she dumped in the recycling bin.

"It's all right," muttered Allison, hurt and puzzled.

"Sure, I know." Noreen inclined her head, neatly framed by auburn waves. "He's so moody this time of year. The Coral Vale Connaughts are all a bit strange. 'Charmed' and 'colored,' too."

Allison was in no mood for quark jokes. Why now, of all times, did this have to surface? "So what's all this garbage?" she demanded, indicating the printouts.

"It's the WEATHERCAST program," said Noreen. "I fixed that ab-end for you—see?"

Allison scanned the printout. "So that's why the program stopped." She threw down the paper with mock horror. "You whiz kid, you—trying to take over my job, are you?"

"Go on, Allison," she responded sheepishly. "Just getting out the bugs."

"The Meeting had better appreciate that infernal program."

Allison checked the radar screen, which showed a small craft steadily descending. "That's it, Noreen. Give Martha a ring, will you? I've got to go."

"Leaving me to miss all the fun."

"Well, some folks have to keep the gears rolling, eh? When I'm back, you can get your sleep, though."

"Go on—me, sleep, after the shock I got from that telex last antinight?"

The Georgeville "landing strip" was no more than a level field just outside the center of town. It had not been used for spacecraft landing since the *Plowshare* was hit by a meteor. Today over two hundred Foxfielders trampled the ground moss, which was damp and redolent from passing showers but fortunately only centimeters deep this early in the summer. The Friends talked excitedly and craned their necks at the sky though it so far contained nothing but undulating cloud banks and Wheelwright's Sun. A stiff breeze blew in from the forest side, ruffling coats and skirts and sending hats flying, to the immense delight of children whose classes had been cancelled for the day.

Allison wore a smart beige suit for the occasion, now to her regret because the pants were bound to pick up moss stains as she wrestled with the microphone connection at the base of the speaker's platform.

"Terribly sorry about this." Lowell looked on solicitously. His tie waved like a flag in the breeze. "Any way I can help?"

She shook her head. "Almost fixed."

At last Allison stood and surveyed the assembly as she stretched. Martha was there, and Doc Frances; and Celia sat in a folding chair, laughing throatily at some remark from Clifford, whose bald cranium gleamed like a moon. The same light brought out the tinge of red in Seth's locks like smouldering coals. The commensal Fractions Ghareshl and Rashernu had their coronal fronds spread wide to catch the sun.

"Do you suppose," someone suggested, "they've all grown radiation-proof scales?"

Bill's eyes were glued to his binoculars. "I see it; I see it!" the machinist exulted. "It's coming down; would you like a look, boss?" He offered Allison the binoculars.

"For the love of God," someone whispered.

A shadow crossed the sun. People gasped, then fell silent, for it was their custom to begin vital occasions with stillness.

To Allison's amazement, the craft landed with no sign of exhaust and little sound. Electrogravitics? Impossible, she thought; they'd practically need a double-star system to supply the power. Still . . .

It was shaped like a spool of thread some five or six meters tall. Not all that big for a spacecraft, really; but then, it was only a shuttle. A dark opening appeared on the lower rim and four figures emerged. They were sheathed in deep green skin-tight suits which heightened their appearance of Earth-born elongation. As they approached, Allison observed some sort of goggles pushed back over their heads. She glanced automatically at their feet, half expecting to see flippers.

"Friends of Foxfield." The woman's voice was amplified by an unseen mechanism. Her tight hood outlined her copper face, long with prominent cheekbones. "I am Silva Maio, Psychosynchronic Adjustor from the Board of Adjustors of United Nations Interplanetary. All citizens greet you with joy today, you brave people whose ancestors accomplished the unique feat of colonizing a new star system during the Age of Uncertainty . . ."

21

Her cadence was a bit distracting, but comprehensible enough. "Unique feat"—was it really? What had become of the other Ramscoop expeditions?

"The past century," the Adjustor continued, "has seen many changes, as you would expect. A critical technological advance was the discovery of a nearly instantaneous means of transport between distant points in the galaxy, based on the Shimuri Effect first detected by Hiroko Shimuri during the last century. This effect will make it possible for all of you to resume active citizenship in UNI.

"My fellow citizens and I will facilitate your orientation and reintegration into our society. Let me now introduce citizen Rissa Nduni, chief medical doctor; citizen Kyoko Aseda, systems architect; citizen Casimir Stroem, biosphere analyst."

She paused at this point, and Lowell took the initiative.

"Citizens, we Friends welcome you to Foxfield. Lowell Braithwaite is my name, and I sincerely hope that your society has not outgrown this time-honored fashion of greeting—" He stepped forward and extended his hand. The Adjustor clasped it firmly.

"May the Lord bless you all," he went on. "We'll try not to inundate you with introductions just now, but we should at least begin with Allison Thorne, who received your first greeting yesterday."

Allison shook the hands of the sea-green clad visitors.

"Such a pleasure, at last, Friend Thorne," said Kyoko Aseda. "I look forward to working with you."

Allison nodded and tried not to stare at the citizen's delicate Oriental features.

"Celia Blyden," said Lowell, "survived the *Plowshare;* she's one of those 'ancestors' you mentioned."

A few chuckles were heard.

"And it is my special privilege to introduce our non-human friends, Ghareshl and Rashernu, commensal Fractions of the One. The One's aid has contributed greatly to our survival on Foxfield."

Seth had been signaling with the Fractions. Each now turned her eye toward the visitors. The humans nodded gravely and did not attempt to shake hands.

"And now," Lowell concluded, "our Committee for Extraplanetary Concerns has prepared an orientation program for you. Martha?" His voice trailed off as he turned from the mike.

Martha stepped to the platform, her hair shifting in the breeze. "Welcome, friends. We will be glad to show you what we have accomplished here with the Lord's grace. But first I have some crucial information for you. We have discovered the hard way that this planet contains high concentrations of certain toxic substances which are rare or unknown on Earth. We have developed antidotes for them, and Medical Director Frances Poyser recommends immediate administration for all of you."

Adjustor Maio exchanged brief unamplified words with the off-world doctor, a nearly two-meter giant with complexion of rich loam.

"We appreciate your concern," said the doctor, "but we've taken adequate precautions. We have extensive environmental data from unmanned probes."

Allison blinked in surprise. How long had these folks been around, then? Had they deliberately kept their ships out of range of her instruments?

Frances stepped forward. "I am pleased to hear that," she observed crisply. "The list of toxins is extensive, however, and some of them we could never have counteracted without the commensals' help. I urge you at least to double-check with me . . ."

"Cliff," whispered Allison, "how can they know all about this planet, no matter how many probes they sent? I mean, we should know; we've lived and died here long enough."

Clifford shrugged. "Why should they trust us? Like as not, Doc is a witch doctor to them."

Citizen Stroem spoke for the first time. "Doctor Poyser, we'll be happy to discuss all your knowledge of this biosphere. We are extremely interested to learn just how it is that you people managed to survive here; from our point of view, it's a miraculous achievement."

Frances nodded. "The Lord has been kind, though I hardly dare claim intervention of that order. We shall assist you in every way."

"That goes for all of us," added Martha. "Our home is yours. We would like to show you Georgeville today, our first settlement, founded ninety-two Earth years ago in 2033 A.D. Like the planet, our town was named after George Fox who began the Religious Society of Friends in England around 1650, and whose *Journal* remains a source of inspiration for Friends. Our first Meeting House and the Medical Center were built here. Also you may care to see our Agricultural Resource Station, and the Technical Services Center . . ."

Clifford chuckled. "Hope they keep up with her better than I can."

"We appreciate your invitation," said the Adjustor. "A word about time scale, though: since your star system lies twelve point two light-years from Terra, and your ship accelerated at one *g* to relativistic speeds—"

The schoolmaster's jaw dropped. "Well, I'll be darned," he exclaimed. "With all my conversions of year length, *that* slipped my mind."

Allison called out, "Add eight years."

"Eight years, twenty-six days," the frog-suited visitor corrected. "Today would have been day one hundred and fifty-one, year 2133, Westerran."

"Great start, Cliff," Allison teased.

"Right, sister. May all our differences prove so easy to resolve."

She winced then and wondered about the other dates, the "real" Earth dates. None had been mentioned so far.

A dozen Friends and their guests strolled the path between tawny fields of Wheat-31. Sheaves from the first harvest dotted the landscape like younger siblings of the Resource Station which loomed on the horizon.

"The first decade was critical for our settlers," Clifford said. "They couldn't just land, after all. A planet had to be chosen, and preliminary biosphere analysis took over two years."

Allison watched the tall visitors whose feet left deep prints in the sod. Yet they walked without effort, and she wondered why the twenty-percent higher gravity did not hinder them. Their hoods were pulled down now, revealing moderately cropped hair, though the Oriental's smooth black coif contrasted sharply with Casimir Stroem's curls, golden as the grain.

Casimir stopped to finger one of the stalks. "Little pest damage," he observed.

"True enough," said Noah Rowntree, the Agricultural Resource Coordinator. "Our crops attract relatively few native species. Though the native chemistry turned out not to be totally alien, thank goodness. In fact, trace metals aside, it was much closer to that of Earth than the specialists had predicted."

"That's generally the case," said Casimir. "On other planets, I mean."

Clifford went on. "Two families made the first attempt to start a settlement on the ground. The results were disastrous. Most died of unexplained illness . . . but certain deaths were particularly disturbing. The bodies were found intact, apparently, except that every drop of blood had been drained away."

Allison suddenly became very aware of Seth and Ghareshl, whose stream of Transac interchange continued.

"Strange creatures were observed," said Clifford, "in connection with some of the 'accidents.' It was discovered that the creatures killed humans by producing a toxic gas, and—well, I'll skip the details; it's obvious that some way had to be found to deal with this menace. At the time, most of the *Plowshare* crew felt that some sort of 'defense' was needed to clear the creatures out of an area for settlement; by then they were really desperate to get out of that cramped ship, you know.

"One person disagreed. Biologist Rachel Coffin believed that the creatures showed evidence of high intelligence and that communication should be attempted. Dissent was very bitter, but the Meeting finally reached consensus for a ten-month moratorium to achieve contact. Rachel did succeed, through the use of visual signals which later were developed into the Transac syllabary. From then on, amazing opportunities unfolded from our interchange with the 'commensal' beings."

"Excuse me, Friend Clifford." Kyoko Aseda spoke up. "You mentioned syllables just now; that implies a spoken language in some sense, no?"

"Since human speech is basically oral, we often find it convenient to interpret the Transac signs in phonetic terms, in teaching and for names and so forth. The 'mensals, I assume, interpret them in olfactory or chemisense terms."

"I see." Kyoko then turned to Ghareshl. She lifted her hands and formed deliberate signs: the raised thumb for *question*, the cupped fingers of *thought*. *"What thoughts on first contact humans?"*

Allison was impressed. She'd picked that up in a hurry.

The commensal extended a handful of corollar tendrils. *"First thoughts of wonderment; expansion of known world-waves. An entity which is One yet not One, blood-sharing yet blood-different."*

Seth translated the response into speech. "They call themselves Fractions of the One Organism," he explained. "She is a hand of many fingers; an eye of many faces."

"As are Christians, united in the Spirit," Anne Crain added. "Friends feel a certain affinity with the outlook of the One."

A pause ensued.

Casimir stroked his youthful chin and turned to Seth. "I gather this 'blood-sharing' phenomenon refers to a friendship ritual of some sort?"

"Far more than ritual," Seth gravely replied. "The exchange of blood for blood enables our survival."

Noah walked closer. "What Seth says was true literally in the early days, more figuratively so now. The commensals were suffering from a scarcity of certain minerals in the soil, particularly iron, which human blood happens to be full of. And, as I understand, they didn't even kill humans deliberately; they simply failed to realize that some of the chemicals which they emitted would interact fatally with any human nearby. Once the body was there, of course . . .

"But after contact, we worked out an arrangement. You see, although commensal physical ability is rudimentary, their biochemical technology seems limitless.

26

Given the necessary elements in any form, a Fraction can produce just about any organic compound you could imagine. So we described basic Earth-type nutrients to them, and eventually even drugs and plastic substances. See out there—one Fraction is spreading fertilizers directly on the field."

Allison followed the sweep of his arm. In the distance a pale green form progressed like a ghost.

"At first," said Noah, "We let the Fractions draw blood from us in exchange. Once we learned the One's precise requirements we substituted some supplements from the *Plowshare's* supply. Today, some folks do continue the direct exchange of body fluids as a special form of communication, most often at the Dwelling. Friend Seth is from Coral Vale; he'd be familiar with that."

Doctor Rissa Nduni looked up. "Surely," she suggested in her deep contralto, "this form of symbiosis has physiological consequences?"

Noah seemed vague on this point. "We do it less, today, since we extract enough minerals from the planet; Lanesbridge, Mawrford and Blydentown are all mining centers. The ores we need have been hard to locate in Foxfield's crust, even with the *Plowshare's* detectors, which we've lacked for some time now. The planetary mass is twice that of Earth, and the mineral composition is more stratified. But at least humans can dig and drill; the 'mensals aren't exactly built for that."

"Speaking of build," Clifford said, "doesn't the Foxfield gravity tire you out at all?"

Doctor Rissa Nduni shook her head. "We train our muscles with metabolic regulators. How is it," she asked Noah, "that the commensal creatures evolved so dependent on minerals scarce on this planet?"

Seth's fingers flew.

"In early times," Ghareshl signaled, *"minerals were enough. Then One needed more, for further growth stages in the Dwelling."*

"The Dwelling is the center of the One's consciousness," said Seth.

Casimir looked up. "Back to planetology; have you

any idea where that unprecedented planetary magnetism comes from?"

"No," said Allison. "Perhaps you folks will find out."

"Yes," Kyoko said. "We'll help you update your mining techniques as well."

"What about weather forecasting?" Noah asked with sudden eagerness. "I'll bet you could really give us a hand on that."

"Of course. The initial phase of climate control might be installed fairly soon, Casimir, no?"

Casimir nodded. "Upon completion of biosphere analysis."

Allison felt annoyed despite herself. "I've a hunch you folks are going to turn me out of a job," she said.

"Absolutely not," said Adjustor Maio. "That is the opposite of UNI's intention."

Kyoko added, "We wish to cooperate with you, Allison, to mesh your social and technical fabric with the UNI System. I'd like very much to see what your Technical Center has accomplished."

"Let's stop off there," said Martha, whose stride was still full of energy. "We've just enough time before supper."

The Center's trapezoidal silhouette stood dark before the reddened sun which now approached the horizon. Patches of plantlike foliage were closing for the night, but Allison heard the cackling witch-vine just beginning to stir.

"What exactly became of the *Plowshare?*" Kyoko asked, as they entered the building.

"Oh, it's still up there," said Allison. "At least it was, the last time I looked. It swings round in a long orbit; shouldn't come down for another thousand years yet."

"We'll dispose of it."

"Thanks," Allison said dryly. "Before it was destroyed we had brought down the essential equipment: Deltron, the manufacturing modules, and so forth. All nice and compact, with providential capacity for self-repair." But they would have given out eventually, perhaps before the Foxfielders were ready. She had wondered about that.

In the computer room Dave sat at Allison's desk and wrote notes on some printout paper. On the shelf by his shoulder his pet lay in a wrinkled heap, one eye stirring sleepily.

The wurraburra came to life in an instant. It flopped down to the floor, waving its eyefeet like a tangle of snakes. It headed for Casimir and climbed swiftly to his chest.

"David!" snapped Allison. "I've told you a hundred times to keep that thing out of here—it *is* harmless, though," she assured the biosphere analyst.

"Mom, I just wanted some company while I do my homework—" The boy stopped and stared at the strange visitors.

"No problem at all." Casimir grinned as he examined the cooing creature. "Never in my life have I seen such a beast! But animals generally take to me, for some reason. It's a useful trait, on the whole."

"Even on Foxfield?" Noah asked rhetorically. "Your gift must be truly otherworldly, then."

Casimir looked at him blankly.

"A spiritual gift," Martha explained.

"Oh, yes, of course."

Noreen now stood expectantly by the desk.

"Sorry," said Allison, "I should introduce you—my son, David Joshua Thorne, and Noreen Connaught, deputy coordinator . . ." She named the four off-world citizens.

"And that there's Rufus Jones," added Dave, his confidence recovered.

"What's this!" Clifford feigned horror. "Young man, have you no better respect for such an illustrious name? Your forebears would turn in their graves."

Dave's cheeks flushed.

His uncle laughed and patted his shoulder. "Rufus Jones was a worthy Friend of the early nineteen hundreds," he told the visitors. "He helped revitalize Quakerism in an increasingly secular age. He was a founder of the American Friends Service Committee, and his own life gave endless witness to the Light. One courageous act was his visit to the German Gestapo, just before the Second World War, when he asked them to curb the persecution of Jews."

"Did they listen?" asked Casimir.

"They were courteous, at least, for Friends had brought relief to German children after the First War. Beyond that . . . The Word falls inevitably upon deaf ears at times."

Kyoko was looking about the machine-filled room.

"Are you familiar with Delphis Electronics?" Allison asked.

"Of course," she replied, "I recall the line. Bloch core; state of the art at the millennium's end."

"It was fairly standard by the time the *Plowshare* left. Had to bring along reliable equipment, after all. What do you use for memory storage nowadays? Electron spin?" she suggested facetiously.

"We're working on it," said the systems architect. "At present, storage is down to the molecular level— crystals of iron chromophores modeled after biomolecules. I'll show you when you visit the ship."

Allison felt slightly foolish. Of course, she knew better; Deltron would be no more than a child's toy for people whose ships could cheat light-speed.

They stayed for pot-luck supper at the Crain farm. Long benches and tables with lamps at the ends had been set out over the field. A hundred or so Friends sat there now, finishing their meal and speculating about their guests from the stars. Children tossed frisbees into the fading light and dodged unusual numbers of commensal yearlings, attracted by the lights and cooking odors.

Allison listened intently as Adjustor Maio spoke.

"The UNI government is quite democratic." Her voice was slightly amplified, as before. "Every human citizen has a say in her future; each has a vote, registered from birth."

"What about nonhumans?" someone called out. "Include any of them yet?"

"I know of no case in which the question has arisen; do you, Casimir?"

He shook his golden curls. "We've tried in every way conceivable to contact potential inhabitants of the

30

planets we explore. So far no nonhumans have proven intelligent enough or aggressive enough to make their sapience known. Four planets are now being thermolyzed and converted for human settlement."

Allison raised her hand for a question, but someone else got there first.

"What kind of rights do you guarantee humans, then?"

"Those which progressive nations have long sought to achieve," said the Adjustor. "Rights to life, happiness, communication . . ."

Allison sighed.

"Tired?" asked Seth as he put his arm around her. He seemed to have recovered from the morning's outburst.

"Tired of old long words. I want to hear about that Shimuri business, the new physics. And I can't wait to get a look at that ship tomorrow."

He nodded. "Should be just the thing for you. Just think of all the new ideas you can get for the Center."

"Please; I feel like a cave man already." She turned to Ghareshl, who stood quite still with her corona closed, but her eye open. *"What do you think of them?"* Allison signaled.

Just enough tendrils extended from the closed leaves. *"The new possible-blood-sharer wave-forms?"*

"Yes."

"Don't smell much. But look nice and green. Do they perform photosynthesis?"

"Good question," Allison said aloud. It was certainly possible, though she doubted it. *"Why not ask?"*

"Uncomfortable. Distasteful wave emissions."

She recalled the One's sensitivity to electromagnetic radiation, especially in the microwave and radio ranges. Rachel Coffin had theorized that commensals monitored their internal biochemistry by molecular magnetic resonances which coincided with those frequencies.

"Those frog-suits," said Seth, "must hide a hell of a lot of equipment."

"Maybe. Ghareshl is more finicky than most, however. That Yshrin, now—I wish *she'd* be a bit more particular. She's up to no good when she gets curious about the Center."

31

The Adjustor was trying to explain just how UNI could guarantee "happiness" to its citizens. "In this century," she said, "the study of the human mind has at last become an exact science. The science is called psychosynchrony. You might try to think of it as the ultimate fusion of politics and psychology, although psychology is to psychosynchrony what alchemy is to chemistry. The function of Psychosynchronic Adjustors is to adjust the psyches of all citizens for attainment of maximal satisfaction in life."

"Well, look here," called a hoarse voice from the end of the table. "Suppose in spite of all that guaranteed happiness, I'm still unhappy? Suppose I just don't want to be a 'citizen' of this United whatever? What can I do about it?"

"I understand your concern," said Adjustor Maio. "After all, we've just arrived here today, after your many years in isolation. Naturally you feel apprehensive. Like all citizens, you have many needs which deserve consideration. I feel confident that once you learn all about our System your fears will be dispelled. To start with, we will set up 'transcomm' units on Foxfield which you may use to communicate with UNI citizens everywhere."

Lively conversations ensued, until Edward Crain asked something which Allison strained to catch.

"I said, what about religion?" he repeated. "Do your people guarantee freedom of worship?"

Adjustor Maio hesitated slightly. "Religious phenomena have undergone evolution over this century, as over any other. But to answer your question, there are no restrictions on 'spiritual' expression, any more than on other types of expression."

"Indeed, do Christians still exist? Or are Friends now extinct on Earth?"

"A group called the Quaker Preservation Society has in fact entered a request to send visitors to your planet."

There were exclamations of joy.

"By all means," said Martha, "let them visit; our heart goes out to them. And I am sure that some among us would like to visit these Friends in return. Do they inhabit other planets now, besides Earth?"

"What's Earth like now?" someone else asked. "Can we go back and see?"

Celia stiffly raised an arm. "Is it true, then, that I can return to Earth . . . that I may see my birthplace once more?"

"Yes," the Adjustor said. "Any citizen may travel when her credit level permits."

"And what about the Holy Land? Can I visit Palestine, the land of the Bible?"

A long pause preceded the Adjustor's reply, but her expression did not change. "You will learn all our history, in time, but let me relate the more painful events now. You recall, of course, the background of the *Plowshare* project. In the face of arms proliferation throughout the solar system, some people hoped to preserve humanity by voyaging to distant stars, and yours were among them.

"But those who remained had to deal with Earth as it was. The Middle Eastern region was particularly unstable then, for political discontent and heavy armaments persisted there long after depletion of the obsolete fossil fuels which upheld the local economy. In 2024, Palestinian terrorists who hoped to break up the Arab-Israeli anti-Soviet alliance hijacked a defective Soviet missile station and set off its warheads toward Israel. Israel then launched missiles against the Soviet Union and the Arab states, while the United States and China in concert took the opportunity for a preemptive first strike against the Soviets. It wasn't quite preemptive enough, however.

"The details are unimportant now. The result of the Last War, as it is called, was devastation for many areas, and the Terran biosphere as a whole was severely strained. Most areas were reclaimed gradually over the generations, but Palestine remains uninhabitable wasteland to this day."

The Friends sat in stunned silence along the lamplit tables. Adjustor Maio surveyed the stricken faces.

"The magnitude of the tragedy cannot be comprehended; but you must hear of its sequel as well. One industrial nation, Japan, emerged relatively intact because she had never built nuclear weapons and was therefore on none of the target lists; with Martian resources, Japan helped rebuild the rest of the world. And since all nations suffered greatly, it became possible for the first time for people everywhere to unite against war and to insure that this war was in fact the Last War."

But at what price, wondered Allison. What price then; and what price now?

The Friends were still for some time. Across the field, youngsters had left their frisbees in the moss and the commensals had disappeared into the undergrowth.

At last came Lowell's voice. "I feel called," he began slowly, "to remind the Meeting of the counsel of our dear doctor Frances, whose voice was so well guided last anti-eve. Until yesterday, we on Foxfield believed that humans were no more on Earth. Today we see evidence that our brethren have not only survived, but have also learned to overcome their evils, perhaps in ways we could never have dreamed of. I hope and pray that this is so."

Silence returned, until Anne Crain spoke. "Ours is not to judge," she said, "but to follow the leading of the Lord. I believe Whittier wrote as follows to Sybil Jones, on the occasion of her mission to Palestine:

> *Oh! blest to teach where Jesus taught,*
> *And walk with Him Gennesaret's strand;*
> *But whereso'er His work is wrought*
> *Dear hearts, shall be your Holy Land.*

Some listeners nodded and exchanged quiet words. But a harsher whisper was heard nearby. "Sinners they are," said Noah. "God forsook them long ago. They should all have perished in their atom fire; if not, then let them burn eternally, for all I care."

Allison frowned at this pronouncement and brushed her hair back. It was getting late, she realized.

"Is . . . anything left of America?" someone ventured.

"Of course," said Adjustor Maio, "much land was reclaimed. My own Peruvian homeland preserved much of her prewar ecology . . ."

Allison rose and stretched her stocky limbs. "Come,

34

Seth," she said, "let's round up that son of mine and head for home. We've some kilometers to walk and a long day ahead tomorrow." She shivered in the night air.

Stars filled the sky tonight, and the moons Providence and Deliverance were both up. The stratosphere must have been calm, since only traces of aurora touched the horizon. On other nights the solar wind dipped into the magnetic field like a paintbrush and spread its colors far across the sky. The auroras were an endless source of fascination for Foxfielders, and although traditionalists frowned on fantasy, some Friends could not resist telling their children that the shimmering lights represented Joseph's coat of many colors, or robes of the angels bearing messages to denizens of heaven. Tonight, however, the lights struck Allison as God's curtain, fallen upon an age.

IV. Gateway

The ground dropped dizzily beneath their feet as the four Foxfielders peered at the view screen in the shuttle craft. Allison stared as the landscape shrank to a globe, then a disk, mottled in cloud masses and darker land areas. The jungles stretched across the southern base of the crescent-shaped continent which held all human settlements. With the exception of Coral Vale, the settlements lay farther north, where the fields yielded more readily to the human plow. They had attempted a sixth settlement near the jungle's edge because of a rich iron ore deposit, but that was long past.

Lowell gasped. "Look there, Allison!"

As the night side of Foxfield rotated into view the auroras appeared—giant spirals, from above, which surged westward over thousands of kilometers. Then the luminous disk shrank slowly away to moon size.

Clifford rubbed his scalp and watched in fascination. Seth, however, was preoccupied with the commensal Ghareshl.

"Allison," Seth called. "Ghareshl is distressed."

Allison turned to speak, but her lips froze in alarm. The commensal's coronal fronds were closed rigid and her frontal folds swelled, nearly covering her honeycombed eye.

"What's wrong, what's wrong?" Allison signaled quickly. She had to get through before the eye completely vanished. Perhaps it had been unwise to bring the Fraction, after all.

Several yellow tendrils poked cautiously out of the closed fronds. *"World is gone,"* Ghareshl signaled.

"That's all she'll say," Seth added.

Citizens Rissa Nduni and Kyoko Aseda stepped forward. "What's wrong with the creature?" the doctor asked.

Allison sighed and felt embarrassed, for she herself, as supposed local expert on such matters, had undertaken to coach her nonhuman friend on the environmental changes to expect from this trip to the *UNIS-11*. She tried the commensal reassurance formula: *" 'I exist, you exist, World exists,' "* she affirmed with a gesture of emphasis. *"If I move away now, my wave-form shrinks, but—"*

"Stay here!" Ghareshl insisted.

"Of course I stay here. World is bigger than it seemed," Allison reminded her, groping for an analogy. *"This . . . is like a gateway to another field."*

"Another World?" Ghareshl's fronds unfolded slightly.

Then it clicked. This sign for "world" also meant "dipole" or "magnet." The magnetic field was what she missed.

"It will come back," Allison assured her.

Kyoko asked, "Would it help to show her the planet close up again?"

"I don't think so . . ."

Nonetheless, Foxfield's image reappeared on another screen next to Clifford, who jumped, startled.

The image expanded and the dense, shrubby forests appeared, then the fields surrounding Georgeville. At last the town's two dozen houses appeared, finally so close that Allison could make out the solar panel junctions on a rooftop.

"How do you watch Georgeville," Allison asked, "after it has rotated out of view?"

"It's all relayed," Kyoko explained, "from the prime ship plus satellite array."

"Satellites?" Allison stared at the slim, viridian-sheathed systems architect. "I've never *seen* any satellites, from the Tech Center."

"They're virtually undetectable. Except for gravity waves."

"Oh . . ."

Her brother frowned. "Sounds like you've already set about cluttering our skies with prying hardware."

"Certainly not," Rissa responded severely. "For safety's sake, the Board of Adjustors strictly limits our orbiting unit population per cubic kilometer."

"Besides," said Kyoko, "your undeveloped planet won't pose problems in that regard for the foreseeable future."

This remark further perplexed Allison, who considered Foxfield's population of eight hundred and twenty-seven settlers an impressive "development."

"Commencing interlock," stated a flat, disembodied voice. The apparent gravitational force lightened suddenly.

Rissa explained, "We've reached the prime ship. Our environment is Terran standard, so you'll find the oxygen a bit low, among other things. For your comfort, then, just set these metabolic regulators behind your necks." The doctor held out flexible oblong objects in her large dark hands.

"What's inside?" Allison demanded. "Microcircuits?"

"It's like a pacemaker, for involuntary neural functions."

Seth shook his head. "I don't need mind control."

Rissa's long face showed annoyance.

"Friend Seth, you misunderstood," said Kyoko as

37

she clasped her hands. "It is only a homeostatic monitor; it has nothing to do with mental adjustment."

Lowell, however, accepted the device. "I appreciate your concern for our welfare," he said, implicitly reminding the Friends that these citizens deserved the trust of guests on Foxfield. Clifford reluctantly followed suit; Allison resolved to pass hers on to Doc Frances later, just in case.

"Interlock complete," the flat voice stated. A wall sector fell away to reveal a bluish corridor which stretched out before them like an ice cavern. Allison guided her steps with care, for she felt as though she might float away.

Adjustor Silva Maio and Casimir Stroem greeted them in the corridor. "Today," said the Adjustor, "we hope to acquaint you with the modern lifestyle which our industrious citizens have achieved."

But Seth still held back with Ghareshl, engaged in Transac exchange. *World still far away,* she signaled. *Many strange waves.*

Allison nodded. "She feels a lot of radiowaves around here, right, Seth?" She glanced at Kyoko. "Must be even worse than the Tech Center; it's as though you had transmitters focused here constantly."

Casimir was intrigued. "A radio sense? What function does that serve? I can't wait to bring that creature up to my lab for observation."

"But wait a minute," said Allison. "She's upset enough as it is."

"There's no need to rush," the Adjustor deftly interposed. "Since 'she' appears to be related to plants, she might feel more at ease in our Garden of Rest. I would like to show you there in any case, to see the facilities which offer the crew of the *UNIS–11* a home away from home . . ."

They managed to coax the commensal slowly down the corridor. Occasional frog-suited citizens passed by without comment. Here and there on the walls curious signs were etched, similar to the markings which Allison had observed on the ship through her telescope.

"Japanese characters," her brother whispered. "They work sort of like Transac symbols."

A sudden burst of light made Allison squeeze her eyes shut. She reopened them cautiously and gazed about the place which had opened before them. Foliage of all sizes and shapes extended over the walkway. The light streamed from above, reflecting brilliantly off the catwalks which crossed the garden on several levels.

"All for leisure?" Clifford's lip twisted. "We can scarcely afford leisure on Foxfield."

"That will change," the Adjustor promised.

Ghareshl actually did seem to perk up a bit. Allison suspected that the rich variety of organic scents attracted her.

Meanwhile, the biosphere analyst pointed out various specimens. *"Asteraceae, Orchidaceae,"* said Casimir, "you name it, we've got it. Our collection is unusually extensive, for a space cruiser."

Allison reached upward to touch an overflowing cascade of petals. Automatically she searched the seeming chaos of undergrowth for signs of order and design, the pruning of a subtle gardener. The scene tantalized her, challenged her as always to seek out the pattern which lay just beyond reach. What use was life without a pattern?

Clifford asked, "Do you have organisms from other planets? Besides Earth, that is."

Kyoko pointed out a flower with tight orange folds at the center, fading to blue at the rim. "These are 'sunspirals,' " she said, "from Vinlandia, system Epsilon Eridani." Her voice was strangely sad.

Adjustor Maio observed, "We have colonized planets in four new star systems, since development of Space Lattice Interactive Transport. SLIT communication unites people everywhere under one government."

"A democratic government?" Clifford asked.

"Yes. All responsible citizens vote regularly on System referenda. If not, they lose System credit."

"A fine for failure to vote?"

"No; *credit* is not a form of monetary exchange. Credit represents social value; the System generates credit levels in such a way as to maintain social equilibrium."

"Government by *machine?*"

"But democratic process sets the credit factors."

Lowell raised an eyebrow. "By 'democratic process,' I assume you mean majority rule."

"That's correct."

There was an awkward pause, and Allison stared at her feet. The Friends made all collective decisions by consensus.

At last Clifford laughed. "That's great. I can just see us running our Meetings in the Tech Center, Allison."

Allison frowned, for her brother's standard joke about her "machines" was a sore point. "When you need a machine, you need it, that's all," she snapped. She glanced uneasily at Seth, who was telling Casimir about commensals. His breathing was labored, and Allison wished that he would try the device Rissa had offered. She understood his aversion, but—they had to start by trusting these people, or how could they get anywhere? She remembered Ed Crain in the Meeting House, speaking through his beard: *if our heart opens not to the stranger* . . .

Allison turned to Kyoko. "I ought to find out more about this 'System.' The Meeting will expect a report from me." She groaned inwardly at the thought of this task.

"As citizens," Kyoko said, "all of you will learn to interface the System. For example, you can use it to contact anyone in UNI at any time."

"Even on Earth?"

"Would you like to *see* Earth, right now?"

Allison blinked and said nothing. She glanced at the others, who seemed in no hurry to leave. Then she followed the systems architect out of the floral maze, back to the bluish corridor.

The two of them stood in a hemispherical chamber. The floor was smooth as glass.

"System call-in," said Kyoko.

"Acknowledged," the ubiquitous System voice replied. "What number?"

The citizen gave a number, and the room grew dark. Against the blackness a bright globe appeared, mottled brown and blue. Allison stepped back invol-

untarily, and nearly lost her balance. Then she remembered holography, one of the fabulous inventions
known to her Earth-born ancestors. The globe swelled;
it looked similar to Foxfield, though paler and
browner. She reached out to "touch" it, and the colors
streaked her hand.

"Day three hundred forty-four, year 82 UNI, Terran
newsview summary," the System voice announced.
"Tsung Corp stratogeyser explodes over Australia,
causing twenty thousand fatalities. African Sector
plans to send one hundred thirty thousand emigrants
to Vinlandia . . ."

Twenty thousand? In one accident? There must
have been some mistake, Allison thought.

"Excavation Europa unveils newly restored work of
a major pre-UNI Westerran artist. Archons battle
Pleiades for Mars Classic. Request details?"

"Call-out," Kyoko said. The chamber lighting returned.

"Direct from Earth . . ." Allison mused. What she
really wanted to see was Pennsylvania, the home of
her ancestors. But that was a desert now, she recalled
with a shudder. "Earth doesn't look quite the same,
now, does it?"

"You'll have to get used to that." Kyoko's eyes
shone with something—pity, perhaps; Allison was unsure. The citizen's Oriental features still unnerved her.

Suddenly she thought of what Dave would ask when
she returned: *Do they still have artists on Earth,
Mom?*

"That piece of art they dug up," she said. "Can I
see that?"

Kyoko queried the System.

An immense metal sculpture appeared which extended in all directions, even meters below their feet,
where the floor seemed to vanish. Allison froze with
vertigo, then collected herself gradually. The tableau
overflowed with bronze human figures entangled in impossible contortions: a man, back arched, about to fall
headlong from the main ledge; women grimacing, crying out; semiskeletons stumbling across the panel below.

"Auguste Rodin lived from two-eleven to one-thirty-four years pre-UNI," the unseen narrator began. "The sculptor's most complex masterpiece, the bronze cast 'Gates of Hell,' was unearthed at the Paris site last year and underwent full restoration and decontamination.

"For nearly forty years Rodin built the portraits of damned souls into the monumental set of doors which lead to nowhere. From Dante's *Inferno* and Michelangelo's 'Last Judgment' he adapted such subjects as the prodigal son, the aged courtesan, and the medieval traitor Ugolino who starved in prison with his sons and insanely devoured their flesh . . ."

The portals moved back, and their structure became clear: two door slabs some ten meters tall, beneath a central corniced panel. Three figurines like Fates crowned the cornice and pointed their arms downward.

"Rodin's view of torment," the narrator continued, "was more than a scene from an imaginary afterlife. It represented the 'hell' suffered by the living in his time, in particular the lack of communication which he saw among his fellow human beings. For none of his subjects seem to notice one another; intertwined as they are, each is utterly alone."

A tone sounded then, and a different voice spoke. "Does this work show that supernatural belief was still a major source of artistic inspiration early in the Age of Uncertainty?"

"In Rodin's time," the narrator replied, "support for Religion was eroding at last as men increasingly sought Reason to order their lives. Rodin's masterpiece reflects this shift, for the central Judgment Seat in the 'Gates' is occupied not by the Christ-god, as in medieval depictions, but by the Thinker."

Of course—Allison recognized it now, from the old bookend on her shelf. Here, the figure rested his chin on his hand with incongruous calm amid the riotous display of suffering.

"Perhaps the 'Gates' foreshadowed the times to come, during which Reason ruled ineffectually over human chaos. Today we may yet admire the sculptor's ability to imbue his still forms with the appearance of living motion. Mobilists should note these details . . ."

The doors moved forward and the figures expanded to life size, as though threatening to take her in.

"Call-out," Allison ordered.

"Call-out," Kyoko repeated.

The "Gates" whisked away.

"It startled me, that's all. I could have told him a thing or two about 'Religion,' though," Allison said.

"You should try that next time, if the questor load is low. You'll need a credometer, to make your own calls." Kyoko handed her a metallic wristband, similar to one which she herself wore.

"A what?" Allison inspected the object. It was made of fine gray mesh with a thumb-sized display which read, "15,000."

"A credometer. It monitors your vital signs, your work performance, your surroundings. The System then determines your credit level up to the minute, and allows you to—"

"I see. Well, thanks, but—another time, perhaps."

"It's perfectly harmless, Friend Allison. All citizens wear them, even infants."

Allison fingered a strand of hair, trying to think quickly.

"You can always take it off; there's only a slight credit drain for off time."

Warily she slipped the credometer over her hand. "Can I really call Earth with this thing? Say, what's happening?"

The number was changing: 20,000, 24,500, 28,200, 31,300.

"That's your credit level," Kyoko said. "See? Already you're doing very well."

"But why? What have I done?"

"You're learning all about the System, so that you can reintegrate into UNI. We assign high social value to reintegration."

The Foxfielder's scalp prickled. She felt uneasy, though unsure just why. "Kyoko, I can't see this. If you folks all want us to 'reintegrate' so badly, then why the devil didn't you contact us a hundred years ago?"

"But SLIT has been practical for less than forty years." The citizen looked flustered. "On a routine basis, that is. Besides, SLIT stations are difficult to construct in certain regions; space fold dynamics, you see . . . do you know anything about elementary particles?"

"Quarks?"

"Quarks, composed of rishons, composed of sliptons. Sliptons bear a property designated 'emptiness.' A slipton with this property may 'slip' through intersecting folds of space and resonate between two loci which may be light-years apart in real-space."

"So it emits gravity waves?"

"Yes, and if enough energy is applied, the locus expands into an 'empty' shell through which the particle may slip out altogether. But the shell remains as a gravity well. It's analogous to an electron, which acts as a well of electrical field, no? The field lines converge at one point and emerge at the complementary point, which contains an antiparticle."

"So if the locus expands enough—"

Just then, Adjustor Maio appeared in front of her, bright as life. "Allison? Your friends are returning to Foxfield now; one feels unwell. You are welcome to stay, of course . . ."

Allison stared for a minute at the talking hologram before the message sank in. Some one was sick; it must be Seth, she thought. "Tell them I'm coming, right away." She turned on her heel and started to run out of the chamber, but she misjudged her weight and lost her footing on the smooth floor.

The next thing she knew, she was regaining consciousness while the ship doctor's face loomed above her. "You must have jarred the regulator," Rissa told her, "since your credometer registered anomalous signals. You'll be all right; but do stop by for a checkup some time, just in case."

Allison and Seth dragged their feet in exhaustion as they hiked up Georgeville Road to the Tech Center Hill. The sun near its zenith beat down without mercy, its heat widening the fissures which scarred the pavement.

"They're not people," Seth said. "They're all machines."

"What?" Allison wiped her forehead, where streams of sweat stung her eyes. "Don't be silly. The 'citizens' are people, just like us; they breathe and eat."

"And sleep? I'll bet they don't sleep. Something has to be wrong, you saw that."

The System didn't sleep . . . Allison sighed. "Seth, you've lived long enough with the commensals; when will you learn some patience? If something *is* wrong, we'd sure as hell better find out what, exactly, before we confront it."

Seth's eyes burned. "I *feel* they're wrong, Sonny. Isn't that enough?"

"Sh." She crossed his lips with her finger before opening the door to the house. She did not like her son to hear them argue.

In the kitchen, Dave's papers fanned out over the table, where he studied for Clifford's exams the next west-day. He jumped up immediately. "Hey, Mom, how was the ship? Did you meet any artists? When can we go back to Earth?"

"Not before bedtime." Allison glanced at the wurraburra on the floor, sucking the remains out of a cooking pot. "David," she complained, "you know that Rufus will eat everything in sight, if you let him."

"Aw, Mom, what's the matter now?"

The room darkened as she drew the dense moss-fiber shades against antinight. "We've had a long day," she said.

"No, you haven't," said Dave. "The 'day' isn't half done yet."

V. Belshazzar's Feast

By the time they awakened, dense clouds had blown in from the northern shrublands. Allison sipped her tea and stared out the kitchen window at the dismal sky. Her head ached because she had slept poorly, her mind flooded with twisted images and unfamiliar ideas.

She remembered the commensal. "How is Ghareshl?" she asked Seth.

He regarded her from across the table. "She survived. She was heading northward, last I saw."

"I see." Allison felt much relieved. "She would know if anything physiological were messed up; commensals always do."

"She'll conjoin soon, though," Seth pointed out.

"That's right. I guess she's more sensitive than usual."

"Also more vulnerable."

Allison tightened her lips. She rose from the table and rinsed out her tea mug. She then reached up above the sink for a jar of scent pods, on the shelf between bottles of cooking oil and ginger ale. She removed one of the maroon-husked pods, replaced the jar and left the kitchen. In the hallway she tripped over the curled up wurraburra, who extended an eye-foot or two and groaned drowsily. She stepped out the door and winced at the thick odor of damp ground moss.

No rain fell as yet, though massive storm clouds hung overhead like an unvoiced question. Allison snapped the pod open and held it upward until the contents had evaporated. The volatile compound was a unique signal for Ghareshl; if the Fraction detected it, she would come when she could. Its effective range was at least a hundred kilometers, but she couldn't have traveled a tenth that far since yesterday.

As Allison turned back to the house she nearly collided with Dave as he rushed out the door, dropping a schoolbook. "I'm late, Mom," he called as he retrieved the book.

"Well, don't miss your exams. Did you feed Rufus, and the chickens?"

"Sure, Mom."

"And don't draw any more portraits of your uncle in your notebooks."

"*No*, Mom. Don't forget your Fifth Query!" He skipped on down the hill.

The Fifth Query called for "simplicity in speech . . ." Allison sighed and wondered whether anything would ever be simple again. She reentered the kitchen and caught sight of that curious wristband on the counter; the "credometer," Kyoko had called it. She fingered it reflectively. The credit figure, now about fifty thousand, had dropped by about five percent overnight.

Seth was rinsing dishes in the sink; he turned to stare at her. "You're not going to touch *that* again, are you?"

Allison frowned and twisted the band into a figure eight. "I want to know how it works. I'll give the Tech Center folks a look at it."

Allison sat at the terminal and tried to concentrate on the numbers as they spewed across the screen. The Mawrford Mine ore location analysis had turned out to be a devilish problem. The results were crucial, since precious time and energy might be wasted if the predicted deposits failed to show up. She massaged her aching forehead as she lost her place on the screen.

She heard the outer door open and wet rubbers squeak in the corridor as her coworkers approached the computer room.

"Hi, Allison," called Noreen Connaught as she shook out her curls and hung up her raincoat. She was joined by Bill Daniels, the machinist who had welcomed with enthusiasm the arrival of the space visitors.

47

"Allison," Noreen exclaimed, "how can you possibly go back to that stuff when the whole world's changed overnight?"

Allison's lips tensed. "Work goes on; we still need iron, you know. Bill, take a look at that." She nodded toward the decwriter.

Bill picked up the printouts. "Test runs on the drill bits for Blydentown?" He scratched his chin.

"Right. The abrasion resistance doesn't look so hot."

He nodded. "I feared as much. That module is a fossil, anyhow. Maybe our new frog-suit friends will replace it for us."

Allison stood up, her features taut. "No, that's *not* the attitude we need around here. They're not to replace *anything*, do you understand?" She rose and walked quickly to the window by her desk, where she forced open the creaking frame. The gust of fresh air helped clear her head, though it still reeked of wet moss. Rain was falling now, lightly but steadily. Allison shivered, for she disliked rain, the implacable flood from the sky; rain swelled rivers and washed away homes and dreams.

Noreen walked over. "Allison, what's the matter?" she whispered. "Just a suggestion."

Allison said nothing at first. Then she turned and raised her left arm. "Can you guess what this is?" she asked.

Noreen blinked, then peered at the object. "It looks like an antique watchband, to me."

"Close—not a chronometer, but a 'credometer.'" She half smiled. "It's from the ship."

"Really? A 'credometer'—what does it measure, your faith?"

"For all I know. Let's see; it measures 'work performance,' whatever that means, and medical state—heartbeat, body temperature, the works. It all feeds into their System, somewhere."

Bill's face lit up at this. "That's got to be the best emergency setup I ever heard of. You could relay everything right back to Doc Frances at the Medical Center."

"Well, now," Allison wryly observed, "don't wish

any emergencies on us just to try out your skill."
Frances had insisted on training one of the Tech Center staff as a paramedic, after the lightning fire on the hill last year.

A buzzer rang from the hallway. "Who could that be?" Noreen wondered. "Nobody stops at the front door around here." The three of them went to see.

Allison's jaw dropped. On the doorstep stood Kyoko and two other citizens—and each of them wore a precisely tailored version of Allison's own beige suit, which she had worn at the landing site just two days before. The outfits matched hers in detail, down to the brownish moss stain on the left pants leg.

". . . and we have come to install your *Shosa-five* transcomm," Kyoko was saying. "Is something wrong? Is our apparel appropriate for Foxfield? I hope we haven't missed something important."

Allison collected her thoughts and shook her head, avoiding the eyes of her coworkers. "I guess we don't usually, er—that is, we don't produce clothes like machine parts here. Besides," she added, "it might help my reputation if you let me launder my things before you copy them."

Now it was the citizen's turn to look sheepish. "So sorry. Shall we go back and—"

"No, never mind. Now, what's this item you've brought?" she asked guardedly.

"A transcomm, as Silva promised, so that you can communicate with anyone in UNI."

They walked out across the soggy hillside to see the structure which the citizens had somehow deposited from the sky. It was shiny and round, like an ice mold inverted from a bowl. There was no apparent entryway.

"How do you get inside?" Allison asked. "Call-in 'Open Sesame'?"

A panel slid aside and a set of stairs extended to the ground.

"Just 'Open' will do well enough," said Kyoko, "if you wear a 'credo.' Let's check that everything's in order."

One assistant monitored the side of the transcomm with some sort of instrument, though Allison could not imagine what she might be checking. Kyoko led the Foxfielders inside; the interior looked similar to the place which Allison had seen on the ship. Kyoko issued commands which caused the lighting to fluctuate; then a luminous cylinder sprang up around the chamber. As if by magic, numerals appeared one by one on the curved surface.

Bill and Noreen were entranced. "Talk about Belshazzar's feast," Bill muttered.

"The System is the ultimate university, or information center," Kyoko explained. "You will soon be using it to learn all about our modern world; for instance, you'll discover all the applications of slipton technology . . ."

Then holographic models appeared in succession: space-lattice interactive transmitters, matter transporters which emitted gravity waves, even gravity converters which tapped the peculiar forces of neutron stars. But the most breathtaking sight was the stratogeyser, which drew energy from the solar surface and funneled it into a reservoir on planet Earth. As the transcomm walls receded, the stratogeyser appeared in the distance; it's collector tower dominated the sky like a giant silver chalice.

Allison remembered something. "Stratogeyser—was that what exploded on Earth, according to your newscast?"

Kyoko frowned. "Yes, partial thermolysis occurred. A solar flare overloaded the collector; it shouldn't have happened, the engineers were at fault. Now I'll get 'credos' for you, so that you may call the System yourselves, no?"

A compartment opened in the seamless chamber surface, spitting out wristbands for Noreen and Bill.

"Questor Lu Ting-yi," stated the System voice, "from China Sector, Terra, requests bimodal interview with Foxfield citizens. Accept call?"

Allison looked uncertainly at Kyoko.

"Well," Kyoko said, "do you wish to talk to a Terran, or not?"

"Sure, why not?" said Noreen. "Accept the call."

The image of a woman appeared and flickered for a moment, then became steady. "Hello, is Allison

Thorne there? I'm so pleased to be able to talk with you at last; we're all so curious about you people . . ." She wore a straight-cut robe of pale violet which struck Allison as exotic, but reassured her in one sense; it was good to see that not all UNI citizens stuck to frog-suits.

"Please tell us," said the woman, "how do you people feel, now that civilization has returned to planet Aurora?"

"Aurora? I don't understand," Allison said.

A few seconds of time lag passed before her face showed comprehension. "Oh, I'm sorry; that's what we call it, because that's what your planet looks like whenever we—" The image flickered once more. "The transmission is poor; you don't yet have local storm control. How do you manage to keep your community together, without a System network? How do you communicate?"

"Well," said Allison, "we visit each other. We have Meetings to talk about things."

"You mean physical translocation? How brave you must be, to rely on that."

Bill added, "We do have telephones."

"Telephones!" The citizen smiled and shook her head. "You must be accustomed to harsh circumstances. We've even seen satellite transmissions of women on Foxfield who bear children alive, as 'floaters' do; is that routine, for you?"

Allison and Noreen exchanged incredulous glances. "Well, how else do you do it?" Allison demanded.

"In foetal incubators; they're so much safer. But of course," she hastened to add, "the natural process is reasonable in your case."

"It's not perfectly natural, with us," Bill qualified. "There's artificial insemination with a gene bank from Earth. Otherwise, we'd see genetic drift in no time."

"Oh." The citizen seemed puzzled. "In that case, why have you reproduced males, in your struggle for survival?"

That left the Foxfielders speechless. Before anyone could come up with a response, the citizen shot a quick look at her credometer. "Excuse me," she said, "I'm near my limit; the Adjustors still keep a high

51

credit barrier on Foxfield calls. Thank you so much for—" She disappeared.

The Foxfielders pounced on Kyoko with their questions. "Are there really no more men left?" Noreen exclaimed. "What's a 'floater'?" Allison wanted to know.

Kyoko held up her hands. "Wait, it's too much at once. That's why the credit is steep—to prevent cultural shock from a deluge of calls."

"If there aren't any men left," said Bill, "I'd just as soon know right away."

"Of course there are men; you met Casimir yesterday, no? It is true that Terrans tried to terminate the male sex after the Last War, because they blamed traditional male values for the history of violent conflict which led inescapably to disaster. Psychosynchrony, however, invalidated this belief—in part, at least."

"Thank goodness for that. What is a 'floater'?" Allison repeated.

"Floaters are not registered citizens and don't wear credometers. It's hard to keep track of such stray people, among hundreds of millions. But foetal incubation is so convenient; the System can tell you all about it."

To keep track of people, of hundreds of millions; was that what credometers were for, Allison wondered. Then her thoughts returned to the workload at the Tech Center, and she gave her coworkers a meaningful look. "I suggest that we tear ourselves away from this feast of technology, for now—at least until the Blydentown order gets done."

Outside the transcomm, the rain fell steadily. Nonetheless a group of determined onlookers huddled together in mackintoshes and umbrellas, at a respectful distance. A couple of commensals were there, too, standing like inside-out umbrellas with their coronas cupped to receive the cleansing moisture.

"Hello there, Friends," called Allison's aunt from across Georgeville. "I hiked all the way up here just to come see your blessed outer-space telephone."

"Well—" Allison wished the news had not gotten

out so fast. But Kyoko said, "Go on inside and take a look. The assistants will take care."

"Much obliged. Do take my umbrella, now, you'll need it," the Foxfielder cheerfully added.

Kyoko declined, however. "I have a rain shield," she explained. Sure enough, the beige suit was bone dry.

Allison squinted at the commensals and recognized one of them. "It's Ghareshl!" she called out, and she ran forward, ignoring the rain. *"Where from, Ghareshl?"* she signaled.

"Forest; colder place. One seeks conjoin-mates." The commensal's outer fronds had thickened and turned deeper shades of green, sure signs that she would conjoin soon, as Seth had indicated. *"Fraction here seeks you,"* Ghareshl went on. She brushed against her companion, a commensal who was visibly shorter than she but had longer foliage. *"She shares memory."*

Kyoko asked, "Did she say, 'shares memory-like'?"

Allison shook her head. "Their interpretation of objects is confusing. The One seems to use adjectives, mostly, so that objects are 'substantiated' adjectives. A 'thing' in our terms would be considered a 'vessel' or a 'wave' of substance."

"I see."

"If they share memory, they must share ancestry several conjoins back," said Allison. *"What name?"* she signaled.

"Thiranne," signaled the newcomer. *"From jungle by ocean. You are blood-sharing wave-form Hand?"*

Allison paused, uncertain.

"Al-lis-on-thorn," corrected Ghareshl.

Thiranne's signals contained unusual nuances characteristic of the far region from which she came. *"One remembers cold place,"* she went on, *"by river; sweeping over land. Brown hand reaches out; five fingers, blood-sharer's hand. It pulls one out of rushing water."*

Allison's scalp prickled. *"My hand?"* she asked. *"How do you know?"*

"Scent is of you."

"Your scent," Ghareshl echoed. "This *Fraction rec-*

53

ognized it," she added with an almost human ego emphasis.

"Amazing," said Allison aloud as she wiped the streaming rain from her face. "That must have been half a dozen conjoins past, at least. They do it every two or three years, each Fraction, and their identities mix. I don't remember her name, just now, but it was a predecessor of Ghareshl whom I pulled from the flood of the Sixth Settlement." After Dave was safe, she had helped others; but some had never been found.

"Her ancestor, too," added Ghareshl.

Taken aback, she reminded herself of these creatures' perception. They picked up human words at times, whether by sound or by lip-reading she was never sure. She watched them sway in the rain, as though to hidden music. At one point they both folded up their coronas.

" *'One exists, you exist, world exists,' "* they signaled formally.

" *'Existence affirmed,' "* Allison responded correctly.

The fronds relaxed.

"You travel far, Thiranne."

"Yes. All go north for seeding."

"Of course. Best wishes for your seeding. Any news from the Dwelling?"

"Great excitement over new blood-sharers from the sky," signaled Thiranne. *"You,"* she added, indicating Kyoko. *"You come from the sky, though frog-skin not visible."*

Allison squirmed at this reference which she knew was derived from conversation with Friends.

Kyoko merely nodded, and signaled, *"Wear underneath."* She unbuttoned her jacket, and the dark suit appeared, snug against her neck.

"Don't you get hot in your long underwear?" Allison asked.

"Only if the thermostat breaks down."

"No rain falls on you," observed Thiranne. *"Why? Energy-wave generation?"* she shrewdly suggested.

Ghareshl quickly added, *"Don't blame rain! Disgusting wave frequencies. Interfere with . . ."*

"Too sensitive . . ." Thiranne began.

Allison said, "I think they've gone back to chemisense exchange. If Seth were here, he might be able to pick up some of it—he's practiced ever since he was little. But it's beyond me."

Without further comment the two commensals flowed off across the tangled ground moss.

Sheets of rain fell, and fiery skeletons crossed the horizon, though the rain poured so hard that its sound nearly drowned out the thunder. Allison raced back to the computer room and rummaged for a towel. There was none, so she wrung out her hair in printout paper.

"Just don't use my latest output," Noreen warned.

Kyoko came in to point out ways in which the System might coordinate services with those of the Tech Center. Allison watched her delicate fingers gesturing as she spoke while her credit number flashed. Noreen's arm also bore a credometer now. As the three women stood together, Allison was reminded briefly of the triplet of figures which had crowned Rodin's "Gates."

"For one thing," Kyoko was saying, "we'll be able to divert inconvenient thunderstorms, once we've got the feel of Foxfield weather patterns—"

An alarm sounded. Allison checked the master plan above her desk; a light was blinking for the Multiform room. "Excuse me," she muttered and hurried out to the manufacturing complex. Water was seeping into the corridors, and in the main room the rain poured through a jagged gash in the ceiling where the roof had caved in. Two of the shop workers were trying to rig a temporary covering, but one lay silent on the soaking floor strewn with solar panel splinters.

Bill looked up. "A piece of glass half sliced Ruth's leg off. I don't know if we can move her—"

"Well, we'll have to try, won't we? We can't do much for her here." Allison's hands clenched and she grew cold as she saw the blood seeping out into the turbid pool. She called the other workers to help drive the victim down to the Medical Center if possible.

Then she had to attend to the machinery, for the

survival of the colony depended upon its function. First, the water had to go; some one had set up the emergency pump, but it was not yet pulling full strength. So she wrenched the valves and unclogged one of them, and the line sputtered and gurgled as it sucked the oil-slicked liquid away. She prayed that none of the precious die cavities would be damaged. Then she climbed to the roof to figure out which of the structural layers had given way. She had repaired some of the solar panels battered by fist-sized hailstones last week, but had not realized how seriously the roof frame had been weakened.

As the debris was cleared away, Allison methodically inspected the equipment to assess the damage. Noreen stopped by after an hour or so to tell her that Ruth was in fair condition at the Medical Center. Seth returned from his sojourn among the commensals.

"How does it look?" Seth gravely asked.

Allison leaned against the dirt-spattered wall and wiped her hands on her coveralls. "Could be worse," she said slowly. "The die casting piston looks intact. But I can't tell for sure."

"Why not?"

"The monitor's completely shot."

Noreen nodded. "The servo link with the computer complex is dead, because the circuitry is jammed at this end. If we can't control it, it's no use."

Seth crossed his arms. "What does this mean?" he asked his niece. "No more nails and screws?"

"Or needles, or scalpels. Until it's fixed."

"If it's fixed," Allison quietly amended.

"You've fixed it before," Seth pointed out.

"It was never this bad, before."

They were silent for some time. Allison reflected yet again on the central absurdity of Foxfield—the colonists had not been expected to make it completely on their own. The original plan had called for reinforcements to be sent if the settlers survived. That fact, buried in the Records, was one which even Clifford rarely talked about.

Noreen looked up. "Well," she declared, "the Lord will provide. Be thankful at least that the storm's moved out—did you ever see the like? I've never seen a storm disappear so fast."

Allison went to the window. She had not even realized that sunshine now streamed into the devastated room. Outside, there was not a cloud in the sky.

A voice crackled. "Questor Casimir Stroem."

"What's that?" Allison was startled; it sounded like the System voice, but Kyoko had left hours ago, and the transcomm was across the hill. The voice repeated, and she realized that it came from her credometer. "All right, I accept," she said.

"Friend Allison, we tried all day to get rid of that storm for you." The biosphere analyst's voice sounded contrite. "We haven't completely solved Foxfield's weather dynamics. It's a shame we failed to manage the storm sooner, since I see how much damage occurred in your shop. But don't worry about loss of function; we'll send you any supplies you need, and eventually . . ."

So they could *see* everything from a credometer, even outside a transcomm, Allison realized. They could have watched her ever since she got up that morning.

In the kitchen, Allison stirred the soup and wondered why Dave was late.

"Will you let them replace it?" Seth challenged.

"I can't say. We'll ask the Meeting." Her credometer was tucked away in another room.

The door burst open as Dave came in. "Mom, I have to eat fast," he gasped. "I'm missing the show—"

"Hold on, now; what's the rush? Feed Rufus and do your homework."

"Homework? But Mom, it's nearly summer." Dave spooned soup into his dish. "There's this fantastic show in the transcomm, all about space ships and—"

She turned and stared at his wrist. "David . . . is that what I think it is?"

"It's a 'credometer.' They gave it to me."

"Well, I'll be goddamned. Take it off."

"What?"

"Just take it off, right now."

57

"Why, Mom?" he cried.

"I said *now."* She grasped his arm, pulled the band off and tossed it onto the counter.

"Ow!" He started to sob.

"David, you don't know what that thing *does.* It lets the whole galaxy watch you at any time—"

"So what?" Dave stamped his foot. "It's not *fair,* Mom. For the first time in ages something fun comes along, and you want to squash it."

Seth warned, "You'd better listen to your mother, now that she's talking sense."

Allison winced but added, "I'll return the wrist-thing right now, so it doesn't drain all your credit away." She picked up the credometer, fetched her own from the other room and marched out of the house. Seth followed and Dave tagged behind, still protesting.

"Open, *Belshazzar!"* she ordered.

The transcomm panel opened, then shut as soon as they had entered. Bill and Noreen stood inside, but Allison could barely see them in the darkness. Her surroundings seemed to stretch out into infinite space, filled with pinpoint stars as if the spectators were floating among them.

A silver comet plunged downward through the starry vault. It approached and grew until it seemed to halt before them, and as it did so the entire cosmic view rotated steadily. Allison saw that the object was a solid projectile with stripes of blue and gold, criss-crossed by dark lines like crackled glaze on earthenware.

"Pleiades ship Darter-seven," a voice announced. "Now let's have a spot with the pilot."

Two luminous bubbles expanded in the darkness. The left one contained the announcer, a man who wore loose-fitting straight-cut clothes. The other inset showed a pilot in a frog-suit striped with blue and gold. He sat before an array of view screens in a control room austerely styled, similar to that of a shuttle craft.

"We're speaking with Ran Dadachanji, pilot Darter-seven for the Pleiades," the announcer told the audience. "Ran, what's your strategy? Do you head for Phobos or Deimos, at this point?"

"Well, Jord, I can't take chances at this point, since half my power's knocked out, so I'll have to head straight for Deimos . . ." His eyes never left the view screen.

"Sounds tough, Ran; good thing the Archons can't hear us. Do you think you'll outrun them?"

"The Archons have lost four ships, so far—three manned, one auto—that leaves three more auto limping out there somewhere, but as I see it a live pilot can outrun three auto any day."

"That's the spirit, Ran; where there's life, there's hope, so give them a run for it. Back outside, now, I see Mars shaping up in the third octant . . ."

Sure enough, a reddish brown disc was expanding below.

". . . and where planet Mars is, moon Deimos can't be far behind. But Deimos *is* behind Mars yet, from this angle, and where are those Archons? Ah, there they are."

Three tiny "comets" appeared above the mottled Mars horizon, which now filled half the chamber and wobbled across the figures of the watching Foxfielders.

"Looks like we've not seen the end yet—and what a ringside seat for the Martians! All up to you, Ran."

The announcer vanished, but the inset of the ship interior expanded somewhat. Now Allison could make out the tense face of the pilot as he watched his own view of darkness.

The blue- and gold-striped vessel veered off to the right as three new ships closed in, twisting their fuel trails in a blazing dance.

A thunderclap hit the ship interior; then another, and another, in deafening sequence. The final explosion tore apart the control board and hurled the pilot across the chamber, landing him in the foreground at a crazy angle. His form was quite still, his eyes stared, and his mouth lay ajar as though about to form sounds which never came. The surrounding debris was streaked with crimson.

The inset winked out while a silent ball of fire engulfed the striped ship. Allison stared in shock at the conflagration. The three comet trails turned as one, back toward Mars.

"That's it for the Darter," the announcer stated. "Our last on-board recorder just gave out. But wait a minute—here's the latest System report: Archon third automatic touched off bounds, that is, within five hundred kilometers of inhabited Martian surface, for just eighteen seconds, and therefore disqualified. The winner of the Mars Classic is—the Pleiades!"

A brightly lit studio faded in, replacing the view of fire-stained space. The announcer sat in a chair across from a woman whose suit displayed the colors of the exploded ship. "Coach Karjanis," he said to her, "tell us how you feel about winning the Mars Classic this year."

She nodded gravely. "The mix of triumph and sadness is especially hard to take, this year. We haven't lost a whole squad in one game since seventy-two. That Dadachanji, now, he was one of the finest players I've seen. You saw him maneuver that Archon out of bounds, and he knew it was a sacrifice, too. Stargo always brings out the best in young citizens."

"True," said the announcer, "but the attrition rate ran to twenty percent last year, overall. Is it really necessary to sustain such losses?"

The coach leaned forward. "The fact is, Jord, that's what draws players to the Stargo games. In the old days, brave young people could get into their coats of armor or their warplanes or whatever, and take on the ultimate test. Now that we proscribe that stuff, what's left to risk your life for? Wasting away on Vinlandia? Policing the floaters?"

"I see what you're getting at."

She pounded her fist on an armrest. "The *competitive spirit*—that's what made our species great. Competition keeps the race healthy; without it, we'd still be stuck back on one little planet for—"

Allison shook herself. "Call-out. *Call-out,*" she ordered in a hoarse voice.

The images dissolved into bluish light. Allison stared ahead, trying to make sense of what she had seen.

At last Bill muttered something about getting back home, since it was late.

"A wise idea," she agreed.

"I'll take the night shift," Noreen whispered.

They straggled outside in the dim evening. Dave grabbed Allison's arm. "Mom . . . he didn't really die, did he?"

"What do you think, David?"

"There was *blood* all over."

She ruffled his sandy hair. "They're light-years away, now, remember? Go on inside, and finish your supper."

"Aren't you coming, too, Mom? I don't want to be alone."

"We'll be in soon."

The screen door clanged behind Dave as he entered the house. Allison paused on the doorstep with Seth, and a thought struck her; *all nations suffered greatly,* the Adjustor had said. But Mars was no Earth nation; Mars had escaped the worst of the Last War.

They sat down together on the cold step. At the horizon Allison watched the faint sunset aurora, violet from nitrogen fluorescence. *Mene, Mene, tekel, upharsin . . . the days of your kingdom are numbered and brought to an end.* Whose kingdom, she wondered.

"Sonnie?"

"Yes?"

"Why are you crying?"

"Because you are, Seth."

They embraced and held each other long after Wheelwright's last light had died away.

VI. Answer the Light

Allison surveyed the familiar faces of Friends gathered for midweek worship. Lowell sat with John Poyser and his two sons; the Crain youngsters fidgeted next to their parents; Noah Rowntree, with his daughter, stared pensively into the middle distance. Her engaged nephew and cousin sat serenely together off to the right, where the side benches faced inward. Allison sat with Dave that day; Seth had departed early that morning for Coral Vale, to commune with the Dwelling, she guessed. The spectacle in the transcomm had been the last straw for him. Nonetheless, she hoped he would collect his thoughts and return soon.

She tried to concentrate, to center down. What thoughts moved the others, today, she wondered. The Light, that inner something that guided one, that held one together, that . . . kept one going? Desultory images filled her mind: level farms, clattering decwriters, the people she loved, working, resting and arguing. Were those daily things what kept her going? In part, yes—but that was not the Light.

The Hall was so still, now, that she could hear her neighbors breathing, a whispering song which rose and fell like the ocean waves. She had seen an ocean only in the video records, but that was how she had remembered it.

> *In vain I send*
> *My soul into the dark, where never burn*
> *The lamps of science, nor the natural light*
> *Of Reason's sun and stars.*

Those words were underlined in a book she had owned once, an old yellowed volume from her grandmother, who had sorely missed the literary world on Earth. Where was that book now? Of course—gone with the flood. Gone with Joshua . . . where was he, now?

An image came to her mind, not of Joshua's death, since they had never recovered his body, but of the stranger the night before, lying crushed and bleeding on the floor of a dying ship. Why? What right did he have to kill himself off that way?

She always seemed to find memories painful, even after many years. The commensals were different; they never seemed to mind. Or if they did feel such pain, they never communicated it to humans.

Perhaps it was because each Fraction had to combine so many details from so many memories, like

Thiranne's memory of the hand. Five Fractions, five memories intermingled each time they conjoined; if there were as much pain as in human memories, how could they bear it? Or did they choose to join the Dwelling when memory's weight grew too heavy?

No wonder they scarcely worried about "individuals" after all that. If an individual Fraction were lost, most of her essence would remain, stored in pieces, at least, among many other Fractions. But the individual who was Joshua was *gone* absolutely, except for the visions which haunted her still, despite her love for Seth. How could she be sure they were even accurate, now; perhaps time had twisted them as artfully as those portraits which Dave drew to infuriate his elders.

He was gone; the Lord had seen fit to take him away. But why, Lord, why so young? *Are you really there, Lord? Hello, I'm Allison Thorne; is anybody there?*

Noah was moved to speak. He rose and crossed his arms. "I've been thinking today about the events of the past three days," he began, "the arrival of our guests from the stars. I feel that we must seem strange to them in some ways. They must want to ask, 'What kind of folks are you Quakers anyway? Why do you all sit there for an hour in those funny little benches twice a week, when you could be out plowing your farms?' "

He paused and swallowed once, then went on. "I'm not sure how to describe something which seems as basic to me as the need to breathe. And as people can only breathe a little at a time, so each individual may hold but a fraction of the Light, precious as it is.

"But what *is* this Light within that we speak of? It is something close to 'conscience' . . . perhaps, the other-worldly part of conscience. George Fox himself offered many names for it: the 'Wisdom,' the 'Truth's Voice,' the 'Love which bears all things.' The phrase which speaks best to me is, 'that of God in every one.' That's what I think of when I seek the Light."

He sat down.

It occurred to Allison that she had given little thought to the way UNI citizens might perceive

Friends. Perhaps they saw her people as backward, superstitious, or simply neurotic. Yet how did they manage *without* the Light? She herself could scarcely imagine life without Meeting.

Edward Crain stood up and walked over to the side door. Dave and the other children rose immediately and filed out after him for classroom instruction. Their patience for stillness was not to be taxed for a whole hour.

Anne was the next to rise. "In seeking the Light," she said, "the crucial element is that of sharing, of putting together so that the whole is greater than the sum of the parts. As Jesus said, 'Where two or three are gathered in my name, there am I in the midst of them.' That is what a Meeting is for. John Greenleaf Whittier described a Meeting in this way:

> *The strength of mutual purpose pleads*
> *More earnestly our common needs;*
> *And from the silence multiplied*
> *By these still forms on either side,*
> *The world that time and sense have known*
> *Falls off and leaves us God alone.*

Allison nodded, recalling those lines, too, from her lost volume. They connected with her own favorite image of silent worship as the purest fraction in a distillation, the most "distilled" form of communication. But how could any of this speak to someone like Kyoko, for whom "communication" was a transcomm? Or to that stranger, thrown across a doomed ship?

Bill rose quickly, almost overeager. "Those words, written centuries ago—it just struck me how timeless they are. 'Forms' could mean any of us: Quakers, non-Quakers, even the 'mensals. God made all of us—and the remarkable thing is that the more we learn about science, the more science shows us just how special is this universe which He built for us."

Allison sighed and shut her eyes. She knew Bill well enough to know what was coming, and she did not like to hear it.

"Consider the background temperature of the universe, which is known to be about three degrees

Kelvin, barely above absolute zero. Now, why should the heat of the primeval explosion, which started the universe, have cooled down to just that amount throughout space? Well, it's obvious that if space were hotter than the boiling point of water, living things couldn't survive at all; in fact, if it were significantly greater than three degrees, even galaxies couldn't have formed very well, because the gravity of all the heat radiation would have outweighed that of stellar matter. On the other hand, were it a bit colder, the primeval mass would have been too smooth to separate out and coalesce into stars. Is it just an accident that God set the thermostat just right for us?

"Another thing: what about the ratio between the strengths of the electromagnetic and gravitational forces? It just happens to be about ten to the fortieth power—an enormous number which none of our physical theories can account for. Yet the age of the universe, about nine billion years, is also about ten to the fortieth times larger than the smallest natural time unit, namely, the time taken by light to cross a nuclear distance. Why should this incredible symmetry be so? Is it possible that the Lord is trying to tell us something?

"Surely the more we learn about the natural world, the more of God's hand we see in it. Science gives endless witness to the Light."

Allison shifted restlessly, and she was relieved when Bill's message had ended. Of course, the background temperature was just right for "us." If it were not, she figured, nobody would be here to worry about it, would they?

As for the present age of the universe, that was also roughly the average lifetime of a star: enough time for some stars to age and spew forth organic elements needed for life to arise, but not so long that other suns had all decayed before intelligent life had time to evolve on their planets. And what property governed the average stellar lifetime? The field strength ratio, of course. So, life had appeared when the time was right.

She checked herself then. Why should Bill's enthusiasm have annoyed her so much? It must have been because at one time, she, too, had worshiped the

Lamps of Science: the Earthly wonderworkers such as Edison, Curie and Einstein, who had seemed as mythic to her as Prometheus or Pandora, or the prophets of the Bible. And now? *In vain I send my soul into the dark . . .*

Breathing swelled and ebbed like a tide. The room's illumination wavered as clouds moved outside. The rain persisted, but perhaps it was trailing off.

"Who has access to the Light?"

Celia's hoarse voice had come from several rows behind. "We all know the answer, Friends," she went on. "Every one of us bears a part of it. Yet with all of this Light, why is there still darkness in the world—and what are we called to do about it?

"Let me tell you something which happened to me as a little girl on the *Plowshare*, just two years out from Earth. We had Meeting on the ship, and I remember the day I was told in class that messages of worship were spontaneous and in fact involuntary in nature, since the Lord used one as a vessel with which to pour out His meaning. This idea terrified me, because I felt sure that I would only make a fool of myself if ever the Lord tried such a thing with me!

"So for some weeks thereafter I refused to go to Meeting. I used to run and hide in the ship's hold among the granaries and chicken coops, and no one could make me come out, not even my parents.

"It was Rachel Coffin who found me at last, for she knew her way down there. She caught me and said, 'Celia, what are you doing down here? What right do you have to keep your own messages hidden away from everyone else? Remember the Sermon on the Mount; don't hide your Light in a chicken coop, but come out and share it with us.' And she took me back to the Meeting.

"Today I realize that 'everyone' means not just Foxfield Friends, but the entire galaxy, every citizen, every form of consciousness in it. Some manifestations of the Light may seem void, incomprehensible to us at first glance, just as the greater and lesser wavelengths of the radiant spectrum are invisible to our own eyes. But ultimately nothing is invisible to the inner vision.

"George Fox told us to 'walk cheerfully over the

world, answering that of God in every one.' So we are meant to go out into the larger world, even where it appears to see things differently from our own way. We must go to answer the Light wherever it may be found, and whatever the shape of its vessel."

Allison felt overwhelmed. How could one answer the Light of billions of people? You couldn't even learn all of their names, let alone get to know them. For that matter, how could she reach even one of them: a pilot who sent his vessel and others to death for the thrill of a game, a war-game among citizens who had forsworn war.

The Meeting was over before she knew it. Hands were clasping one after another, the children returned, and brief words were exchanged before Lowell rose for announcements.

"No infants born yet this week," Lowell said. "But of course we do have our UNI guests, as we all know by now. The crew of the *UNIS–11* extends an open invitation for us to visit the ship, and prophylaxis for oxygen shortage will be provided on request; if interested, please see Martha.

"Furthermore I've just been notified that a delegation of UNI Quakers expects to arrive on Saturday. A half-dozen individuals are expected, so if you've extra room in your home for a few days let me know.

"Other UNI-related matters will come under care of the Committee for Extraplanetary Concerns, which Martha will convene next Tuesday. Anything else?"

Letitia Mott, a Coral Vale woman, stood then. She was tall for a Foxfielder, and gaunt, and her eyes were dark like Seth's. "Friends know," she said, "that this is the time for conjoining among Fractions of the One. Her numbers are greater than usual this year, so I remind everyone to take care in your travels, especially northward, so as to avoid harm either to yourselves or to the new Splints."

"We appreciate your counsel," said Lowell. "Anne?"

Anne announced the spiritual retreat to be held at midsummer.

Then people flowed into the aisles, waving and chatting. Allison tried to reach Lowell, but Frances Poyser accosted her.

"Allison, I haven't seen you for days." Frances embraced her, then looked at her sternly. The doctor's features were sharp and economical, like the tip of a pen. "Ruth is in bad shape. She'll be in bed for a while."

"But she will be all right? I'll stop by, before I head back."

Frances nodded. "I'll be out by then, on a case of chicken pox."

"Business as usual?"

"More or less. Rennie's foetal karyotype looks normal, praise the Lord; she was so worried about Down's syndrome."

"That's a chromosome defect? Like Gordie Daniels last year?"

"Quite rare; his was the first case I've seen. But the chance does rise for mothers your age, or Rennie's. And there's nothing I can do for it—nothing."

The mother's fear, Allison thought, would be especially sharp in any case; the father's genes, supplanted by the eugenic sperm bank, were never in question. "What about the UNI folks?" she asked. "Could they treat it, somehow? Or do they still practice ..."

"Heavens, no. They screen genetic defects at the *earliest* stage. In fact, they pick out their genes from a catalogue, if this Doctor Nduni is to be believed." She paused to give weight to her skepticism. Allison tried not to smile; it had been years since anyone had told Frances how to run things.

"That reminds me—Allison, I must get out to see that 'transcomm' gadget before long, since they insist on installing one at the Medical Center."

"Another one?" The programmer pressed her head, suddenly anxious.

"They say it is invaluable for emergencies. They would have brought it today, but I put my foot down; that's your corner, my dear, so I'll await your verdict. By the way, that Casimir Stroem showed up again, too; the young biosphere analyst, remember? At least he looks young to me, though looks are no guide any more, from what Rissa tells me."

She folded her arms. "Allison, do you know what else she told me?"

"I can't imagine."

"She said I won't have to wear glasses any more!" Frances glared through her sparkling lenses.

Allison blinked. "Well, Doc, that sounds like good news to me."

She threw back her head and laughed. "Of course, dear, don't mind me. All the same, why do you suppose I got into medicine in the first place? As a child it fascinated me to be afflicted with such a rare form of astigmatism. I understand they replace eyeballs at the drop of a hat these days—a profligate practice, to my mind."

She lowered her voice. "To change the subject— Allison, you can take a word from old Doc, now, can't you? About that Connaught girl. She burns the midnight oil too much these days; she'd do anything for you, you know, at the Center. But frankly, when's she going to start her family? Moderation, that's all; even you had your chance. It's not just her duty; she'll be sorry later."

Allison was saved from need to reply by Anne, who caught the doctor's arm.

"Frances," said Anne, "you've got to speak to her— Grandma Celia, I mean. She's gotten some crazy ideas into her head, mostly my fault, I'm afraid, but I know she'll listen to you . . ."

Allison then stepped backward, smack into Noah Rowntree.

"Whoa, there!" he warned. "Might spill a precious burden."

His daughter Becky squealed and bounced on his broad shoulders.

"Pardon me. How's she doing, these days?" Allison asked.

Noah set the child down gingerly. "Sleeps through the nights, but not the antinights, yet." His wife had succumbed to sunstroke while repairing a burst pipeline at high noon.

Allison squatted before the child so that their eyes were level. "Hi, there, Becky. Did you make that in class today?" she asked, noting a decorated apple in her chubby hand. Apples were among the few fruits successfully adapted to Foxfield, though the trees grew as stunted bushes.

Becky nodded.

"It's very good, Becky." The apple had a carved face and a black paper hat.

"It's a Quaker apple," the child volunteered.

"Oh, a Quaker doll, I see. Like the old Earth Quakers, who wore black clothes, right?"

"Quakers freed black slaves, too."

Noah grinned with pride. "Isn't she the learned one?"

In a fit of shyness the girl buried her face in his trouser leg.

"Thanks for finishing up WEATHERCAST," Noah added, referring to her latest program for the Resource Center. "It will serve us well for the next planting season."

Allison smiled. "Always glad to be useful."

Finally she left the Meeting room and found Lowell and Martha sipping tea in the annex. They listened gravely as Allison poured out her account of the catastrophe at the Tech Center, and the citizens' reaction to it. "The citizens want to help us out, but I'm beginning to wonder what we're getting into."

Lowell considered this. "It's only natural that they should help us. All people are one."

"Remember the Charter," said Martha. "They should have sent us help long before now, if they were able to do so."

"But that's not the question." Allison twisted her fingers, trying to find the words. "Can we live with them, Martha?"

"Live as Friends? We'll see. The Quaker citizens are coming; let's find out how they manage."

Allison still was determined to get rid of David's credometer. When she returned to the transcomm, however, this task proved unexpectedly difficult.

"Request unacceptable," the System voice told her. "Citizen David Thorne is not deceased."

She tried to control herself. "No one is more aware than I," she replied with outward calm, "that my son is alive and well. How does that fact relate to my request?"

"Each citizen at birth is issued a System credometer which she or he retains until moment of decease, as determined by the System monitor."

"But David didn't receive it at birth, so why can't he return it now? Things are different on Foxfield."

"Correct. You are referred to 'Special Status Foxfield,' UNI Board of Adjustors registered document three-one-one-zero . . ."

A pale wall of light encircled her, and the "document" spread out hieratically upon it.

Allison lost her patience. "I asked for an *explanation,* not an Egyptian tomb."

"Please rephrase your question."

"All right. In ten words or less, why can't I discontinue my son David's credometer?"

"You can, you did, and the action cost you credit."

So that's why her own credit level had dropped to the low thousands. Allison muttered an imprecation.

"Please rephrase your—"

"Cancel. Is Dave's 'credo' now permanently inactive?"

"No, David Throne is not deceased."

"I can't inactivate it?"

"Only by lethalization, which incurs extremely high loss of—"

"Cancel. In ten words or less, why can't I or anyone else *inactivate* a credometer before, er, decease of the wearer?"

"Because communication is an inalienable right of all intelligent beings."

Allison stared for some minutes. She took a look at the Special Status document, but gave up on the first sentence.

"All right," she decided. "Request communication with Kyoko Aseda, privacy level ten."

"Request holding . . . Request accepted."

A furnished room materialized over precisely half the chamber. Kyoko wore a straight-cut robe of floral design and sat on a mat before a very low table beside a painted screen. To her right sat two young girls with alert eyes and smooth black hair. The three of them rose immediately and bowed in unison.

"So pleased to see you, Allison," said Kyoko. "These are my daughters, Keiko and Michiko. We are at supper, now."

"I'm terribly sorry," Allison said, for she had no idea of what schedule the ship crew followed.

"Never mind," said Kyoko, "I'm glad to see you again. What can I do for you?"

"Well, I . . . it's about the credometer which you gave my son," Allison began. "As his mother I'm responsible for him, and—well I would have been happier if you'd spoken with me first, that's all."

"Oh, I see. Have I missed another local custom?"

The girls watched Allison gravely. The elder, Michiko, might have been Dave's age, perhaps a year or two older.

"Excuse me," Allison said, "I'm not sure I understand. Is parental responsibility a 'local custom'?"

"Some aspects inevitably are. The community also bears some responsibility, no?"

"Exactly. That's why I'd like to have Dave's System connection inactivated until we have considered the issue in Monthly Meeting."

Kyoko sipped from a small teacup. "Allison, it might help if you could describe your concerns for me. What might the Meeting have to fear?"

"Well the privacy problem is one thing; it takes time to learn how the whole thing works, to sort it out. And the strain of all these new things can be especially hard on a youngster like Dave. Two days ago he watched a show in the transcomm where the violent aspects were most distressing, and afterward he couldn't get to sleep all night. Furthermore, the 'credo' seems to permit direct input from anybody anywhere, who could call and tell him who knows what, and—I just can't allow that." Allison brushed down her overalls decisively.

"I see." Kyoko set down her teacup and clasped her hands. "I understand your concern now, and I would like you to understand the perspective of the greater UNI community. Each citizen is connected to the System from birth and remains so throughout life;

one grows up with it and accepts it. The System performs many essential functions, but its key role is to synchronize the needs and desires of two hundred million citizens."

Allison absorbed this number. "But don't you have the right to choose not to 'connect'?"

"Not if you're a citizen," Kyoko replied, "because you would interfere with the rights of other citizens. As on Foxfield, all UNI citizens depend upon one another. It's like the right to life."

"What about that show we saw? They were all blasting each other in spaceships. Or wasn't that for real?"

"If you renounce your right to life, that's another matter entirely. I assume you refer to the Stargo games; in that case, the players must release consent under well-specified conditions."

"You mean they can throw their own lives away like that, but they can't say 'no' to constant surveillance? How does that square with *inalienable* rights to life and freedom?"

"Communication is the first right. Life *is* communication. What is death but the irrevocable absence of communication? And the System keeps ninety-nine percent of our citizens within minutes of life-support at any moment; that's our affirmation of the right to life. Freedom, too, is communication. How can anyone be a prisoner when she can contact any person in the world at any time? Privacy is a luxury by comparison, though it's easy enough to raise a credit barrier, or to remove a credo for a limited time, as you did for David."

By now Allison felt thoroughly confused. "So what difference does it make, then? Suppose I just forget about Dave's credo?"

The System interrupted. "Questor Silva Maio," it announced. The scene in the transcomm split in two, with Kyoko on the left and the Adjustor on the right.

"Greetings, Friend Allison." Adjustor Maio's words, like her face, were polished as usual. "I see a possible short-term solution to your problem. Under Special Status provisions I may raise a special credit barrier against contact with undermature Foxfielders. This would prevent contact without parental consent, with perhaps ninety percent efficiency. Would this allay your fears?"

"Perhaps," said Allison guardedly, somewhat taken aback by this turn of events.

"Think it over. I could of course suspend further issuance of credometers on Foxfield."

"No, that wouldn't be fair. People have a right to choose, as I did, but they should know about the strings attached."

The Adjustor nodded, without a wrinkle in her smooth suit. "I thought you would feel that way. After all, why should such productive citizens as yourselves wish to hide the fact?"

Allison flushed as Adjustor Maio signed out. She was left alone with Kyoko and the two round-faced little girls, who kept perfectly still but seemed to take in everything. She reflected for some minutes in silence.

"Your silence is a strange thing for me," Kyoko observed suddenly. "The silence of your people when our shuttle first landed; even more so, the silence of your Meeting this afternoon."

She looked up. "You mean you were there today? I didn't see you—" She caught herself.

"I was there, nonetheless."

"No, you weren't," Allison coldly replied. The citizen seemed hurt, so she added more softly, "You have to participate to understand. You should come, next time."

"Will you trust me, if I come?"

Allison smiled in spite of herself.

"It reminded me of a Buddhist meditation hall," Kyoko went on, "but there, no communication is expected among the meditators."

"But communication is the key thing. *You* do it through 'emptiness,' we through 'silence.' "

Kyoko laughed in delight at this analogy and caressed the hair of one of her daughters, who were showing signs of restlessness at last.

Allison let them return to their supper. She wondered about the Buddhists and Quakers in UNI, and whether they lived "in the world, but not of it," as George Fox used to do. Of course, the modern Quakers would be very different from Foxfielders, as different as Foxfield was from the world George Fox knew. Still, they were Friends; how would they answer the Light?

VII. Informal Education

On Friday Allison continued the roof repairs and tried to catch up with the Tech Center backlog. Seth's absence depressed her, and the System relayed calls which unnerved her. People would call from bizarre places with equally bizarre questions which meant little to Allison except distraction from her work. After a while she placed a twenty-credit premium on acceptance, and was pleasantly surprised to find that it succeeded with little effect on her own credit level. The only questor who ignored it announced a referendum of some sort on a "Senior Self-determination Factor." She had no idea what that meant, either, and was too busy watching Deltron to bother to find out.

That anti-eve, Dave sat on the floor with Rufus, trying with little success to tie the wurraburra's eye-feet into knots.

"Dave?"

"What, Mom?"

Allison crouched beside him and held out his credometer. "Dave, I think you can have this back now. There will be certain restrictions, though—"

The boy tensed and gripped the wurraburra till it squealed. "I don't want it, Mom."

"You don't? Listen, Dave—"

"I don't *want* it. What if they come to kill me in there, or Rufus?"

"Now, Dave," she began softly, "you know that can't happen. It's all just images in there, like the videocaps, right? Besides, you don't have to go near the transcomm if you don't want to." And besides, she thought, no one could get away with calling her son an unproductive citizen.

By Saturday, a warm, summery air mass rested like a blanket over Georgeville and surrounding fields. It was a good morning to clean out the chicken coop behind the house, as Allison was doing.

She paused to stretch a moment and wiped her hands on her muddy overalls. Around the house, bushes seemed to have sprung up overnight, alive with rustling shapes and flying creatures which swarmed over the hill. The fibers of ground moss had grown into a tough, springy mass which became tricky to walk upon. Above the Center complex the radio telescope dish gleamed, a tantalizing reminder of projects which she had set aside for now.

Noreen's weekly newscast carried over from the radio in the kitchen. The UNI encounter took up most of this week's coverage, followed by the Tech Center accident. "Influenza outbreak," it went on, "sends six children home from school in Blydentown . . . 'Mensal Fractions converge in record numbers in the northern fields . . . Our latest forecast made possible by the new WEATHERCAST program: rain will hold off as warm front moves in, but electrical activity will shoot up early next week . . ."

The broadcast closed with the regular theme, an old American Shaker tune. " 'Tis the gift to be simple, 'tis the gift to be free . . ." Dave had a good ear, and he sang along with the radio as he mopped the kitchen floor before hiking across Georgeville to give a hand on Aunt Anne's farm. As Allison shoveled yet another load of organic filth into the recycler, she reflected that he had good reason to be cheerful, since she had let him off on this job for once. Those hens produced more dirt than eggs, that was for sure.

A bright object caught her eye as it settled downward through the sky. Allison stared in dismay at the shuttle; was Kyoko back again? Why had she not used the transcomm? Allison ran inside to rinse off and changed into a denim skirt and blouse. She slipped out the front door in time to see Casimir Stroem, the biosphere analyst, walking up the hill. Why should he be here, she wondered; to check out the storm damage which he had failed to prevent?

The citizen's cherubic curls shone in the rising sun. Wings on his ankles would turn him into Mercury, Allison thought, as she twirled a wisp of her own brown hair.

"Hello," she said, "I'm sorry; I had no idea you were coming. I was tending the hens; hope I don't smell too bad."

"No problem." His grin was infectious. "I would have called, but you raised your credit barrier to such a level that I figured it wasn't worth the expense."

She half smiled. "Got to get work done somehow. Tell me what else I've been up to lately."

"Not sure I dare. I heard about what Kyo did to you the other day, though. The clothes, I mean."

"Oh, that." Allison shrugged. *"Most* impressive."

"We had a good laugh over it. On Kyo's account, I mean; she's so particular on details. I could have warned her off, though personal taste is a slippery business. Hope I haven't done any worse, myself."

She examined his "local" outfit: short brownish jacket, trousers nondescript gray, of uncertain material.

"I fed in data," he added, "on a hundred specimens observed, then asked the System to generate a 'typical' suit and . . . you don't like it."

"Oh, it's not bad. For a first approximation. You might try Jem's place sometime. He's the tailor in Georgeville."

They both laughed. Casimir asked, "Is Friend Seth here today? I'd like to learn more about those commensals."

"Seth is away." Allison looked intently into his face. "Some of us feel . . . unsettled by recent events."

"Of course." He quietly added, "You must have expected that."

"We had little chance to 'expect' anything. It's you who've been watching us for ages."

"Just four years, from hundreds of kilometers out —no substitute for good fieldwork. Did you say you were tending poultry? Do you keep any other livestock?"

"Only chickens, for eggs. We've got a vegetable garden, too. Would you like to see?"

She led him around back to point out the rows of tomato plants and scrawny bean stalks, with a few meter-long yellow beans dangling. "Have to get after Dave to pick those," she apologized. "But it's nice to have extra greens when in season. Here are the chickens."

She unlatched a wire gate and three hens waddled out into the enclosure. "Come on, Abby, that's a good girl . . ."

Casimir clicked his fingers at them, and one came over to investigate.

"That one's Shadrach. She's the ornery one."

"Quite a name for a fowl."

"David named them Shadrach, Meshach and Abednego after he left them out one antinight and they nearly fried to death." Allison sighed. "They *are* a nuisance. Resource Committee periodically urges us to give them away because we can't get them to lay more than once a week. But Dave always throws a fit. He's lonely out here."

"Most of your families are larger, aren't they?"

Allison frowned. "That's what Ministry and Counsel gets after *me* for."

Casimir attracted the clucking birds like a Pied Piper. "Do you eat their meat?" he asked.

She shuddered. "No, we recycle them, like human bodies. Do you?"

"We have something called 'cultures' which are roughly like animal flesh grown as a plant; there are many varieties. You have no burial rites, then?"

"In the ground, you mean? Heavens, no; that stopped when they left on the *Plowshare*. Of course all fertilizer goes to the ground eventually, including the 'mensal stuff."

"I see."

"I'm sorry Ghareshl's not here; I think she's up north, conjoining at last."

"The mating process?" Casimir asked. "Why do commensals all migrate northward before conjoining?"

"Because that's where the Splints have to be 'born.' Splints form as seed embryos within a postconjunctive Fraction, who deposits them in the ground. They

78

sprout and grow like plants until autumn, when the daylight hours wane. This signal induces root conversion to motile pseudopods so that the organism can pull free from the soil.

"But if she sprouts too far south, where the sun varies less, limiting daylength will occur too late or not at all."

"So what happens then?"

Allison winced. "I've never witnessed a case, myself. Seth has. I understand it's a very slow death, like asphyxiation over a month or so."

"So they really did evolve from plants, then," Casimir mused. "But why the mind's eye would a plant evolve to be motile, and more incredible still, intelligent as well?"

"That's hard to say. I think plantlike species in general are more complex here than on Earth."

"Which is complex enough."

"But you should read Rachel Coffin's essay in the Records. She thought that at the time of the last ice age the uprooting of plants in the north would have enabled migration to warmer climates, and provided greater access to secondary nutrient supplies by scavenging."

"Couldn't be otherwise," Casimir agreed, "as far as nourishment goes, since true plants can't ever get up enough energy by photosynthesis to move around like animals."

Allison sighed. "I know the feeling. At times I'm convinced that *I'm* a 'true plant.'"

He chuckled. "Join the club: *Homo iners,* 'lazy man,' first true plant to evolve from a higher mammal. Coffin's theory sounds good," he added, "although it fails to explain why similar phenomena have not been observed on Terra or other planets."

Just then Rufus scampered over the ground and climbed like a monkey to Casimir's shoulder.

"That beast really does go for you," Allison observed. "It tends to avoid me, as a rule."

He pushed an eyefoot away from his face. "As I said, there's no accounting for taste—" As he tried to settle the creature, his foot caught in the web of moss,

79

and he nearly lost balance. He bent down to pull at the fibers. "This stuff is deceptively strong," he said.

"That's right," Allison agreed, "and its roots reach many meters down. Even commensals can barely digest it, with all their fancy chemistry."

"What sort of digestion do they have?"

"It's like a chemical factory which performs millions of chemical transformations on demand. Give a 'mensal a few molecules of virtually any organic compound, and she'll produce it in quantity, usually within minutes."

"Mind's eye, how do they manage it?"

"You tell us. You're the modern scientist," she pointed out. "Rachel thought that they might use magnetic resonance to observe chemical reactions. You familiar with that? The atomic nuclei and electrons align like magnets with an applied field, in two or more energy levels—it's a quantum effect. Then you induce transitions with radio frequencies, and the spectrum is highly sensitive to chemical composition."

"Yes," said Casimir, "we still use the technique as a diagnostic tool. But how would a commensal make a radio transmitter, or a high-field magnet? The planetary field? Granted a hundred gauss is strong as planets go, but still the resonance energies would be very weak."

"A biologist thought this up, remember."

"Thanks a lot."

"Commensals can sense a magnetic field," Allison pointed out.

"So can Terran magnetotactic bacteria," said Casimir. "They grow tiny crystals of magnetite, and the cells orient along field lines. But that's a far cry from what you propose."

"The Dwelling," said Allison, "is located over a region of anomalously high field strength. Why do you suppose that is—a matter of taste?"

He smiled as he tucked down the restless wurraburra's eyefeet once more. "I wouldn't put it past them. What maximum does the field strength reach?"

"We don't know. We've never been allowed to measure it, since electronics of any sort interfere with Dwelling purposes. We do know that commensals communicate by chemisense; that is, bursts of volatile compounds with structural information tags which convey complex networks of ideas in an instant."

"That sounds like a flexible system, with fewer linear constraints than human speech. What sort of 'brain' do commensals have? Are they smarter than we are?"

Allison shrugged. "Who knows? They think differently, more in terms of probabilities than of discrete events."

"Have they got families? Culture? Formal education?"

Allison laughed. "Formal education? What a quaint idea. Do you have 'formal education'?" she challenged.

"Not that you'd recognize," he admitted. "Everything works through the System. Children pass a series of tests, usually by age fifteen to twenty-five, and then they become 'mature citizens.' Beyond that there are endless forms of education."

"Life is endless education," she agreed.

The wurraburra refused to keep still, but would not be put down, either.

"Does a commensal have a brain, a central nervous system?"

"I guess so. I've never cut one open; don't suppose anybody has."

"Something taboo? For a corpse, I mean."

The question irritated her. "I don't know. We never see them dead, for one thing."

"Do they bury their dead?"

"Of course not. They would scavenge it, probably. But they don't usually——" She stopped.

"Yes?"

"Commensal Fractions rarely die up here."

"Where do they die?"

"I'm not sure that I would call it 'death,' exactly."

The citizen raised an eyebrow. "A supernatural state?"

That hit a nerve. "What are you trying to say?" Allison demanded. "What do you think of us, just because we're religious? There's plenty of mystery in the natural world——"

He threw up his hand. "All right, all right, I stuck my neck out. Truce?"

Allison nodded. "We still don't know much about the Dwelling, the central core of the One. Coral Vale was founded fifty years ago in order to increase our understanding of it, but so far they've made little headway."

Rufus flopped to the ground and scampered over to the back door. The wurraburra flung itself against the door, screaming in terror. Allison promptly let it in to the house.

"What was that all about?" Casimir asked. "Did I hurt it, somehow?"

"I doubt it." She looked up and surveyed the hill. Sure enough, she caught sight of a familiar Fraction approaching around the house. "Yshrin is here! Rufus is scared to death of Yshrin, ever since . . ."

Allison took a closer look. "I take it back; she's not Yshrin, at least not entirely."

"What do you mean?"

"See the deep fissure down the stalk? It's not fully sealed yet. She must have conjoined yesterday or the day before."

"How far north? They don't seem to travel fast."

"Georgeville is just far enough north, unfortunately, and farther north there's still frost this early in the season. One spring a conjoining started just outside of town, and the whole settlement had to be evacuated. Do you know Transac yet?"

"Yes," he said.

"Good. Let's find out who she is."

"Which Fractions conjoined, you mean?"

"Sure; which memories she has. Conjoining is a kind of education, you know, especially for a Splint who does it for the first time."

"So much for formal education," he muttered dryly.

Allison gazed at the creature's eye, set like a jewel in the frontal fissure. She saw her own image reflected a thousand times over in its mirrorlike components, and recalled a saying of the One, *"The One Eye has many faces."*

"Know me?" Allison signaled.

The commensal responded, *"Remember odors, form, Plant-spike."*

"Name *Al-lis-on Thorne (Plant-spike). What is your name?*"

"*One Organism.*"

"*Which Fraction?*"

"*Lherin.*" A coronal fold opened to reveal a cluster of new scent pods.

"Marvelous," said Allison aloud, "that's one less thing I'll have to explain all over again. David?" she called. "He must be out by now. I'll be back in a minute."

She ran off to the kitchen to fetch a jar for the new pods. When she returned, Lherin was conversing with the biosphere analyst.

"*You new from sky,*" signaled Lherin.

"*How do you know?*" asked Casimir.

"*Strong energy waves.*"

Allison asked, "*Waves disturb you, Lherin?*"

"*Disgusting, but tolerable,*" the Fraction reassured her.

Casimir asked, "*What do you know of ship in sky?*"

"*Place where World goes away.*"

"*Comes back,*" Allison reminded her. Ghareshl for sure, but who else?

"*No matter,*" Lherin signaled. "*Some world-forms fun to make disappear.*"

Allison groaned; *that* was Yshrin. "*Remember Tech Center, place of many wave-forms? Place of* Danger *for Fractions.*" And to be a nuisance at times.

At this point Lherin folded up her whole corona except for several inner tendrils which escaped at the tip to signal, " *'One exists, you exist, World exists.*

" *'Existence affirmed,' *" Allison signaled. "You have to reply correctly," she told Casimir, "or else she'd go away. Well, two down, three to go."

She drew a blank on Friends Meeting and other subjects which Rashernu might have recalled. That was inconclusive, though, since not all memories would be retained by each postconjunctive Fraction.

"*Know far jungles?*"

"*Place of warm darkness. Strong World. Dwelling. Wide water.*"

"I knew it!" said Allison. "One must have come from far south. *Recall hand in river?*"

"Hand of five fingers."

"It *is* Thiranne. She was from the jungles; she might even have been a Guardian."

Casimir asked, "Will other, er, conjoin-mates come back to see you?"

"That depends. Rash and Ghar did last time, though Ghar was always closer. One year half a dozen called on me from different conjoinings, remembering me in various bits and pieces. It felt very odd."

"I'll bet it did."

"Plant-spike?" queried the Fraction at last.

"Yes, Lherin?"

"Why do blood-sharers ask endless questions?"

Taken aback, Allison tried to shape a reply, but Casimir began to laugh. "What is your problem, Friend Casimir?" she demanded.

He went on laughing, then abruptly began to cough and choke.

"What's wrong? What's the matter?" She grabbed his arm to steady him. Then the fumes hit her; she turned in an instant, fingers flying. *"Lherin, stop that! Stop now!"*

The air cleared in a few minutes, and Casimir's coughing subsided.

"Are you all right?" Allison asked.

"Guess so. What in space was *that* for?" he asked, wiping his streaming eyes.

"I'm not sure." She turned a stern face to the commensal.

"One tried to help," Lherin explained. *"He looked ill."*

Perhaps. No harm had come, after all.

"Seeding time," Lherin observed.

"Good," Allison replied, *"take care to seed away from travel roads."*

But Lherin was already moving off down the hill.

"Was she offended, somehow?" Casimir asked.

"No, that's how they are." She sighed. "Sometimes they 'affirm existence' in the course of exchange, but they don't say anything like 'hello' or 'goodbye.' "

He nodded. "Speaking of which, I suppose I've taken enough of your time by now."

"That's all right. Though I do have a couple things to get done, before the Quaker citizens arrive today."

"Yes. Say—what are those?" He pointed to a swarm of tiny creatures which rose from a bush nearby.

"We call them 'copterflies,' because they whirl up and down. Their swarms darken the air by midsummer."

Casimir watched the shimmering forms, entranced. Allison bit her lip; she had a question to ask, but was unsure how to begin. "Casimir . . . you love all of these living things, even though they're not Terran?"

"Yes," he said, "that's why I came here."

"But sometimes you thermolyze whole planets, like Vinlandia."

He continued to watch the copterflies. "Vinlandia was uninhabitable," he said at last. "Ask Kyoko about it sometime; she took part in one of the earlier expeditions."

"But it wasn't uninhabitable for native things, like those 'sunspirals.' "

"We save as many samples as possible. That's why we keep ecological preserves, like the garden you saw on our ship."

"Is that what you did with people after the Last War —pick the best samples?"

Casimir turned, and anger creased his face. "You don't know what you're saying, citizen."

"Don't I? What are *you* saying?" Her pulse quickened. Casimir seemed to check himself, and he sighed. "Allison . . . suppose you ask the System for a UNI census."

She did so, and her credometer announced a number over two hundred million.

"That's a lot of humans, isn't it?"

Allison frowned. "Millions" were fine for stars or atoms, but she had trouble connecting such numbers with people. "Still," she recalled, "I thought Earth used to have billions."

"Earth is not the same," he reminded her. "We can't support that many. Only a fraction of Terran farmland has been reclaimed. We farm the oceans, too, and Vinlandia will help. But it's never enough."

She shivered. She thought it might be better never to see Earth again, but to keep the Records, crude and imperfect though they were.

"We need good planets," he added, "to settle future generations. Our population is expanding."

"That's a social concern. Can't you use 'credit' or something to regulate growth?"

Casimir chose his words carefully. "That is less simple than it sounds. Incubators and increased life-span make it possible for a citizen to have two or three families in one lifetime."

This puzzled Allison. She felt relieved to know that the System could not control the incubators outright, but was surprised that such an advanced society would have a population problem.

"Look at it this way," he said. "When you plow a field under for crops, you destroy the preexisting community of organisms. Does that disturb you?"

"That's different. We don't kill off entire species, much less a planet full."

"But, always, some things must die so that others may live."

No immediate answer came to mind, and Allison was confused. Casimir stood there on the moss, relaxed as before, and a breeze ruffled his hair. "I've taken enough of your time," he said at last. "Thanks for the help."

Allison nodded. "Come back next Tuesday, for the committee on Extraplanetary Concerns. Seth will surely return by then."

"I'll do that."

As the shuttle ascended, a thought struck Allison. She had not yet passed any UNI "tests," to her knowledge; did the System consider her "undermature"?

The atmosphere of a picnic pervaded the scene at the landing strip. The turnout was even larger than when the first citizens had arrived, since many Friends had come from other settlements. Allison and David joined the crowd.

"Yes," Martha was saying nearby, "I understand transcomms will be installed in all settlements soon."

"Allison," called her aunt, who had come to the

transcomm the other day. "Do you know, I accepted this gadget from the frog-suits that day, and it's given me nothing but trouble since? Day and night folks call me from Lord knows where, just to talk to a 'Real Quaker from Foxfield' or a 'Pioneer from Aurora,' whatever that means, and I just can't turn them away."

"Just raise a credit barrier for privacy."

"But how can one refuse them?" asked Ed Crain. "They're calling from light-years away; it's not right."

"They don't see it that way," Allison tried to explain.

Frances said, "Nonsense. Just take off the infernal thing; that's what I did, as soon as they were out of sight."

"But credometers will be invaluable for emergencies," said Allison.

The doctor tilted her head. "That may be. What I'd like to know is, if our UNI friends are so clever, why don't they invent an answering service, hm?"

"Why, I hadn't thought of that. I wonder if—"

Dave yanked her arm. "Mom, when are they *coming?*"

"Soon, very soon." She wondered why the UNI citizens didn't inform them of some of these simple things. Was there just too much to tell? Or did they want Foxfielders to learn from their own mistakes—like children, undermature? An informal education, to say the least.

The crowd hushed as a shuttle craft appeared and settled to the ground. The first of the Quaker citizens stepped out.

He wore a cloak of deep gray with white collar and cuffs. His dark shoes were square-toed with large brass buckles. Under a wide-brimmed hat his hair was cropped level, and ruddy cheeks graced his smile.

"Greetings, good Friends," he said. "I am called William Penn, of the Quaker Preservation Society."

Lowell gasped. "Surely not . . . *time travel?*"

"No, indeed, Friend!" The citizen beamed. "I thank thee for the compliment, nonetheless."

One by one the six of them collected outside—for all the world, thought Allison, like so many "Quaker apples" all in a row.

VIII. All the Kingdoms of the World

Allison found it difficult to concentrate this morning among the silent Sunday worshipers. She watched the shadow patterns which danced across the next bench back. She glanced furtively at the Quaker citizens, whose features were composed almost to the point of self-righteousness, and wondered what thoughts filled their prim heads.

She missed Seth badly. To gaze into his fierce eyes, to touch the dimple of his chin, to hold him until she gasped . . . He was right; it was not good for them to be parted so long. But it was he who had left again so soon.

Rennie Fuller, Allison's cousin, raised herself with care. Just about everyone was related to everyone else on Foxfield in a tangled web, a continuum of flesh; an expanding continuum, to which Rennie would soon contribute. And thousands of other mothers in the galaxy at the same time—no, Allison corrected herself, incubators now.

"I've something stirring in my mind today," Rennie began conversationally. "I've been mulling over desire and temptation. Now, I know some of you are going to squirm in your seats and think, well, here she's going to preach at us about sin and all; but that's not what I'm after, really.

"In fact, 'desire' in general can't be a wholly bad thing, since if we didn't desire anything, we wouldn't ever do anything, would we? I mean, if we didn't *desire* to live, we'd just curl up and die and that would be the end of it.

"But sometimes the things we desire do not help us

to live, not in the long run, and that's when we need our conscience to help us out, to tell the light from the dark. That's what temptation is, and often it's just a simple little thing; like when my alarm rings early and I just want to lie in bed instead of getting up to send the kids to school, to stew the beans, to start the tractor..."

Allison closed her eyes and conjured up all the perverse things *she* would like to do. Forget the Center and lose herself in the moss fields, watching the clouds chase the sun. Take off somewhere with that cute biosphere analyst and find out whether UNI citizens had learned any new tricks in the past hundred years, besides how to kill planets. Probably not, she decided. So why not just leave Foxfield for good and spend the rest of her life figuring out how "empty" quarks fit in with the strange, charmed and colored?

"These things are minor worries," Rennie was saying. "Sometimes we resist, sometimes not; more often than not, I hope. But what happens when something really important turns up; which of us can know how we will act then? Jesus was starving in the wilderness when the Devil came upon him and offered him all the kingdoms of the world. How can we be sure to do right when the real trial comes?"

Indeed, thought Allison, perhaps we would eat our own children, were we starving like one of Rodin's damned souls. That, too, was human.

A loud beep shattered the stillness. Allison caught her wrist. "Hold," she hissed, acutely embarrassed. She got up and walked down the aisle, burning with shame and annoyance. This had to be the limit, the very limit.

"All right, who's calling?" she demanded when she reached the annex.

"Questor Zeba Dadachanji, Chandrabad, Mars, registered 024717008. Accept?"

"Oh, all right, go ahead."

A woman's voice began. "Friend Allison, I'm terribly sorry if we interrupted something, but you could have set up a credit barrier, you know."

"I thought I did."

"Oh, did you? It didn't seem so—in any case, my mates and I have heard of the great interest you've taken in the Stargo games, and since our whole family is into them, we'd just love to view with you and see what the Lost Colony thinks of our modern spectacles. I'm sure they're quite tame by your standards, but—"

She broke off, and whispered voices were heard.

"Oh, yes, Mithua, I forgot that—" She muttered about something like "pacifist."

"Can I call you back later?" Allison suggested. "I'll use the transcomm, then."

" 'Sponential, Friend Allison."

"Good. Good-bye. System call; raise present privacy level by a factor of a hundred."

"Done. Privacy level ten thousand credits per minute."

She checked her credit level; it was dropping, now, but would be O.K. for a while. She hurried back to the hall.

At the rise of Meeting, Lowell read announcements, and the Quaker citizens introduced themselves again. All their names were touchstones of Friends tradition: William Penn, John Woolman, Aelfrida Tillyard, Rufus Jones . . . At the latter name, Dave elbowed her with a question.

"No, it's *not* the same one," she snapped. As attenders rose and mingled, Allison went to hear what the citizens had to say.

"The spirit of thy Meeting," said William Penn, "the feeling of it impressed us wondrously."

"In faith," agreed Aelfrida Tillyard, "it appeared so authentic as to ring truer than ever I imagined those Meetings of old. Thus spake my namesake: 'The spark of spiritual apprehension is kindled into flame by contact with the gathered fire of many souls together.' "

William adjusted the brim of his hat. "True enough, thee's hit the mark there," he said.

"Let me see, now," said Clifford, scratching his scalp. "I'd say William Penn was quite a renowned statesman, even outside Friends circles, wasn't he?"

"Truly he was. As a young Englishman, his trial for 'preaching to the people' became a landmark precedent for the right to trial by jury. He founded a major colony in America—verily, a brave task in those times, not unlike that which faced thine own twenty-first century forebears. And he paid twice for the land thereof: once to the English sovereign, and again to the Indian natives of that new world."

Clifford nodded. "A master of politics and of conscience, he was both."

"But thee knows, alas," said Aelfrida, "that Penn was not the *most* renowned Quaker politician who ever lived."

"Really? Who else, I wonder; not John Woolman?"

She shook her head. "One who led all the United States, but fell for scandal."

"Oh no. *He* was a Quaker in name only. Philadelphia Meeting disowned him, I recall," Clifford finished lamely.

"A sad story," Aelfrida commented.

Allison shuddered. She could not imagine such an action taking place on Foxfield; for if it did, it would be a death sentence.

Martha said, "You praised our 'authenticity' before. I'm curious to know what you had in mind. Did you expect something different?"

"Thee is direct," said Aelfrida, "in the true manner of Friends. But I see that you all have more than the 'manner' of worship; you people possess true belief in the Spirit, as well, do you not?"

"Lord willing, yes," said Martha.

"Amazing. I've not seen the like elsewhere in my lifetime, nor expect to see again. We of the Society exist but as a mirror of the supernatural culture whose history is long past."

A stunned silence fell.

"Not quite past," William corrected, "as thee sees here, my dear. Friends, our Preservation Society is like a museum, a 'cultural museum' if you will, which preserves historical tradition for the edification of the citizenry. Our activities are registered, of course."

Someone muttered, "Well, I'll be, just like a zoo."

"Are there other 'Preservation Societies'?" asked Allison.

"Oh, yes. There are Catholics, Jews, Moslems. The Catholics even tried to refuse sterilization; now, that's carrying authenticity a bit far. Then there are various African tribes, and the Youth Cultists of the Age of

Uncertainty, all in relatively small numbers, of course."

"But still," Martha persisted, "you no longer value *faith* as we know it, any of you?"

"Well, now," said Aelfrida, "faith *per se* is an entirely different matter. Faith in something—life, hope, whatever—is essential to the human condition. That is a principle of psychosynchrony. The brain pathways which produce faith, hope and suchlike have been discovered and are regulated chemically when the need arises." She smiled under her bonnet like a demure sunflower.

"I see." Martha's gray eyes never wavered.

"Good Friends," said William at last, "you all have shown us wondrous hospitality, and I heartily welcome you to visit us at any time, in the once-green land of Pennsylvania which is our home. Our doors are open to all, of course, in the manner of Friends; and truly, we have received many callers of late, have we not, Aelfrida? Fascination with Friends is the great fashion, it seems."

"My dear," Aelfrida objected, "speak not of *fashion* with such glee. For fashion is frivolity; and frivolity, thee knows, is a sure path to perdition."

"Mom, let's *go,* now," Dave whined.

"Okay, I'm coming." She let him pull her away from the group and out of the room. As they walked the scarred road back to the Center, her thoughts were far away, and she nearly sprained her ankle in a pavement crack.

In the transcomm Allison prepared to return the call which had interrupted her during Meeting. She had to admit she was curious to hear from someone involved in the "games."

"Call Zeba, holoview."

"Registered number?" the System asked.

"Ah . . . the 'questor' from this antimorn." The surname escaped her recollection.

"Zeba Dadachanji, Chandrabad, Mars, registered 024717008. Interstellar call, bimodal or direct?"

"Direct, I guess."

She found herself within a plush living room. Two women and a man sat before her on a semicircular divan. They all wore robes of pale violet gauze. They faced one another with strained features, and did not seem to notice Allison.

"I don't know what's come over you," said one, her voice like that of the questor earlier. "What *is* wrong?" she asked the man.

Allison cleared her throat. "Excuse me, citizens—"

"Zeba, let him be," said the other woman, extending an arm. "Truth-telling won't come off, this way."

"Posit. Come on, Shujaath, what's eating you?"

"You know," he said. "Shul, Reza, now Ran . . . they've all gone in glory, I know, but—I just want Chen to be different, that's all."

Zeba threw her hands up in exasperation.

Allison realized they had not heard her yet. This seemed to be a mighty long time lag. Perhaps she ought to call back later?

"You're fucked out, that's all," Zeba decided. "Tell him to get a new psychormone, Mithua."

"He's our baby boy," the man insisted, "our only one left."

"*Balls.* Chen's sixteen standard, expects to pass next year, and he's got more of *that* than you ever had."

"Zeba!"

"Mithua, I'll handle this. Now, look, Shujaath. Chen's our child, too; he's got my genes and Mithua's genes as well as yours, and we want to give him his chance when the time comes, just like the others. We raised them all to expect it, so how's it fair to draw the line here? Besides, Shul nearly made it to Coach, and Chen's as good as she was in training, so maybe he'll even—"

A siren began; the living room vanished.

"Your credit is negative ten thousand twenty-six," stated the System above the din. "Please acknowledge."

Allison exclaimed, "What the devil—"

"Please acknowledge."

"Okay, I acknowledge, for heaven's sake."

The siren stopped.

"For first occurrence, please file explanatory statement, one hundred words minimum."

"Listen, I don't know what's going on—"

"Please file explanatary statement."

"But I can't—"

"Please file—"

"Emergency override. Call Kyoko Aseda, UNIS-11."

The machine paused as if to think this over. "Thirty minutes' extension," it allowed. "Request accepted."

An immense hall reached out around her. Open tiers of floor levels spread across the far side, while giant stairs curved downward from the right and left. Figures moved here and there, like ants in the distance.

In the curve of the left stairway stood Kyoko and another woman by a screen covered with equations.

Kyoko bowed. "Allison Thorne," she said, "I am pleased to introduce my honored colleague Hiroko Shimuri."

The woman bowed low. Her figure seemed small and shrunken, and her hair was white, but her features glowed. "I am honored to meet you, citizen Thorne," she said. "I have heard, of course. The outer world does not completely pass me by."

"Thank you," said Allison, who wondered just what the citizen had heard.

"You see," Shimuri went on, "Aseda and I are concerned here with the inner world of physics; to be specific, the teleplasticity gap. Aseda's ideas intrigue me, as they may clear up a troublesome discrepancy." She glanced at the screen.

Kyoko said, "I should explain, Allison; I am consulting Shimuri at the Shimuri Institute in Osaka, Japan. I've a part-time affiliation there, as I told you."

"This," said Shimuri, "is the Hall of a Thousand Cranes. Look upward, if you will."

Allison stretched her neck back and saw them: hundreds of angular white bird-forms were suspended invisibly, and they moved slowly about the domed space as though in flight.

"A Thousand Cranes," Shimuri repeated. "The symbol of eternal life and peace."

"Peace and eternal life? You believe in those?" Allison asked before she thought.

The woman's smile broadened very slightly. "The Institute was built during the rebirth of United Nations. Many then still knew what it was to long for peace.

As do your people, I understand. I recall the year your well-named ship left for the stars."

Allison thought, she might be older than Celia, then. "But citizens aren't religious any more?"

"Religious? Some, perhaps. Myself, I am religious as any true scientist. Kepler, Newton, Einstein—all worshiped the music of the spheres. But the outer world—" she shook her head. "The outer world cares but to turn sliptons into transcomms."

Allison frowned as she remembered the original reason for her call.

"What is amiss, Allison?" Kyoko asked.

"Well, I guess I've had an accident with the transcomm."

"Did it break down? They do, on occasion."

"I'm not sure. All I know is, the System told me I'm negative ten thousand and keeps demanding a 'statement.'"

"I see."

The two colleagues exchanged glances. Shimuri bowed and said, "You've other duties, Aseda."

"The discussion—another day, perhaps."

"Of course. I am honored to have met you, Allison Thorne."

The Institute vanished. Kyoko was left in a bluish cavern typical of the ship.

"Allison, this happens to the best of us at times. Just file a statement and forget it for now. The Adjustor won't call you on it until at least the third time."

"The *Adjustor?*"

"Don't worry; Special Status, you know."

"But I don't even know what happened," said Allison. "It was fine this morning. I did set the privacy level high, and took a gradual loss from that."

"It must have been something more sudden, to get you ten thousand below. Did you make any transaction without knowing the rate?"

"An interstellar holoview, just now. But they asked for it."

"That should have been safe, unless—System call, itemize cost of last holoview, questor Allison Thorne."

"Direct view," said the System, "two credits per minute. Conference barrier, by Dadachanji parentcorp, fifty thousand per minute."

Kyoko looked puzzled. "Allison, it appears as if you were monitoring an intimate family affair."

"I beg your pardon." Allison flushed. "They called me this morning, and I said I'd call back."

"But direct view would not have worked for that. You need bimodal exchange."

"Is that what we're doing now?"

"No, local calls do not enter the SLIT station. Interstellar calls require coordination of energy flow in both directions. A slipton well allows passage in one direction only; remember, sliptons must be 'negative' or 'positive.' So one-way calls are cheaper, when appropriate."

"But it was neither, in this case." Allison felt like sinking into the floor.

"It was a simple mistake, then," said Kyoko. "Just explain to the System, and that will be the end of it."

"I see." A hundred-word explanation to an omniscient machine; a statement of why she, Allison, had dropped in on a set of parents striving for the fate of their child. She wanted to ask whether Kyoko had ever considered such deadly choices for her own children, but her nerve failed her.

Allison also wondered why Kyoko had chosen to come here, to have given up so much time from her physics just to instruct some ignorant settlers. And Casimir had mentioned her connection with another frontier planet. "Kyoko," she asked, "were you a pioneer on Vinlandia?"

The citizen hesitated and clasped her hands. "Yes, I was on the first expedition, with my family; that was thirty years ago. We were less fortunate than your people. I myself lost my . . . sister there, near the end."

"Yes, I know how that is." Suddenly Allison saw her in a new light. "My husband Joshua died in the Sixth Settlement. It's not easy on Foxfield, either."

"But your people survived on Foxfield. I think your approach was different from ours."

Allison sighed. "You all tell us how 'different' we are. That caller this morning said we were 'pacifist'; but isn't UNI pacifist? You don't have—"

"The word must have been 'passivist.' This refers to a culture which defuses both aggressive and creative energies with high efficiency."

"Wait a minute. Is that supposed to be us?"

"That's what the experts are saying."

"But that's unfair," Allison insisted. "We put all the energy we've got into working to survive."

"Precisely. That is why Foxfield Friends are passivist."

"But why do you link the two—aggressive and creative?"

"Societies can be aggressive without great creativity, like the Spartans or the Nazis. But creativity is a special manifestation of aggression. Cultures noted for artistic and intellectual brilliance have always been strikingly violent. Japan, for example, is renowned for the beauty and serenity of her art forms, and for her progress in science, although her history is as bloodthirsty as that of any Westerran state."

"But what about—"

"Extension terminated, Allison Thorne," the System interrupted. "Adjustor Silva Maio will handle your case."

Kyoko's image vanished, and to Allison's dismay she found herself alone with the Adjustor. The tall bronze woman eyed her calmly. "Allison, I'm sure you will have no trouble with your statement. Nonetheless, I think that it might be useful for us to get together at this point to share some of our concerns about Foxfield reintegration. I understand your preference for personal contact, so why don't you visit me in the ship tomorrow?"

Monday afternoon found Allison once again walking the bluish ship corridors. She wore her one good outfit, which she had laundered since the incident with Kyoko.

"Turn right," directed her credo. "Enter now."

She faced a door with no handle. When she tried to touch the surface her hand plunged through. She caught her balance and stepped inside.

Silva Maio half rose from her seat by a low table.

"Allison, good to see you. Please have a seat. You like gingerale, don't you?"

"Yes, thank you."

The center of the table opened, and a glass of sparkling liquid projected upward.

"Kyoko tells me the Shosa-five is in good order." Silva's tone was uniform, matter of fact. The cast of her features evoked the image of an Incan chieftain on Earth long ago.

Allison nodded and raised her glass. She had never seen such a narrow base for a vessel as the stem of this glass, and wondered why it was made so fragile.

"Excellent," Silva said. "One local week has now elapsed since contact, and orientation has progressed steadily. I'd be interested to hear your impressions."

Allison swallowed. "It's so hard to sort things out," she said. How could she describe it all: no war, and yet no peace; caring, and utter callousness; communication free, yet treacherously expensive. "So many conflicting signals," she added at last.

Silva nodded. "You must expect diversity, among two hundred million individuals."

"The uniformity amazes me more. Everyone accepts one System, and people everywhere speak English." That had jarred with her knowledge of the Records.

"A slight correction, there. We do speak English for your sake, but many citizens speak only their native tongue. The System translates automatically among all languages."

"Really." She was intrigued. "Even in the trans-comm? Facial expression and all?"

Silva waved a dismissive hand. "Image processing. It contributes to time lag, but the systems architects are working on it."

"Then it *is* still a Tower of Babel."

"Excuse me? Oh, yes, of course. Major spoken languages are Spanish, Hindu and Chinese, for reasons of demography. Japanese is the lingua franca of commerce and space travel; you really should learn it, you'll pick it up in no time. That aside, the only 'universal language' is SYSTEMIC, for data processing."

Allison's credometer interrupted. "Referendum update. Senior Self-determination Factor One-Two-Six, five point increase: vote for or against. Issue level four, due within one hour."

"Just a reminder," said Silva. "It's pointless for a citizen to lose credit from absentmindedness if she does want to vote."

She hesitated. "Do you really run everything by majority rule?"

"Yes."

Allison shook her head. "I can't imagine any means other than consensus, for us. If it weren't for consensus, I doubt whether any of us would be alive today," she added, recalling Rachel Coffin with the commensals.

"You're right, for such a small group. But for larger populations—tell me, Allison: what is the precise function of consensus?"

She tried to describe it without reference to the Light. "For consensus, each individual must break down the issues into their essential parts on which all of us can agree. Then together we can build a decision which is not just yes or no, but tailored to fit the given situation."

"Exactly so. Our voting system achieves the same end on a larger scale. Instead of holding a few elections on large issues, as in the primitive stages of democracy, we generate referenda on numerous minor issues. Statistically, this does for a large population what consensus does for a small one."

"Wait a minute. That misses the whole point. Exchange of ideas is what makes consensus work; where do you get that with simple voting?"

"Correct choice of referenda removes that requirement. Through psychosynchronic feedback analysis, we determine which issues need further clarification and what questions to ask to achieve this. System data processing makes it practical. Practicality is the key, Allison; you can't solve a sixteen-digit multiplication problem in your head, and you can't run UNI by consensus."

That sounded unanswerable. Allison wished her brother were there; she knew he'd have a fit. "What is the current issue about?" she asked.

"Self-determination for senior citizens. You can always ask the System to tell you in ten words, or ten thousand. Essentially, a vote to increase Factor One-Two-Six widens the options for older citizens to choose how to spend their remaining years of life."

"Well, I'll vote for that. I'm for anything that gives one a greater say in one's own future."

"As you wish." Silva's long fingers curved about her glass as she sipped. "What other aspects of our modern lifestyle disturb you?"

Directness appealed to Allison, and she decided to return it. "The one thing that really gets me is those Stargo games. I don't care what anyone says, it just isn't right for people to kill each other, even if they do agree to the rules beforehand. And why in heaven would anyone want to do such a thing?"

"Allison, you surprise me. Surely you know of the innumerable attractions which physical conflict has held for mankind over the centuries. For womankind, too, although participation tended to be vicarious. Only in the twentieth century did untamed warfare become more than just a deadly game, but a game whose stakes threatened to break the house.

"Our modern arrangement channels warlike instincts and eliminates innocent victims. And System transmission provides wide access to vicarious participation; it's an important social service."

Allison stared into her glass and twirled the crystal stem. She recalled the sumptuous living room of the Dadachanji parentcorp. She looked up. "Have you ever played, yourself?" she asked.

"I did, one season. The last game I emerged sole survivor. That was enough for me."

The glass slipped from Allison's fingers and shattered. Brilliant shards and droplets covered the table.

"No matter," said Silva. "You'll get another one."

The table top reopened to swallow the debris. It then produced a full glass.

Silva continued. "Creative pursuits are the finest channel for aggression. Advances in science and technology, even in medicine, have always occurred during explosive times. Your ship the *Plowshare* was based on missile design."

"Yes, that's where the name came from—'swords into plowshares.' But things don't have to work that way."

"But they usually did, in your Records of Earth,

100

didn't they? What about literature? The greatest of epic works centered on colossal wars. Artistic inspiration from ancient vase-painting to Picasso's 'Guernica'—"

"What about the 'Mona Lisa'?"

"The Westerran Renaissance society," said Silva, "was a treacherous one. Patrons of art were warring princes; the works they commissioned furthered their competition."

"Or the cathedrals of the Middle Ages?"

"And the Crusades? Christianity inspired both. Tell me, Allison: what great event was it which drove the unprecedented rise of Christianity in the West?"

"The life and teachings of Christ."

"Or the Crucifixion?"

Allison said nothing.

"The drama of the Crucifixion carried immense power. Violence makes a strong message."

"So does silence."

Silva fell silent, as though testing the idea. "That may be so," she said at last. "I shall attend one of your Meetings soon."

"You are most welcome." Allison wondered how many times she had heard or expressed that sentiment during the past week.

Silva nodded. "I've also heard interest on the part of Foxfielders to visit other worlds. This should become practical in the near future."

"Why, yes, I would hope so," said Allison, for lack of anything better to say.

The Adjustor set down her glass. "Friend Allison, I understand that you do not feel entirely at ease with UNI as yet. I accept this because I know that Foxfield cannot reintegrate without overcoming perceived conflicts. Our task is to brush aside the superficial differences and to illuminate our basic consonance of purpose within. The most obvious of the differences lie in technology, and for that reason I hope that you, with your technical background, will be most able to help bridge the gaps between Foxfielders and the rest of our citizens.

"You can imagine the opportunities which will unfold before you in UNI—new sciences to discover, new

101

worlds of art for your son. All the things you once dreamed of are real; you called us, and we are here, Allison Thorne."

IX. Aurora

Allison watched the violet-tinged clouds dribble over the horizon as she walked from the Center back to her house. Already this evening the heavenly lights were out in force; quite a storm must have raged up in the stratosphere.

She blinked as she entered the kitchen. The air reeked with other-worldly odors from the stove, where Dave scraped at the frying pan.

"Hi, Mom," he said, not looking up. The pan juices sputtered.

"Um." Allison dropped her notebook on the table and began to review her report for the Committee.

"You'll never believe what I saw in the transcomm today," Dave said.

"The calls I checked, you mean?"

"Yes. There was this little girl, see, some weirdo Earth name—"

"Japanese. Michiko Aseda."

"Anyhow, she says she runs a whole fleet of cargo ships, like a school project, you know. She showed me some of them."

"Um. Cargo, you say?" Allison flipped a page.

"Yeah, they run everything from antigrav earth-movers to loads of 'audiovisual apparel.' She transports things for people, and then her credit goes up, since it's socially useful, and then she goes to hunt lions in Serengeti. Real lions, like Daniel in the lions' den."

"I see."

"She said I could do it, too, Mom. All I'd have to do

102

is pass a System course and get enough credit to register a transport vessel."

"Sure you can, son. It's your life."

"But *then* I visited this mobilist—that's a kind of artist that makes all these amazing effects with sounds and images and moods. It's like a painting or a song that goes on and on, filling the whole world with things you never thought you could imagine even . . ."

She looked up and sniffed. "Dave, I know you like to surprise me, but what in heaven *is* that concoction?"

"It's called Indonesian shrimp crackers."

"*What* crackers?"

"Indonesia—some new planet or other."

"Country, an *old* country."

"Anyhow, I got the recipe from the Library of Cuisine."

Allison frowned. "I don't recall checking any 'Library of Cuisine.' "

"Oh, no? Well, anyhow, you make this paste out of shrimp—that's a kind of sea worm—then you just—"

"Shrimp? Where'd you get shrimp?"

"This frog-suit lady came and knocked on the door, and had all this stuff, and I got some."

"A *traveling salesperson?* All the way from Indonesia?"

"Easy, Mom. I think she's just from the ship; a frog-suit, like I said. I didn't lose much credit; I checked first."

Allison made a grim note in the margin of her report. She glanced at the window, half expecting to see another 'salesperson' lurking in the shadows. Instead she saw a familiar silhouette, a figure climbing the hill.

"Seth's back!"

She left the house and skipped over the matted fibers to meet him. They embraced tightly.

"Seth, love," she gasped, "you'll crack my ribs one of these days."

"Never," he said.

She kissed his chin, then the eyelids, saving the lips for last. "I missed you so," she told him.

"I know, Sonnie."

"You're lucky in one way, though; you missed all the trouble I've been getting into of late."

"I'll hear soon enough."

"That you will. Come on in for supper," she said, leading him to the house.

"Sorry for the bad timing," said Seth.

"Never mind. It's Dave's night, and you know he always makes enough to feed an elephant."

"Elephant?"

She laughed lightly. "Surely you know what that is. Don't they school you at Coral Vale?"

"We school in other things."

In the kitchen, Dave set down a platter heaped with what looked like bricks of browned Styrofoam.

"That's shrimp?" she asked.

"Crackers," said Dave. "They start out like little hard cakes and then blow up like a flat balloon when you fry them."

She broke off a corner and popped it into her mouth. It crunched and melted away, leaving a spicy taste. "Great," she said. "Look, I'll also whip up some eggs, since Seth is here."

"That's extravagant, Mom," he mocked.

"Smart aleck. Why don't you feed that stuff to Rufus?"

"Aw, Mom."

"Dave," said Seth, "sit down and I'll tell you a Dwelling tale."

"Wow, a new one? What's it about?"

Allison thanked him inwardly.

"It concerns the Great Migration, many planet-tours past, when the day was cold and the One young and without form . . ."

Clifford spoke with Allison and Seth in the bustling Meeting House. "Quite a turnout, for a committee," he remarked. "Allison, you look a bit peaked. Nothing wrong, eh?"

"Not really," she said, shifting her hair to the other side.

"Overwork, I'm sure. I used to think machines were supposed to run themselves."

"Some do." She glanced at his wrist. "Joined the citizens' club, I see. Watch any Stargo lately?"

"Not funny, Allison."

"Sorry."

"Just think," said Clifford, "I've got a century's worth of history to catch up with. Not that Foxfield has no history, but this is like opening an Egyptian tomb."

Allison shrugged. "Earth always did sound like an Egyptian tomb, to me. People would spend entire lifetimes collecting elaborate artifacts, while Earth itself was set to become a giant tomb at any moment."

"My, you're cheerful tonight. Don't tell me Seth's got you down already."

"Of course not, Seth's just fine," she said, patting Seth's arm. "It's just that . . . Clifford, is it true that a creative culture has to be a violent one as well?"

"Well, *there's* a thesis you could write volumes on, and folks have. Would help to define your terms. But a couple of exceptions come to mind, right off: Pueblo native Americans, West Indian island groups . . . Such populations are small, as a rule, and tend to be overlooked. When they overcrowd, the violence sets in. How's that for a thesis in a nutshell?"

"You're getting as good as the System."

Clifford groaned. "Thanks for nothing, sister."

Allison saw Kyoko and Casimir approaching.

"Good to see you again, Allison," said Casimir. "What do you think of us? The clothes, I mean. We took your advice and went to the sartorial establishment of one Jeremiah Crain, number four, Georgeville Road."

"Cas insisted," added Kyoko.

Allison said, "Why not? You both look perfectly gorgeous."

"It's great," said Casimir. "I haven't felt this elegant since I left Mars."

"Is that your home?"

"For generations. We Martians are perversely loyal to our homeland, perhaps because, next to Titan, Mars has the most undeserving of climates: Death Valley and Siberia rolled into one. My grandson's family still lives there."

Taken aback, Allison raised her estimate of his age by a decade at least. "Excuse me," she said, "you both know Seth Connaught?"

"Yes," said Kyoko, "I remember you well, with the commensals last week."

Seth nodded. "You were good at Transac," he admitted.

"Friend Seth," said Casimir, "I've been hoping to run into you again. As you know, I hope to study the commensal Fractions in their natural setting and I wish to propose—"

Allison motioned them to be seated, for the Hall had grown still.

Martha rose. "The function of the Committee for Extraplanetary Concerns of the Georgeville Monthly Meeting is to address matters which involve visitors from worlds other than Foxfield, and to promote our relations with these worlds as Friends see fit. Yearly Meeting will convene an analogous committee this fall."

Allison shuddered. Yearly Meeting committees were notorious for inertia.

Martha read the agenda. "Questions or additions?" she asked.

"I've a concern," called a man who rose in back. "Since all those wrist-antennas folks are starting to wear let people listen in and call in from anywhere, should they really be allowed at committee meetings?"

Martha considered this. "Conduct of monthly business has always been considered open to the public, and this is an open committee."

"But that was when the 'public' was only Friends. What about closed committees, like Ministry and Counsel?"

"We may recommend a ban on credometers in closed meetings."

Noah rose and said, "I for one think this whole credometer thing needs looking into. They're more than just another gadget, and some folks might've thought of the Meeting before accepting them."

Allison bit her lip.

Martha only said, "These concerns come on the agenda under Technical Services. Anything else? John?"

John Poyser rose and said, "In view of the evolution of sexual attitudes in modern society, I ask Friends to reconsider the question of homosexual marriage."

106

"The concern is valid," said Martha, "but to my mind it is purely a Foxfield matter, and therefore outside the scope of this committee; Ministry and Counsel might be more appropriate.

"Well, let's put *that* on the agenda, then."

"Are Friends in accord? Very well. Anything else? Then we'll hear from Casimir Stroem, biosphere analyst from the *UNIS-11,* who asks our help to study the commensals."

Casimir then rose to explain his interest in Foxfield's native inhabitants. "I believe they are the most complex non-Terran life forms yet discovered," he said. "In particular, the conjoining behavior is of great interest to UNI scientists, and we hope that it might be possible for us to observe a conjunction event. I bring this up now because I know that the season is short."

Some Foxfielders shifted in their seats. "Such a notion, indeed," whispered one. "They'll be peeping in *my* bedroom window next, I shouldn't wonder."

"The first thing," said Edward Crain, "is to ask the One. I see Rashernu here."

"Comprehend?" signaled Martha. Seth was translating as usual, though Allison suspected that the Fraction often did not require it.

"Yes," the commensal signaled, while humans craned their necks to see. *"No harm for One within usual wave limits. Blood-sharer safety uncertain."*

Frances spoke up. "The danger for humans is serious. Our leafy friends protect themselves well indeed throughout the mating process, which takes some thirty hours. They exude a battery of neurotoxins, some deadly within a hundred meters; the response is instinctive, so they can't control it. And the composition is never the same, though we keep a long list by now: new compounds crop up all the time."

"We'll protect ourselves, doctor," said Casimir.

"Seth," Martha asked, "what do you think of the project? Can it be done safely?"

Seth shrugged and stood up. "I often come across conjoining Fractions. Bring filters, and a chemical monitor. Bring common sense, too."

"Would you guide such an expedition?"

"When?"

"A week to prepare?" Casimir suggested.

"All right. Might have to go north a ways by then; conjoining won't occur this far south again, this season."

Martha said, "Why don't the two of you work out your plans; if need be, we can always call a brief business session to approve. If no further comments—"

But Rashernu signaled once more. *"One invites new blood-sharers to Dwelling. One expects you soon."*

"What was that?" someone asked.

"The One," said Martha, "would like to see our new friends visit Her at the Dwelling. That also should interest you, Casimir."

"Excellent; we'd be delighted to do so."

Kyoko asked, "Do they consider us 'sharers of blood' in the same sense as yourselves?"

"Seth?"

"Humans," said Seth, "are assumed to be blood-sharers. The transaction must occur, for one to contact the Dwelling."

"Transaction?" asked Casimir.

"An exchange of body fluids," Frances explained. "The amount needed is small—a mil, or so—when it's done with a Fraction, that is."

"Yes," said Martha, "but there are psychological effects as well. That's the whole point, is it not, Seth?"

Casimir said, "I'm sure we can work something out."

Allison smiled to herself. He'd have a lot to work out—especially since nothing electronic, not even a finger-watch, could get within a kilometer of the Dwelling before the Guardians stopped you. What recorders would they use? Picture a UNI citizen trying to use a manual camera, or even a pencil and paper.

"We'll hear next from Technical Services," said Martha. "Allison?"

"Er, yes." She collected her thoughts in a hurry as she stood up. "The first thing is that Kyoko Aseda and I have reviewed the various functions of our Tech Center—power storage, manufacturing, radiocommunications, and so forth—to make best use of the System facilities. The original concept was to try to interface our Deltron network with the System somehow, but frankly, we've come to see that that's about as practical as to hook up an abacus."

She took a deep breath. "The fact is that UNI could absorb all our needs overnight almost, at little cost. In practice, of course, we'd prefer a gradual transition so that personnel can be trained; but with the new hypno methods . . . Frances?"

The doctor was rubbing her glasses in vexation. "Allison, my dear, I hate to see us rush into a quantum leap here. These new gimmicks all look enticing, but it's an old rule that any new operation tends to drag along with it at least as many weaknesses as that which it replaced. For example, last Sunday a perfectly healthy young man burst in on me scared to high heaven because his 'credo' assured him he'd just suffered a coronary."

Kyoko said, "Please, doctor, the defect was corrected immediately, as you know—"

"Darn good thing, too. Nearly gave him a real one."

"You see, we usually set credometer units for infant metabolism. For Foxfield we had to modify the program for physically mature individuals—a delicate adjustment."

"I'm sure it is. But won't some of these other 'transitions' prove even more delicate? What guarantee do we have against further slip-ups?"

Allison asked, "What sort of guarantee do you expect, Doc? Heaven alone knows how many slip-ups *I* perpetrate each year."

"Now, now," Frances demurred. "We'd not last a day without your work."

"That's just it. From now on, we can't get on without UNI, either." She bit her lip; she hadn't meant it to come out like that. "I mean, we're all one world, right? Of course we'll take care—a gradual transition, like I said," she finished lamely. She chafed at the role of UNI apologist, but saw no alternative.

"Noah Rowntree," said Martha, after a pause. "Have you something to add?"

He stood and folded his arms. "Something we've not considered as yet: the commensals, our relationship with them, our interdependence. What will become of it? Will we just replace our whole economy with an interstellar push-button dispenser?"

Allison felt glued to her seat, and she avoided Seth's

eye. Long seconds passed, until Edward Crain rose.

Edward stroked his beard thoughtfully. "I believe that our relations with the One include lasting, spiritual qualities beyond mere 'economic' exchange. If our friendship is distilled by time, it need not be weakened."

Martha nodded. "These are things for us all to think on," she said.

Then Friends seemed to feel a unified need for silence. Some minutes passed. Allison glanced at the commensal Rashernu in the aisle by Seth, her outer fronds half closed. It was nighttime, after all.

At last Martha looked up again and asked Allison to continue her report.

"All right," she said, "about the credometers: a lot of folks have accepted them, now, and plugged into the System, but they should be clear on what they're getting into. For one thing, UNI considers the deal permanent; the System won't take back your 'credo' if you change your mind."

"Until death do us part?" said Clifford.

"Well—that's about it."

"What if you just pull it off?" demanded a woman from across the room.

"After a few weeks, your credit level will decline and start to run negative—another point to beware of, by the way; perhaps Kyoko will explain—"

A man's hand shot up. "That's right, I heard you on the 'space news.' First Foxfielder to go in the red, eh?"

People muttered and clucked their tongues. Underneath her embarrassment, Allison was worried. Couldn't they see the point of what was happening now?

Kyoko rose to explain the Adjustment procedure which applied to credit problems. Some discussion of details ensued.

Clifford leaned back and clasped his hands behind his head. "It's good old Earth, that's all. Everyone likes to tell you what to do, and why it's best for you, if you holler about it. It's called 'democracy.' "

Noah rose quickly. "Clifford, I learned my history, too—from your own mother, right here in the Meeting House. Friends used to die in 'prisons' rather than obey laws which did violence to their Light. I remember what 'prisons' were, as well."

110

There it was. Stony looks appeared. With some hesitation, Kyoko rose. "I assure you that UNI no longer has 'prisons,' nor any similar incarceration facilities. They are unnecessary in the Age of Psychosynchrony."

"Thank you," said Martha, "we're all glad to hear that, I'm sure. Noah, do I hear a concern on your part that credometers violate Friends principles in some way?"

He turned to Allison. "Why don't you tell us, Allison? You know the nature of the beast."

"That's just what I'm trying to do. The most serious risk, to my mind, is that children of any age can acquire regular, unrestricted credometers despite the fact that UNI considers them officially 'undermature' until certain tests are passed. Now, Special Status provides—"

"Excuse me," said Martha. "Question, Lowell?"

"At what age do they take the tests?" Lowell asked.

"I don't think it's specified . . . Kyoko?"

Kyoko explained, "The tests are not formal examinations in your sense. They form a part of the System program base, and 'testing' goes on automatically, so long as the credo is worn. I understand that all Foxfield credo-wearers have 'passed,' so far."

Allison stared. "What about David?"

"He passed yesterday."

"But he just turned twelve."

"It doesn't surprise me," said Kyoko. "Children always take on responsibilities at earlier ages in frontier societies."

No more parental control? That sent her back to square one. "Listen, folks," Allison warned. "Children who wear credos can encounter programs which upset them, and they can get visited by all sorts of strangers, like this 'salesperson' who came to Dave today."

Kyoko shook her head and pressed Allison's arm. " 'Provisions supplier,' " she whispered.

"Allison," called Anne. "Where is David tonight? Perhaps we should hear from him."

"Well—he's at home. Doing his homework," she added defensively. "Besides, he's on call in case the late shift needs a hand."

"Perhaps the Tech Center needs volunteers to fill in occasional nights," Anne suggested. "Dave is certainly old enough to contribute to Friends business."

"Well. Of course."

Martha said, "Perhaps we may agree that considerable self-education in these matters is indicated for us all. Anything further, Allison?"

"The question of voting by credometer is significant, since UNI does not run by consensus. I did talk with Silva, the Adjustor, about this yesterday. She explained the philosophy of voting, and how it works for such a large population."

Clifford nodded. "Friends have abided that, historically. But who are the 'candidates'? Robots?"

Allison was irritated; such nonsense only made things worse.

Lowell asked, "Allison, would you tell us more about your talk with Friend Silva? I for one would be glad to know her feelings at this point."

She cleared her throat, mindful of the credometers. "We exchanged views on, er, contact so far. Silva said she thought that we were making good progress but that . . . conflicts were bound to crop up along the way. She also said that Foxfielders were going to find many wonderful things in this new, expanded world."

Lowell nodded. "It is well that you have developed such a close rapport with our new friends."

"But, of course," said Clifford ironically. "They rule their whole society by machine—they must think my sister does the same."

"*Clifford,*" said Martha, "such talk is hardly helpful."

For her part, Allison was stunned. She had not seen things in that light before.

Martha saw that Allison had had enough. "I suggest we ask the next Monthly Meeting to consider whether credometers violate our Light, and if so, how. Are we in accord?"

Kyoko looked like she wished to say something, but refrained.

"So noted. Frances will now tell us about modern medicine."

"Back to 'wonders' and 'adjustments,'" said Frances. "Wonders first. To my mind, the biggest advances are in limb regeneration and in control of aging. And in vitro foetal development has revolutionized family planning. I could go on about this, but—don't let me get started.

"Now, here are the caveats. One—the body of each UNI citizen becomes property of the state upon decease, for purposes of study, organ culturing and so forth. Secondly—" She paused and turned. "Friend Casimir, am I correct in saying that permanent sterilization is required of all citizens upon physical maturity?"

"Yes," said Casimir. "But all personal genotypes go into permanent storage."

Several hands shot up.

"Let's see," said Martha, "Bill?"

"Well," said Bill, "I happen to think we can live with those terms just fine. We encourage organ donation, anyway. As for in vitro pregnancy and all, why it sounds like a mighty fine thing to relieve our women of such a strain, especially when we're aiming to double our numbers each generation."

"Now that brings up item number three—"

"Frances, please," said Martha gently.

"Sorry."

"Anne?"

"The question of choice concerns me," said Anne. "Each of us should have the right to control his or her own body. Many women find child-bearing to be a fulfilling, rewarding experience . . . I confess I don't know why this is not the case for other UNI citizens, but I see a definite problem here."

"True enough," said Martha. "Edward?"

Edward said, "Friends have never sanctioned organ donation against the conscience of the donor. We have always held this to be a private decision."

A woman jumped up, back several rows on the left. "You folks have all missed the point. It's plain as day they don't *care* about our conscience, any more than our Light, so why are we wasting our breath?"

"Martha," Frances demanded, "I must insist. UNI will have something to say about our growth rate from now on—which will include immigration . . ."

113

"Immigration? How much?" Clifford demanded.

"A thousand per year was suggested. But the fact is—"

"What?" He jumped out of his seat. "Do you know what that will do to us in five years? In one year, for that matter."

Frances glared at him. "Well *I* didn't write the Charter. What option do you suggest? Those of us who took credometers may already have lost what little choice we had."

Kyoko objected to this. "You haven't lost anything; you've only gained the privileges of citizens. And the Special Status provision gives Foxfielders extra flexibility, for now."

Indignant murmurs returned nonetheless. Someone asked what "Special Status" was, and Kyoko explained. Rashernu sat sleepily in the aisle, and Allison wondered what the commensal made of it all.

"I think," said Martha at last, "that one question demands an answer before we proceed further. Friend Kyoko, from your viewpoint, just what choice have we in any of the issues raised so far?"

Kyoko rose and spoke with care. "These issues are complex. Our first priority is consistency: fair and equal treatment for all citizens everywhere. So we must maintain uniform standards. You as citizens have one sure way to influence those standards: your vote. For example, present credo-wearers will recall a recent referendum on the Senior Self-determination Factor."

"Yes," said Frances, "the Self-*term*ination Factor, I call it. That was fourth or fifth on my list. With lengthened lifespan, it seems, some folks get tired of hanging around waiting for their eternal reward, so this Factor makes it easier for them to choose their own—"

Allison clapped a hand to her mouth. "You mean," she whispered, "I voted for *that?*"

Noah stood and cried out, "How can Friends abide such wanton extinction of the Light?"

The night sky blazed with aurora as Allison and Seth walked home. Silent sheets of flame undulated far above them as charged particles from the solar

114

wind surrendered to the planet's magnetic vortex and rained upon the stratosphere. Electrons struck gaseous atoms of oxygen and nitrogen, causing "forbidden" quantum leaps to higher energy states, whose decay produced bursts of electromagnetic radiation at precise frequencies throughout the spectrum. Two oxygen shifts were most visible: the green singlet-singlet transition at 5577 angstroms, and the red triplet-singlet at 6300. And so the long curtains alternated heavenly pastures and hell fire.

Allison also knew of thousands of lesser transitions in the visible region alone; not just oxygen, but also nitrogen, nitrogen cations, nitroxide radicals . . . The human eye could not distinguish these, but a good spectrograph would reveal the lines for each species' fraction of the light.

Seth walked as though in a trance, unable to turn his eyes from the sky. Allison had to pull him from the brink of a pothole more than once. She swore and muttered to herself that, say what they liked about the Center, it was high time the Meeting sent a roads crew to fix up the fragmented pavement which made her one-kilometer hike from the Meeting House a perilous journey. But she knew as well that given the unhurried cycle of Wheelwright's sun, the road would never stay smooth for long.

"Look there." Seth pointed out over the bank. A dim glow hovered over the bushes, like a smoky campfire.

"Is it—can we go see?"

They walked down from the road across the springy ground moss. A cluster of commensals stood in the hollow. Their coronas were closed but they sent aloft colored streams and blobs of phosphorescent gases, as if responding to the auroral lights.

"Awake, or asleep?" Allison whispered.

"Both." He stared in concentration.

"What are they saying, Seth? Can you read the scents?"

After interminable minutes, Seth began. " 'Waking . . . in dark, damp . . . cold roots cry out for . . . time cuts rooted things . . . greatest energy wave of sky draws out roots . . . changes gases to sugars and sugars to . . . but forbidden to return, and time sheds a tear for each level more before forbiddenness ends. . .' The branches tangle, Sonnie," he concluded.

Allison watched on dreamily. "Do they really shed tears, Seth?"

"No," he said, "but it's the nearest thought I can find."

The gases and the sky lights seemed to intertwine as she watched; they became wheat fields bending before the wind, dolphins breaching the crests, mobilist shows in the transcomm. What need had Foxfield of mobilists when auroras danced in the night?

Then her eye caught a bright object near zenith, too small for a moon, but unwavering amid the folds of red and green. She recalled what it was. "Seth, look—like a star, see? That's the *UNIS–11*."

Seth's face slowly darkened. "I think we should send all those frog-suits back where they came from, ship and all."

"Seth! What kind of attitude is that?" She stared at his taut features.

"Realistic. We don't get along and never will."

"Nonsense. How could we 'send them back,' even if we wanted to?"

"The One can."

She paused at this unexpected suggestion. "How? What can commensals do about all those humans?"

"I think it's all a fake. How do we know that world really exists out there? Maybe it's just the one ship, escaped from the holocaust."

"That's preposterous, and you know it."

"I don't know," he whispered. "But I wish it were so, Sonnie."

Abruptly her mental vision transformed. The world on which she stood, the world of Friends and Fractions, was not solid but utterly fragile, a crystal glass with a narrow stem, set on the dark floor of the universe; while the lights above were not streams of evanescent particles to disperse by dawn, but the ponderous robes of a God who strode the ways above, heedless of a glass caught at the hem and shattered below. She felt an impulse to reach up and tear aside the folds; but what then, if only darkness lay behind?

In her mind a decision was taking shape, as a planet coalesces from the eddies of a young star.

She found both Bill and Noreen in a state of agitation at the Center.

"Noreen, what are you doing here?" Allison demanded. "It's Bill's turn, isn't it?"

Noreen looked up, her orange curls askew. "Thank God you're back. Allison, we've lost everything—not just the short wave, but the long wave, AM and FM, the whole works. The ion shower's emitting all across the spectrum, from radio to x-ray; I've never seen the like."

"Worse than the last one," Allison admitted. "But does it help to run around like a chicken with its head cut off?"

"Boss, you've got to do something," said Bill.

"What am I, a magician?"

"But that's not all," Noreen went on. "The magnetic field lines have gone crazy, shifting hundreds of gauss; it's messing up every circuit in the Center."

Bill snapped his fingers. "Let's call our citizen friends; if anyone can help us out, they can."

Noreen tossed her head. "What do you think credos run on—neutrinos? Allison, we're completely wiped out; we can't reach the settlements or anybody. What if someone gets sick, or has an accident? What will we do? We can't *communicate*."

Allison sighed and leaned back on her desk. "I know an old saying that'll solve everything."

"What?" they chorused.

" 'This, too, shall pass.' "

If only her own dilemma were that simple. Martha was the one; by Thursday, perhaps, Allison would be ready to face her.

Silva Maio made an unexpected appearance at the worship meeting on Thursday. At its close, she rose and announced, "I apologize for last night's temporary contact lapse. Aseda is upgrading our ionosphere

117

stabilizers to deal more effectively with Foxfield's unusual planetary magnetism. She also proposes installation of a graviton network for emergency use."

Gravity waves? Allison couldn't wait to see how that would work—but no, she mustn't think of that now.

The Foxfielders soon swarmed about the Adjustor. Allison found Martha and tapped her on the shoulder. "Please; a word with you in the annex, when you're done?"

"Of course," said Martha, noting the programmer's bare wrist. "I'll be there shortly."

Allison worked her way down the aisle, but Frances caught her.

"Allison, have I got a case for you. Remember that poor fellow who used to live on the hillside?"

"The 'tooth-radio man'? How could I forget?"

Frances nodded. "Used to pick up all the Center transmissions in his teeth."

"Gold fillings, wasn't it?"

"Oh, no; helped a bit when I replaced them, but not much. That's why he moved to Coral Vale, but he's back for a few days to see the ship, and he was moaning and groaning away in the infirmary all night. Said it was like thunder rolling in his head all night—"

"The aurora?"

"Right. Don't get those down south, either, lucky for him."

"Imagine. Not the fillings, you say?"

"Nope," Frances assured her. "Some chemical interaction. A few cases on record in my old Earth texts, but no definitive explanation. When I find out, I'll put you out of business."

"Still need a transmitter."

"Ah, well." Frances shrugged. "Back to medicine, then. I won't keep you, dear, you look distracted."

Allison got out at last and went to the side room. It was a plain room, with a timeworn desk and some very old books on the shelf. There were two chairs; she sat in one and tried to steady her hands.

Martha entered, and closed the door. "So what can I do for you, Allison?" She took the other chair.

"Well, I—" She kneaded her hands together. "I

118

think I have to resign from the Tech Center, and I want to tell you why."

"I see." Martha's eyes were deep gray pools. "We all feel a great strain at this time. Your brother's words were unfortunate, the other night."

"Oh, it's not that, really—" She stopped. "The fact is, I feel that the position I've fallen into now requires a person of greater faith . . . to serve Foxfield's interests at this time."

"I see," said Martha. "I am sorry to hear that these feelings trouble you again."

"No, no, *that's* all long past."

"Is it, Allison?"

"Of course, eleven years," she went on in weary recitation. "The river was white and wild, like a Van Gogh—my folks had no chance, they lived down the bank. I got out with the baby, but Josh was never found. I didn't kill him just by not finding him."

"Of course not. But the memory bears down on you, nonetheless."

"Not really. It's been eleven years," Allison repeated.

"But you limit yourself all the same."

"What?" Allison frowned, taken aback. "You mean with Seth? Seth doesn't want any more ties. That's why he takes off at odd times; Coral Vale folks are like that—" She stopped, recalling that confrontation the morning the shuttle had first landed.

"I won't speak for Seth," said Martha, "but you do limit yourself now, because of our visitors. Why don't you trust yourself?"

"That's different." The programmer shifted in her chair. "These people—they're so powerful, and I can't deal with them. The Meeting seems to think I know what's going on, but I'm afraid I'll make some ghastly mistake."

"The Meeting will manage. As for yourself, I thought you were getting on rather well."

"Well . . . frankly, that Adjustor gives me the creeps."

"I see." Martha digested this pronouncement. "Now, why do you say that?"

"Well, for one thing, she told me she used to play the Stargo games. You know about the 'games'?"

"A little."

"They're like games, only the players get killed for real. Supposed to channel aggressive drives."

Martha nodded.

"She said she *played* in them, do you understand?" Tears started down her face. "She *killed* people, that makes her a *murderer*," Allison sobbed, "and *I never shook hands with a murderer before*."

She buried her face in her hands, and Martha rocked her shoulder gently. "So sorry," Allison muttered, unconsciously picking up Kyoko's inflection.

"Don't be, at all," said Martha. "You have to let it out, now."

She rubbed her eyes and looked up once more.

"Allison. There are many different . . . ways, different paths in life, some of which you or I may never understand. And because we've been isolated so long on Foxfield, the differences may seem unbearable just now."

"But killing is never 'right,' ever. Is it, Martha?"

Martha reflected. "If you really believe that, why are you afraid of yourself? You began by saying, or implying, that your own faith was weak. Do you fear that you might become like Silva; that you might 'sell us out,' in some sense?"

Allison stared dully across the desk.

"You know that self-questioning is nothing to be ashamed of. George Fox was but the first of many great Friends who have agonized over faith."

"Yes, but the fact is I've *lost* faith, Martha."

Her sister-in-law said nothing, so she went on quickly. "It began a long time ago, I think, before the Sixth Settlement even. I never did have the kind of faith that the Crains do—they'd stake their lives on the Lord. And now it just seems gone, altogether . . . I could never tell this to Anne; she wouldn't understand. Maybe you don't, either."

"Allison," Martha suddenly asked, "you're a scientist, aren't you?"

"I guess so. I try to be, sometimes. Not that that's any excuse; great scientists have always been religious, like Newton, or Einstein. But then, I'm no Einstein, either."

"Allison, I won't speak for Anne, but myself, I've always been amazed to think how much faith a true scientist must have."

A puzzled frown crossed her face.

"Let me ask you something. Do you believe the sun will make it over the horizon tomorrow morning?"

"Of course. That doesn't mean anything."

"You're absolutely sure, then?"

"Well, no, if you press it, like the commensals do. There's always Heisenberg. But the chance of the sun simply hopping to another galaxy, say, without invoking a SLIT or something, is pretty small; considerably less than the reciprocal lifetime of the universe."

"Why?"

"Because . . . well, we assume the laws of the universe are everywhere invariant."

"If you can make that assumption for the outer world," Martha asked, "for parts of the universe billions of light-years away, then why not assume the same for the inner life?"

"It's different," Allison muttered. "You can't test the 'inner life' at all." She looked quizzically at Martha as the fading sunlight from the window cast shadows across her square cheeks and the pools of her eyes.

"The life of the Light is always within us, yet always just beyond our reach," Martha explained. "One can test it only by living it. Faith means insisting on living the way of the Lord, no matter how little evidence is revealed in the outer world—because life without the Lord is just another form of death. Am I reaching you?"

Allison heard the words but still did not understand.

Martha leaned forward suddenly and clasped her hands together. "Even the smallest amount of this kind of faith is a miracle," she whispered. "At times in my life I have wished that I could know even a fraction of the faith you hold in your outer universe."

Then Allison saw the creases at the banks of the gray pools, the eyes she had long felt to be pillars of strength. "I think," she began slowly, "that you're telling me we're all in the same boat and I can't get out."

"It is not easy to live 'in the world but not of it.' I can't carry your Light for you, Allison, any more than you can carry mine."

X. Commensal Watch

Days passed and turned into a week. Allison saw the shuttle come to and from the Center hill as though weaving an invisible fabric across the sky, or a spider web, she thought at times, depending on her mood.

On Thursday she looked out on the silvery pylons which had sprung up for a new power station—just a test model, Kyoko had said. Allison reminded herself to read up on it in the transcomm, some time. She might try that new hypno-process, too, though the description of it alone made her head ache. Her thoughts wandered.

"You look serious today," Kyoko remarked.

Allison shook herself. "An old book I've been reading. I don't read books much since Grandma Ruth died; it's too distracting. But Martha recommended this one: *The Stranger*, by Albert Camus." She recalled Ed Crain's words, *if our heart opens not to the stranger . . .*

"Ah, yes," said Kyoko. "Premillennial Westerran classic."

Allison frowned. "Why do you always frame them off that way, 'Westerran' works? As if they're foreign, somehow, and irrelevant."

"Sorry, I meant no offense—"

"You never do," she observed dryly.

"It is true that Westerran culture has receded since the Last War."

Allison shrugged. "Are you coming to Meeting this afternoon?"

"I think so, if Michiko and Keiko can manage to hold still. They love to come down here, you know, after months of being cramped on board."

Cramped quarters? More room by far than the *Plowshare,* and that had lasted nine years, subjective time. But the girls seemed nice enough. And now that school was out, Dave enjoyed having *yujin* on his occasional days off from work on the Crain farm. *Yujin,* a word she'd picked up from Kyoko, meant "friend" or "companion." Japanese, like Transac, had no explicit plurals. But *yujin* had a good ring to it, like "Three Musketeers."

"Will your husband come today?" Kyoko asked.

Allison started, then she relaxed. "You mean Seth. We're not married."

"Oh, I thought—" The citizen flushed.

Allison had never seen Oriental features redden before. The effect was interesting. "Dave was Joshua's son."

"Yes, of course."

"Marriage is a very special commitment. For life, hopefully."

"Yes, I know. In any case, I was about to invite you both to our Midsummer Lantern Festival in the ship Garden, next week."

"Oh—well, thank you. Is it 'midsummer' by current reckoning?"

"More or less; it coincides with UNI Day, now. The festival tradition stems from a midsummer Buddhist observance in old Japan. They hung lamps outdoors and floated them in boats down the river at night, to bear away the spirits of the dead. The holiday is purely secular, now, just a big party, really."

"I see. Well, maybe Noreen and some of the young folks'll be interested. Which reminds me, we'd better round up the kids if we're going to Meeting." She pressed her credometer. "David Thorne. David?"

"Call rejected."

"What? Call direct, then."

There were sounds of scuffling and crackling undergrowth. "Keep quiet," a faint voice called, dissolving in laughter and unidentifiable sounds.

"Directional finder," said Kyoko. With a few commands, her wrist began to beep, and she followed its intensity across the hill.

They found them behind the house. The smaller girl ran forward, her sandals flapping, as she shrieked in Japanese. Dave and Michiko were tugging at a net which contained a writhing mass.

"She says they caught a creature," Kyoko explained.

"But *she* sniffed it out for us." Dave pointed to the commensal Lherin, who stood complacently nearby.

The trapped creature looked decidedly uncomfortable.

"Don't think you're going to keep it," Allison warned.

"Aw, Mom." Dave's hair flew in tangles as he clung to the net.

"What is that thing, anyway?" Allison peered closer as it twisted and flailed its stubby legs. "A *stickwort?* Get away from it this instant."

"But Mom, Michiko's going to build a cage."

"Posit, Friend Thorne-san," said the girl, "a commodious enclosure with permaplast life support—"

"It's poisonous."

"But Mom," Dave insisted, "the stingers aren't out yet; Lherin said—"

"The hell with Lherin."

Kyoko spoke to them.

"Come away, Keiko, Michiko," translated Allison's credometer in Kyoko's voice. "Remember your maturity indicators."

"Mama, mama," whined Keiko, as Michiko reluctantly dropped the net.

Dave said, "Why can't we, Mom?"

"Suppose it got out and stung Rufus one night. Then how would you feel?"

"Well . . ."

The stickwort tore itself free and crawled off hastily, though it left several leg stubs behind. The crestfallen youngsters went off to the house to clean up for Meeting.

Allison turned to the commensal who stretched her

fronds to soak in the sunlight. *"You be ashamed,"* she signaled. *"Foolish to endanger our Splints."*

"Danger?" replied Lherin. *"Danger insignificant above universal noise-level."* With that, she flowed away over the thickening matrix of ground moss.

"So Lherin's back," Allison muttered to Kyoko. "Yshrin always did like to play tricks on me."

Allison lay back on the warm hillside and watched the clouds chase the anti-eve sun. On the northern horizon towered rough masses which detached into scattered medallions like fallen leaves on a pond, as viewed from the watery depths.

"Sonnie." Seth lay beside her.

"Mm?"

"I've found a convergence, a hundred kilometers north."

"You mean, Fractions conjoining?"

"They've just started."

"So what else is new?"

"Your friend wanted to see it," he reminded her.

"My friend? You mean Casimir?" Allison stretched her arms. "Fine. Call him and set off tomorrow."

"Martha did. He's bringing the frog-suit doctor, so we need Doc Frances, too."

"I thought you said it was safe."

"Not with a frog-suit doctor around."

"Seth, that's not nice. You don't have to wear a credo, but you should try to be civil at least."

He said nothing, but grasped pensively at the moss fibers.

"Anyhow, Doc's too busy for nonsense. We'll spare Bill, if you like."

"You, too."

"Why should I go?"

"It was all your idea."

"The devil it was."

"I won't go, if you don't."

"What? Seth, you're impossible."

For answer he pulled her over across his chest. She laughed as her hair fell between their faces. Their lips met at last, and the moss settled quietly beneath them.

The Deltron terminals hummed and clattered. Allison said, "Noreen—could you spare an hour with Kyoko this morning?"

Noreen looked up from the decwriter. "I think so."

"She wants to go over the power line proposal, you know. Sorry to leave you in the lurch, but—"

"I'll manage. I've been studying it through the hypno-process; I really think I'm getting the hang of that thing."

"You'll steal my job yet," Allison warned.

"Go on. It's UNI that's stealing all our jobs, so far."

"That reminds me. Call Bill Daniels," she told her credometer. "Bill, you in yet? Come over a minute, please."

In a few minutes the machinist arrived. "What's up, boss?"

"Bill, you're the paramedic. You're joining the 'commensal watch' today."

"But there's a whole load of circuits due."

"Never mind. UNI will ship ten thousand chips in by the end of the week."

Bill's jaw dropped.

"That's right," she said. "Would have been sooner, too, except they had trouble duplicating our antique design."

"But Allison, a whole *year's* supply?"

"Why, yes, Bill," said Noreen. "Don't you think it's just marvelous, all that new technology?"

"Okay, okay," said Allison. "There's more to the world than circuit chips. For today, Bill, let's go watch the Fractions conjoin."

The expedition assembled on the hill. Casimir and Rissa arrived in a sleek electrograv vehicle that looked more like a space cruiser than a surface car. Dave wandered over to gape at it before setting off for the farm.

Seth demanded, "What's wrong with the jeep?"

"Heavy equipment," said Casimir.

"Fully sealable environment," said the doctor. "The shuttle would be better still—"

"No." Seth shuddered. "That thing drives the Fractions crazy. You'd land on them, like as not."

126

"Are you all protected?" Rissa asked. Both citizens wore frog-suit uniforms.

"I think so," said Allison. "We have filter masks, and our skin is treated. Bill, you've got the kit, and the air sampler?"

"Right here." He tapped the black box and grinned. "Also some of life's other necessities."

"I'll bet. I guess that's it, then."

They piled into the vehicle. The seats were not in rows, but faced inward in a spacious oval.

"Now," said Casimir, "let's settle directions—"

"Oh, dear," said Allison, seeing Dave's wurraburra climb in and head for the biosphere analyst as usual.

"Too bad, Rufus," Casimir said, "you and your seven eyes can't come with us today." He stopped and frowned. "Seven? Do I need memory boosters already?"

"No, it's grown a couple, that's all. One more, and it'll split in two. Dav-ie!"

"Here, Mom."

She grabbed the squealing wurraburra and hurled it out to her son, who caught it expertly.

Casimir chuckled. "Binary fission. Poor fellow misses all the fun."

A glassy bubble slid down to enclose the passengers. The vehicle lifted half a meter and raced off down the hill.

"Whoa, there, folks. Keep to the road, okay?" Allison called, uncertain who was driving. The vehicle slowed a bit.

When the directions were settled, Casimir opened an air vent. The rich fruity scent of the northern bushlands slipped in. "Beautiful countryside," he rhapsodized. "Never seen anything like it."

The vehicle streaked across the moss-field expanse where Foxfielders had dug a rough travel road. At times the path penetrated clumps of stubbly forest where the dense plants seemed to strangle one another in their passion for the vital sunshine.

Bill ventured, "I missed your remark about Rufus. What strikes you about our local 'fauna'?"

"Or 'flora,' perhaps?" said Casimir. "Hard to tell around here."

They rounded a sharp bend, but Allison felt no accelerative force; the scenery simply turned, as it would in the transcomm. It felt disconcerting.

"It's always amazed me," Casimir was saying, "how many different forms sexual reproduction can take. On Terra, 'true' plants tend to be the most promiscuous, you know, spreading their pollen to the wind."

"True," Bill agreed. "But then, they don't have much fun either, without a nervous system."

"Well, I've never asked a plant, myself. But animals do all right. Lions, for instance, spend all day at it, coupling every fifteen minutes when in heat. Though they bear surprisingly few offspring."

"That sounds a lot closer to humans."

"Lizards, now, are most curious," Casimir went on. "Male lizards each possess a double set of ejaculatory organs. They can only use one at a time, however."

"What a decision to make," said Bill.

Rissa spoke up. "Would you prefer no choice at all? In some fish species the male members exist only as new 'sperm,' which after 'birth' go directly to fertilize the females again."

Casimir groaned. "You Ultrafeminist."

Allison laughed. "Sounds like *those* females know how to run things."

"Well, how do you like that?" Bill exclaimed. "You'd feel pretty lost without a couple of males I know."

"Perhaps," Rissa suggested, "she prefers 'sisters.' "

A brilliant shower of copterflies engulfed their view. The vehicle raced on, unperturbed.

"Homosexual behavior," said Casimir, "is hardly confined to *Homo sapiens*. Numerous species of birds and higher mammals indulge, including chimpanzees and dolphins—"

"A mark of intelligence?" asked Bill.

"I've always wondered," said Allison, "how dolphins and other sea-dwelling mammals managed to survive at all, much less copulate underwater. What an alien environment for mammals—but then, I know nothing about oceans, even on Foxfield."

Casimir nodded. "Dolphins manage, all right. They have tremendous lung capacity. They also enjoy lots of foreplay."

128

"Well, there's one choice the 'mensals don't have."

"What, foreplay?"

"No; homo or hetero. Their 'foreplay' lasts for hours, though."

"Days," Seth corrected.

Seth observed the air sampler. "All right," he said, "close enough."

The vehicle slowed to a halt just outside a bush forest. Seth pointed out something in the distance, half a kilometer away, Allison estimated.

Casimir said, "Can we get closer? The car really doesn't need a road, and we can seal off the interior, as Rissa mentioned."

Seth looked as if he would have a heart attack.

"No," Allison explained, "the north lands are thick with seedling Splints."

"Oh, that's right."

The glass bubble peeled back. Bill pulled out his old binoculars.

"Surely we may walk closer," said Rissa, "if we're careful."

Seth nodded. "I'll guide you." He put on his filter mask.

"Good," said Casimir. "Let's get out the bio-scans."

The rear compartment opened, and three pieces of equipment rolled out. Casimir's pink face and Rissa's sepia both disappeared under their goggles. They all waded off clumsily over the rubbery moss, following Seth like a troupe of robots. Allison fought back her giggles until they were out of earshot.

"Allison?"

"Yes, Bill?" She already had her calculator out to figure some ore assays.

"How about a hand of gin?"

She looked up. "Is that a 'game of chance'?"

"I guess so. Picked it up from the System."

"Hm. Seems to me the Ninth Query might apply here."

"Aw, come on—just for pennies. Not credits; the System takes a percentage."

Allison paused. "How does it go?"

Bill pulled a deck of cards out of his box.

Wheelwright's sun rolled steadily down the sky. Clouds gathered and rain began to fall, but the droplets parted and fell aside above the vehicle, deflected by its rain screen.

"Questor Casimir Stroem," squeaked her credometer.

"Accept." She slapped down a card.

"Allison, I left an infrascan attachment in the car. Would you mind bringing it out for us?"

"Won't it walk by itself? I'm busy." She slapped down another card.

"Friend Allison. What *would* your Meeting say?"

"At least I'm no voyeur. Gin. All right, what's your infernal gadget look like?"

"You'll know when you touch it."

She climbed out of the vehicle and started to rummage through the assortment of artifacts in back.

Bill called, "Hey, wait a minute; you have to give me a chance to recoup."

The objects were labeled in Japanese characters; Allison spotted a *tai* here, a *ka* there. When she touched one of them, her wristband beeped. "That's it," said Casimir's voice.

She put on her filter mask, opened an umbrella and took the attachment out to the observers.

"Thanks," said Casimir. "Now let me get this straight," he told Seth. "Each of the five Fractions opens at the frontal fissure, and they fuse in a ring, at the frontal folds . . ."

Allison had never seen it up so close before. The ring of Fractions, just a dozen meters distant, looked like a giant tree stump with a leafy top, drenched in the rain. She could see no seam or ridge to indicate where one Fraction left off and another began.

"Yes," said Seth, "They fuse into one organism to form the seed. The neural nets intermingle gradually."

"Like the Dwelling, in microcosm," Allison added.

"Curious," said Casimir. "We're picking up some new bursts of electrical activity now."

Allison peered over at the equipment. "So what does it all mean?"

Rissa said, "We'll require much more data; this is just the beginning. Then follows analysis." The tall, goggled doctor looked like a mythical sea monster as she spoke.

Casimir added, "We must study more individual Fractions, as well. In fact, we'd really like to take one—invite one, that is, back to the ship for detailed observation. Can you recommend any ways for us to make the ship environment more comfortable for them?"

"Rig up a strong magnet," Allison suggested. "Ghareshl swooned as the planetary field strength diminished."

"That reminds me," said Rissa. "You promised to come back some time for a modern medical checkup, after your blackout on the ship two weeks ago."

Allison winced. "So I did."

"What's this?" Seth glared through his filter mask. "Not enough for you to spend a day prying at the One, so you have to poke at Allison, too?"

"It's okay, Seth," she reassured him. "Frances said I should go ahead."

Toward evening the Fractions began to disjoin, and the humans returned to the surface vehicle. The sun was low on the horizon as the vehicle took off across the long plains. Bill unpacked drinks and sandwiches. Casimir and Rissa argued over their data, and Allison dozed off against Seth's shoulder.

A System alarm roused her with a shock. "Medicalert, medic-alert . . ."

The Foxfielders automatically grabbed their masks. The vehicle plunged and buried its nose in the moss.

"We're sealed off now," said Rissa, "but the air vent was open next to Casimir. Cas, are you okay?"

They exchanged some Japanese. Casimir's credometer continued to sputter.

Bill said, "The air sampler—something got in, allright—"

"But we're far off by now," said Allison.

"Look there," said Seth.

Outside, commensals were gathering at a spot some distance behind; a hundred at least, already, converging from all directions.

"And we're off the road," Seth noted. "Why the hell are we off the road?"

"We're stuck," Rissa added. "That ground moss must have incredible tensile strength."

Casimir slumped in his seat.

Rissa adjusted his position and continued talking with the System. Allison caught the word for "shuttle." She grabbed the doctor's arm. "No, you *can't* have the shuttle! Don't you see all the 'mensals out there? They'll go crazy; there's no telling what they'll do."

Rissa eyed her severely. "Casimir is acutely ill; his life may be in danger. I must get him to the ship."

"We're all in danger," Bill corrected. "The air sampler shows three or four distinct components, and chances are they're all deadly—even Foxfielders, with some immunity, can expect delayed effects."

"What are the toxins?"

"Who knows? Doc has a catalogue. Call Frances Poyser," Bill told his wrist.

"On the ship," Rissa insisted, "the System will analyze his blood in minutes, and devise an antidote within hours."

Bill shook his head. "Permanent paralysis, by then. Doc? Doc, we got a problem and we're stuck out here . . ."

The vehicle groaned and shuddered as Rissa issued futile commands to pull it out. Casimir was muttering, semiconscious.

Frances's crisp voice passed judgment on the air samples. "No good," she told Bill. "I'm fairly sure of one, but the others—thousands of possibilities."

"The One knows," said Seth. "We must have run over a Splint, and she sent a distress signal."

"Then ask a Fraction. Keep in touch, and I'll make the antidote right away."

Rissa was skeptical. "You expect one of those creatures to tell you what the poison is?"

"Poisons," Frances corrected. "Any Fraction in the vicinity will know what was emitted."

"I'll contact one," said Seth.

"Very well," said Rissa, "it's worth a try. I'll try to pull us out again, but my legs are growing numb, and I don't know how much longer I have." She pulled down her goggle mask and Casimir's, before opening the vehicle.

Bill looked up from the air sampler. "The stuff is dissipating, whatever it is. Say, Seth—take my credo, and hook up directly with the Medical Center."

Rissa shook her head wearily. "Credos aren't transferable, citizen."

"Come on, Seth," said Allison, "we'll use mine."

They left the vehicle and headed for the crowd of commensals. Allison stumbled in the dim light, and wondered whether she, too, was affected. Seth began signaling, and finally caught the attention of one of them. *"Splint distress signal; please tell composition, urgent."*

Allison did not know the chemical signals, but Seth did. "Three-methyl, two-hydroxy quinoxy . . ." There were four compounds in all, and he read them out for Frances.

"Well," said the voice from Allison's wrist, "there's good news and bad news. Good news is that three of them are common; Bill's kit has appropriate neutralizers. Bad news is, the quinoxy one's new to me. I'll add it to my list as usual, but that won't help you now, I'm afraid."

"Then what'll we do?" Allison whispered. She half expected Frances to say, *am I a magician?*

"There's only one thing," said the doctor. "Ask *her* what her own neutralizer is—and get her to make it."

"But what about dosage?"

"I'll guess-timate. Best I can do."

Seth nodded, and signaled once more with the commensal. Precious minutes passed.

"Got it," he said. He told her the formula, and added, "I think she'll make some more for us."

"In pods?" asked the doctor.

"That may take a while," said Seth, "an hour, perhaps, but I can't be sure."

"Never can."

They waited twenty minutes more in the damp field, as a fine drizzle soaked their skin. The sky was dark, now, and the commensals glowed like ghosts as they mingled about the accident site. Allison wondered again just what had happened. The moss was nearly a meter deep in some spots; had it overgrown the road? Or had a seed sprouted right on the road? But the vehicle must have lost its bearings somehow, to have veered off the path like that.

At last the Fraction dropped a pod into Seth's hand. He and Allison hurried back to the vehicle, which was now fully lit.

They found Casimir somewhat more awake, as Rissa adjusted a half-moon-shaped instrument over his chest.

"This should stabilize his condition," she said.

Casimir's forehead was damp with perspiration and his eyes stared as he spoke broken phrases, some in English, some unintelligible.

Bill had the rest of the neutralizers prepared, and with a syringe he withdrew some fluid from Seth's pod. "Quite sterile," he assured the ship doctor. He picked up Casimir's arm. "How do you pull back the sleeve of this—"

Rissa knocked his hand aside, and he cried out in pain. "What do you think you're doing?" Rissa demanded. "I'd lose my registration."

"Well, don't break my radius over it, for God's sake," said Bill as he nursed his forearm. "That's a good antidote; what else can we do?"

"You don't even know the dose."

"That compound," said Frances, "will cause a bit of queasiness, at worst. What alternative do you propose?"

"His condition is stabilized," said Rissa. "My legs are paralyzed, but I'll call the shuttle and—"

"What," said Seth, "with all those Fractions out there?"

"Aren't you young for Senior Self-termination?" Frances inquired.

Meanwhile, Bill had prepared similar injections for the others. Rissa looked on in horror as he administered them to himself, Allison and Seth. Allison smiled and tried to look as healthy as possible, although she felt nausea rising.

"Where . . . shuttle . . ." whispered Casimir.

Rissa exchanged foreign words with him.

134

"A *witch doctor?*" blared Frances' voice. "Is that what he called me? Well I never—"

"Now, Doc," Bill soothed, "you must have misheard; he's speaking a different language—"

"Young man, I'm not deaf yet, and I heard him in plain English. Listen, Friend Casimir—"

A stream of Japanese translation came from Casimir's wrist, ringing strangely in Frances' tones.

Rissa's face was scandalized; then her expression changed, as if to stone. When Frances stopped talking, an awkward silence fell. Then she faced Bill.

"Citizen," she said levelly, "the Medical Code authorizes none but a UNI-registered doctor to administer medical therapy to non-Special-Status citizens. Please hand me the syringe."

Bill did so without a word. She expertly injected Casimir, then took the last one for herself.

Allison reached out of the vehicle and vomited. The others soon followed suit.

XI. A Midsummer Night's Dream

Half the drill press lay in pieces on the floor. Allison reached deep into the machinery with her wrench and swore softly, while Bill looked on.

"Allison?"

"What?"

"Did anyone ever tell you you've got the vocabulary of a 'sailor'?"

Allison grimaced as she pushed stray hair from her forehead with the back of her left hand. "Now where did you pick up a phrase like that?"

"The Terrans still have sailors on ocean ships. They used to seek continents the way the *Plowshare* sought Foxfield. But now they're mostly for sport, like hunting whales and things."

Her credometer interrupted to announce Casimir Stroem. "Hello, Allison," he said in his usual exuberant tones.

"It's good to hear from you," she replied. "You sound so much better."

"Yes, we've recovered. But you should take Rissa up on her offer, you know."

"That's right," said Bill, "we all ought to get modern checkups."

"Sometime," Allison added.

Casimir said quietly, "I'll never be able to thank you all, you know—"

"We did what we had to."

"Besides," Bill pointed out, "our credit levels all doubled afterward."

Allison said, "It wasn't all your fault, either. The roads were overgrown; that happens in early summer, and they should be kept up better."

"The Fractions stay out of your roads?"

"Not always, but they almost never seed there. The paths are odor-marked."

"But our auto-guide strayed from the road." Casimir sighed. "Oh well. How is Seth, by the way?"

She grimaced. "Haven't seen him, lately."

"Rather upset, I understand."

"Rather."

"Where does he go?" Casimir asked. "He doesn't wear a credo."

"That, citizen, is the type of question that makes Foxfielders refuse credos."

"Thanks, I'll keep it in mind."

"Seth follows the commensals, mostly," she told him, "just as some Fractions come to Meeting. He keeps us in touch with the Dwelling."

"The Dwelling poses even greater hazards for human visitors, doesn't it?"

"Hard to say. The Dwelling is more powerful than the separate Fractions, but more self-controlled, as well."

"And more sensitive," he pointed out.

"More complex entities usually are."

Casimir paused. "This Dwelling is not really a building structure, is it?" he asked carefully.

"It is, in part. The skeleton or framework is built of 'coral'—you know, that orange porous stuff, like the paperweight on my desk."

"Yes, I remember."

"The Guardian Fractions secrete it, and it hardens. It's surprisingly sturdy stuff. The composition's on file in Deltron."

"I see," he said. "Might one then say that this, er, structure is in some sense analogous to a temple of worship?"

Allison considered this. "Fractions don't 'worship' there, as far as I know. They do maintain the needs of the central consciousness, and they visit for 'advice,' or some such communication."

"They all go there in the end," said Bill, "like a permanent conjoining. Why don't you go visit, like Rashernu said?"

"I'm afraid I must agree with Rissa that considerable further study is warranted, before we undertake another risky expedition. Well, I won't keep you from your work. See you tomorrow, at the UNI Day Festival."

"The what? Oh, yes, that," said Allison.

Casimir chuckled. "Friday anti-eve, seventeen hours east. Don't forget, now."

"We won't," Bill assured him.

Allison approached the ship garden, which she had visited less than a month before, though it seemed much longer. Several adventuresome young Foxfielders accompanied her, including Bill and Noreen, and her engaged nephew and cousin, all self-consciously dressed up. She felt somewhat out of place among them.

The entrance was open wide and strung with colored lanterns. Two strangers in bizarre costumes greeted them. "Colonists! How marvelous," the woman exclaimed, as she clasped her hands amid piles of ethereal material. "That's your word, right—'marvelous'? I hope you enjoy our Lantern Festival. This year we've also added a Westerran midsummer theme, to help you feel at home. So, call me Queen Titania, tonight; and this is Bottom, of course."

Her companion spoke in a deep voice, muffled by a monstrous head which he wore, a beast which Allison had seen images of but could not place. A horse head?

"Balaam's Ass, did you say?" Noreen ventured.

"No," Titania corrected, *"Bottom,* the Ass. A figure from Shakespearean mythology. Don't you know your own heritage?"

Allison remarked, "We didn't know to wear costumes, either."

"Never mind, you look exotic enough for me. What do you say, Bottom?"

Another muffled reply.

"Oh, yes, quite right." Titania raised a finger. "Check your credos at the door, everyone."

For once, Allison found herself reluctant to surrender her omniscient wristband. But the Foxfielders all did so, and stepped inside.

The Garden was darkened, but lanterns hung everywhere and bright shapes flitted through the patchwork of foliage. Some were clearly people, actually present at the party, but others seemed to be insubstantial, holographic transmissions, perhaps. Sounds and spicy scents mingled bewilderingly.

"Hello, hello, who are you?" A group descended upon them, jostling about in Elizabethan skirts and trains.

"Tell me," said one, "are you really Lost Colonists or just costumes? Yes? 'Sponential—I am Yoshiko, from Tsung Corp; we supply stratogeysers, you know."

"Have you heard," said another, "about our latest line of psychormones? 'Byronic Fever' heads the list; it induces the most scandalous moods, just the thing for this season."

"You're the technical folks!" said Yoshiko. "How very fortunate, I've got just the thing for you. We can direct a SLIT into your ocean to boil off the water— and there you have an inexhaustible supply of rainfall, where and when you want it."

Allison managed a guarded response. "Wouldn't the tides destabilize it somehow?"

"We'll see. No problem is too tough for Tsung Corp." The supplier vanished.

Bill gasped. "What the—"

"Look here," called Noreen as she pointed off in another direction. "What's happening?"

Allison turned and blinked at a pair of man-sized dragons, scaled in red and gold. The beasts emitted high shrieks as they feinted and clawed at one another. Behind each one stood a person with a panel supported like a music stand; the controller moved his or her hands and fingers above the panel as though manipulating a puppet on invisible strings.

One of the controllers stopped and motioned to Noreen. "Here," she said, "come have a try."

Noreen went to one stand, and Bill to the other. They placed their hands as instructed.

In an instant, both dragons had fallen on their backs and were writhing about the arena.

The original controllers laughed. "I'll show you," said one. "Keep your hand steady," she told Noreen, "then move one finger, then another . . ."

Noreen's dragon rolled over and put out one scaly forepaw, then another.

"Allison." A voice called, like Casimir's voice, but she saw him nowhere and there were no credometers.

"Allison. Follow me."

"Is that you, Casimir?" She did follow it, and stumbled down a narrow path, dodging the partygoers on her way. She was beginning to distinguish the solid ones, now; they glowed a trifle less.

"Over here, Allison."

She pushed aside the branches and ran straight into an ocean which roared as the waves rushed past her. She cried out in fright; but of course, there was no water, only an illusion which she could neither feel nor touch, though the waves' "surface" foamed and eddied about her waist. Farther out she saw lithe blue sea-creatures dancing impossibly on their tails.

With one final crash, the waves dissolved and receded into the surrounding foliage.

"How do you like it?" Casimir stood with Kyoko on an arched bridge above. He shone in gold from head to toe, and raised a golden glass.

"What do you think?" he asked. "The ocean, I mean."

"Oh, it's . . . dramatic, thank you," she called up at him. "Were those dolphins?"

Then her eye fixed on Kyoko's robe. The line was straight like a kimono, but the material swirled with colored patterns, a hypnotic kaleidoscope. How could that work, she wondered; liquid crystals, or . . .

Casimir was saying, "They look just like people when they do that, don't they? Legend has it they used to throw themselves onto the shore, hoping to become men."

"Is that right? I thought it was the other way round."

A flock of fairies sailed by overhead, leaving behind a trail of glitter.

Kyoko said, "Why don't you come up, Allison?" She pointed out the foot of the bridge.

Allison climbed carefully and held on to the rail, for she was still unaccustomed to the weak ship "gravity"; it made her feel as though she might take off with the fairies. Rissa's pills did seem to take care of the oxygen problem, at least.

"A drink, Allison?" Kyoko offered. "Some gingerale, perhaps?"

"Thank you." She gazed at the robe as its colors flowed and disappeared around Kyoko's slim form.

"Do you like it?" Kyoko asked. "I picked it out from my daughter's last shipment of 'audiovisuals.' It reminds me of Foxfield auroras."

"Oh, yes, you're right."

Casimir shook his head. "I know something better than ginger ale, much better, to celebrate New Year UNI 89. Something Westerrans used to drink for their New Year. Ever had eggnog?"

"Egg what?"

"Eggnog. Lots of eggs in it," he promised.

"And what else?"

"Oh, good spirits, milk and cream, touch of— what's wrong?"

"Milk? You mean a mother's milk?"

Kyoko laughed like a bell. "She thinks you mean *human* milk, Cas. No, it's all cultured," she said.

"Bovine formula, originally," he added, "with a few enzymes thrown in to take care of lactose and other irritants." He handed Allison another golden glass.

She swirled the creamy substance on her tongue. It tasted surprisingly good, she thought.

Explosions and crackling noises filled the air as the space above filled with fireworks. The bridge allowed a good view of the people below as they laughed and cheered, vanished and reappeared.

Several partygoers straggled toward the bridge. "Casimir," called one, "we've found you at last. You must come settle this question. *I* say it's a yellow chrysanthemum, but *they* say it can't be a Terran plant because—"

"It's a Vinlandia 'plantoid,' isn't it?" called another.

" 'Plantoid' is not a word," replied the first.

Casimir's metallic features creased apologetically. "Excuse me, Allison; glad to see you here." He left the bridge and went off with them.

"Sunspirals," murmured Kyoko.

"What?" Allison was feeling lightheaded, from sensory overload, she thought.

"They're called sunspirals. I know them well."

"Oh, the Vinlandia flowers. Let's walk a bit, I feel dizzy up here."

Kyoko nodded, and they walked slowly down to the path. Allison watched the shadows of her face and her sleek, black hair. *A sister on Vinlandia* . . .

"She wasn't really your 'sister,' was she?"

Kyoko flushed deeply. "You understand, then."

"I think so," said Allison. "Yes, I do."

"Forty years ago we tried to settle Vinlandia. Nothing would grow, people kept dying; we just couldn't make it work. Iva was among the last to go. I saved her genes for my children; perhaps that was foolish—"

"No, I would have done the same. It is something, for one to have . . . a continuum."

"But you kept your planet, as well. Vinlandia was thermolyzed to be seeded with Terran forms; only specimens were kept for—I'm sorry," she said, "I shouldn't distress you—"

"No, believe me, I do understand," said Allison.

"I remember with Joshua, how many times I wished it had been myself instead."

"Yes, that's just how it is."

They walked on in silence. Allison heard more fireworks muted in the distance. Then she tripped over a low branch, and Kyoko caught her arm to steady her.

"Your bone structure is unique," Kyoko observed. "All of you who have grown for generations on Foxfield seem to have firm, solid limbs, like unglazed earthenware."

Allison turned and looked her over. "Earth people seem to come in all different forms. You look like crystal."

Kyoko laughed again; it was an irresistible sound. "You have such a refreshing way of putting things. It is true, among our millions you must find bewildering variety. Yet even from that perspective, Foxfield is unique." She paused and grew serious again. "Allison, I'm so glad to know you, and to know that people may learn to keep a place like Foxfield, somehow, without . . ."

"Yes," said Allison, "we've been fortunate. Now that you're here, your System may help make our existence less precarious than it has been."

"Do you really think so?"

"Yes, I do."

Then Allison found herself embracing the citizen, and their lips pressed together. Allison felt something hot rise within her, then flow away. Slowly she drew back.

With a shudder, she turned and broke away. The lanterns flashed by overhead as she stumbled back down the path.

XII. The House Divided

Allison sat in the transcomm Sunday afternoon and stared at the white wall peppered with equations. She tried to grasp the essence of these abstruse hieroglyphs. The universe was but a sheet, a "Shimuri sheet" which twisted and folded about itself and through itself, in another dimension or in infinite dimensions? And where the folds met, yet did not seem to meet . . . *"One is visible and tangible and our senses find it, the other is invisible . . . but close to us as breathing . . ."*

She shook herself. Friend Rufus Jones had had something quite different in mind, a different set of worlds.

A hand tapped her shoulder.

"Oh!" She started violently.

"Scared you, huh?" said Dave.

"Don't creep up on me," she snapped. "I'm trying to concentrate."

His muddy footprints faded away on the self-cleaning floor, as efficiently as had that shattered glass on Silva's table three weeks ago.

"Hey, what's eating you?" Dave complained. "You've been cross ever since that weird party that you won't say a word about. Bill talked enough, though." He smiled slyly. "I bet you made out with some neat guy up there and are scared to death about when Seth finds out."

"David, you really are getting to be too much. What a thing to say about your mother."

"Okay, it was someone you knew already. Of course; that Martial fellow, the one that looks like a kewpie doll."

"Martian," she corrected, and shrugged. "Go ahead, make up stories."

"Why shouldn't you like him? Rufus does. Anyhow, I promise not to tell—if you let me see this program now, that Michiko told me about."

"Michiko, eh?"

"She says we're all *in* it, Mom! Isn't that fantastic?"

"What else is new?" Allison dryly observed. "Our 'Lost Colony' is the talk of the galactic town, these days."

"This is different, Mom. It's a 'documentary;' that's a genuine scientific study, right?"

Allison's interest pricked up. "A 'documentary' program on *us?*"

"On Foxfield," Dave said.

She was sick of Shimuri, anyway. "Call-out," she ordered.

"Oh boy! Call-in Social Newsviews, number zero-one-six-four-three."

"Program two minutes in progress," said the System.

A gray-robed narrator appeared. "—societal phenomena of interest and importance to all citizens," she was saying. "Today we visit a cohort which evolved for one hundred and three years, subjective time, completely isolated from the mainstream of civilization. These people call themselves the Foxfield Religious Society of Friends. The title of our feature is— *Foxfield: Pastoral Passivists in Transition.*"

An open moss field faded in around them, the "landing strip" near Georgeville. From somewhere, a squeaky chorus sang:

'Tis the gift to be simple, 'tis the gift to be free.
'Tis the gift to come down where we ought to be ...

"Mom," Dave whispered, "that's our Sunday class."

"This," said the narrator with a sweep of the hand, "is Foxfield, the fertile, tranquil planet sustained by Tau Ceti, a sun slightly cooler than Sol, twelve light-years distant from Terra. And here ..."

The scene shifted to Georgeville Road, before house number four, home of Jeremiah Crain, tailor. Number five, Cliff and Martha's place, was just visible down the road.

144

". . . is Georgeville, the capital of Foxfield, both named incidentally after George Fox, the founder of the Quaker system of supernatural belief over five hundred years ago. The planet was, of course, settled toward the end of the Age of Uncertainty. Note the delightful styling of the townhouses and the quaint solar-paneled roof tops, a major energy resource during that period.

"What sort of people are these Quakers? Why did they leave Terra during the 'stone age' of space travel, and how did they survive on an alien, albeit hospitable, planet? To answer these questions . . ."

" 'Tranquil' and 'hospitable,' indeed," Allison grumbled. "She ought to fry down south one antinight—"

"Sh, Mom," Dave whispered.

". . . a brief look at the Terran roots of Quaker supernatural belief."

A gray Meeting House interior appeared, full of "worshipers" in black hats and bonnets.

"We are speaking with William Penn, leader of the Quaker Preservation Society, registered, which resettled in the Pennsylvania Desert after postwar decontamination. William, what can you tell us about the early Quakers?"

Allison exclaimed, "Not the 'Quaker apples' again—"

"*Sh,* Mom, you're embarrassing me."

". . . an offshoot of Westerran Christocentric mythology," the sanguine "Quaker" was saying. "The key feature of Quakerism was that every individual possessed equal access to the divine will or 'message.' This personal 'gateway to the supernatural,' as it were, enabled each person to minister unto his fellows to some degree. In the earliest Meetings for Worship this ministry was often accompanied by violent trembling —hence the term 'Quaker,' invented by outsiders."

"William," the narrator asked, "the Quakers had a hard time fitting into the rest of society. Why was that so?"

"Maya, the curious thing was that all of those individual messages seemed to agree upon principles of behavior which clashed with the prevailing social codes of that time. Examples include *simplicity,* meaning abstinence from alcohol, ornamental attire

145

and the arts; and *pacifism,* a form of peace-worship, which means denial of war and warlike needs. Such principles did lead Quakers to free slaves and found mental hospitals, but these services were not then recognized as socially useful behavior."

"But later, William, Quakers found their niche as prosperous capitalists, did they not?"

The broad-hatted head nodded. "They settled into Quietism."

"Also known as *passivism,*" said the narrator. "Thank you, William Penn, of the Quaker Preservation Society."

The Meeting House vanished.

"Then, in the year UNI minus one hundred six, the world changed."

The horizon exploded in a blinding mushroom cloud. Allison let out a cry and covered her ears until the roar died away.

"Hiroshima," the narrator calmly continued, "ushered in the Age of Uncertainty, an age in which men developed the capacity to destroy the biomass of an entire solar system. This feat was prevented ultimately by the Ultrafeminist uprising which followed the partial catastrophe of the Last War.

"Since Quakers failed to foresee this fortunate turn of events, some grew fanatical in their peace-worship. One group from Philadelphia launched a discarded United Nations Ramscoop vessel to settle at Tau Ceti. Without SLIT it was a desperate mission, for even astronomer Wheelwright, who had detected and studied Tau Ceti's planets, gave the star but one chance in ten of possessing a planet habitable by humans."

"Gee, Mom," said Dave, "we sure lucked out, didn't we?"

"So did they."

Foxfield returned: a level brown farmland, etched in infinite rows. Two commensals were spreading fertilizer, and a human farmer drove by on a tractor just behind the ubiquitous narrator.

"Here we see a typical Foxfield farmer, plowing her field. We also see two of those bovine native creatures called *commensals,* whose discovery made human survival possible on this planet. Commensals generate essential nutrients for humans, much as cattle and other domesticated animals once produced milk and meat for—"

"What the hell—"

Dave stamped his foot. *"Mom,"* I can't hear a *thing!"*

The narrator said, "Other typical occupations include mining and parentcorporal maintainance. Parentcorps average three point four children per woman; Foxfielders still practice in vivo foetal development, as do other noncitizens. Nonetheless, an even sex ratio was maintained for 'religious' reasons, despite the obvious sexual disparity in survival value.

"System monitoring of the twenty-three current credo-wearers suggests that the average Foxfielder spends eighty percent of her time on survival needs, ten percent on formal education, and most of the remainder on religious ritual. The religious center of life is also the political center, the Meeting House, where Quakers conduct both government and religious ritual.

"How does Quaker government function? Let us find out."

The main room of the Georgeville Meeting House appeared, with people milling about socially. In the foreground stood Clifford, Anne and Celia, sipping tea with the narrator.

"Friend Clifford Fuller. You are the principal Foxfield historian, are you not?"

Clifford nodded. "In between stuffing kids' minds and chickens' gullets."

A couple of youngsters ran screaming past the narrator as they played chase among the bench rows.

"Is it true," the narrator asked, "that all Quaker decisions are made by consensus?"

"Of course," said Clifford. "How else can you find the real truth of the matter?"

"So everyone has to agree on the 'real truth' before taking action?"

"That's right."

"You must have long meetings."

"Too long," Clifford groaned.

"What happens when a strong disagreement arises?"

Celia spoke up. "The Meeting is like Balaam's

Ass," she said with a glint in her eye. "It may see truth's sword outstretched in the path ahead, when an individual who would lead it is blind."

"What a colorful image," noted the narrator. "I take it you're saying that peer pressure intervenes. . ."

"Not necessarily," said Anne. "It is possible for one person at a given moment to see a much greater fraction of the Light than anyone else in the Meeting. When that happens, the force of the individual vision may become the will of the Meeting."

"A supernatural leading, I see. Tell me, Friend Clifford, do you foresee any difficulties in reconciling your tradition with UNI System voting?"

"No," he said, "so long as we continue to run our own affairs according to the Light within."

"Thank you, Friends of Foxfield."

The room vanished, along with the narrator's tea-cup.

"As you see, Friends show initial resistance to the concept of UNI Systemization, as have other populations. But change is coming to Foxfield. Just twenty-four days ago, or twenty-eight 'half-days' local time, Adjustor Silva Maio of the Board flagship *UNIS–11* reestablished contact with the colony."

The initial landing scene appeared. Allison stared into the crowd of Foxfielders, as viewed from the shuttle. Even then, the credos had been watching.

The scene dissolved, and the narrator stood with the Adjustor. "Adjustor Maio is best known for her adjustment of the neofascist movement on Titan."

Silva nodded. "A very different task."

"At this point in time, how do you assess Fox-field?"

"Foxfield is unique in that the colonists have no experience of System evolution up to today. That is why the Board enacted the Foxfield Special Status Act. I think that reintegration is progressing well. The fact that a number of Foxfielders already have accepted credometers and are active, voting citizens speaks for itself."

"Do you foresee any significant change in the Friends' way of life resulting from reintegration?"

"UNI maintains that all humans have the same

basic set of physiological and social needs, and equal right to fulfillment of those needs. The Board of Adjustors will uphold that right for all citizens."

"Thank you, Adjustor Silva Maio, of the *UNIS–11* stationed at Foxfield. *Foxfield: Pastoral Passivists in Transition* has been a feature of Social Newsviews zero-one-six-four-three; your host, Maya Wotumbu. Join us again next week as we present, *The Floating-World Subculture: Fact or Fiction?* See you then." The narrator winked out.

Allison stared off in thought.

"Mom, I forget," said Dave, "what is 'cattle,' anyway?"

"Uh . . . they were sort of overgrown four-legged chickens." She was more interested in what the program had not mentioned; the Silence, for example . . . and Aurora, the nickname which citizens seemed to give this planet. It was all so puzzling. "Maybe we should bring this up in business session this anti-eve."

" 'We'? Aw Mom, I don't have to go, do I? I'd rather do homework."

"But Dave, you don't have homework in the summer, and I got someone else to watch the Center for once. So," she added cheerfully, "that's what you get for being such a precocious young citizen."

Half the population was here tonight, and the Hall resounded with voices. Monthly Meeting Ten was a Third-Month Meeting, when delegations came from other settlements to discuss matters of concern to all. Of course, Georgeville's usual agenda would be full, as well . . . she had to admit some sympathy for Dave's reluctance to come.

Anne approached Allison before she had found seats. "A word with you, Allison. Your name has come up in Ministry and Counsel, and it was felt that a brief talk might clear up the matter."

Allison grew cold inside. "Of course, Martha has discussed our . . ."

A faint uncertain look crossed Anne's face. Then she pressed Allison's arm. "Oh yes—that. Allison, we are at ease on that matter, though since you brought it up I'd like to let you know how glad I am that you

149

and Martha have opened your hearts together on your feelings. Each of us agonizes over the Spirit at times, and such trials are hard to bear alone. My present concern is a far lesser matter. The Fifth Query, you know."

Dave spoke up. "Okay, what's my Mom done now?"

"David," said Allison, "go sit over there by Doc Frances and save me a seat."

"Aw, Mom . . ." He headed for the bench.

Anne said, "Our standards of outward simplicity have taken on new importance since credometers have blurred the distinction between private and public behavior."

"I see. Can't let UNI think we're uncivilized, right?"

Anne shook her head. "The point is, we must consider more than ever before the example we set for our children. Now that credometers expose them to a bewildering array of lifestyles, how are they to know what Friends sanction? You yourself first pointed out the danger, Allison."

She nodded.

"That is why," Anne continued, "even the appearance of thoughtlessness in word or action should be avoided when possible. Moderation, that's all."

"'In speech, in lifestyle and in choice of recreations,'" Allison added. "That's all fine, but frankly, Anne, I think the problem's a lot bigger than that."

"I'm sure it is, and we'll deal with matters as they arise. I think folks want to start now—"

Most were already seated in silence. Allison hurried to sit by Dave. Lowell opened as usual, and Martha reported the accounts.

Then Anne brought up the request, originally raised in the Extraplanetary Concerns Committee but referred to Ministry and Counsel, for reconsideration of homosexual marriage.

"At this point," said Lowell, "I ask leave of Friends to transfer clerkship temporarily to Martha Fuller, during consideration of this issue."

Frances nodded. "Lowell's been pushing for it, though," she muttered to Allison. "He's lived with my brother for years. But you know as well as I how many closet traditionalists are among us."

Overt reactions were mixed. Some spoke to the issue, while others felt that it more properly belonged to Yearly Meeting.

"Indeed," observed Frances, "then Yearly Meeting will stall on it forever."

Edward rose to speak. "Over the years," he said, "Friends gradually came to accept homosexual feeling as a valid expression of human love. Myself, I fail to see how we can stop there and deny this form of love the highest recognition which we bestow upon heterosexual union."

Then Noah rose from his seat in the center row opposite Allison. "Friends came gradually to accept nonmarital heterosexual relations, as well. As far as marriage goes, I still feel that sexual preference, like other desires, must be restrained at some point in deference to higher needs. The Lord said, 'be fruitful and multiply.' On Foxfield, the wisdom of those words is practical, as well as spiritual."

Frances shot up. "A successful family requires *parenting* as well as procreation, and in my experience the former takes far more effort than the latter. Homosexuals have adopted at least a dozen orphans over the last generation alone. There are children who lose more than *one* parent, Noah."

Allison winced. Directness was fine, but Doc could go a bit far sometimes.

"Furthermore," Frances went on, "you may recall that we now face UNI population quotas."

Bill Daniels' jaw dropped in that typical way of his.

"That's right," said Frances, "you young folks had better let this sink in. Population quotas, and immigration: the price of the security which large numbers bring."

"How much immigration?" Bill wanted to know.

"That's not set yet," Martha told him.

"But the *minimum*," Frances pointed out, "for a habitable planet is one thousand per year."

Clifford shook his head. "Forget it. I tell you, we'd have to be crazy to accept that. The first year alone

151

would swamp us. We'd be left with a Foxfield Preservation Society, at best."

Allison cringed at the thought of her own planet overwhelmed by a sea of faces. Why, she wondered, should citizens want so badly to come here? Anxiously she searched the others for answers.

Anne asked quietly, "How can we turn them away?"

Someone else called out, "What about the Lanesbridge Motion?"

Lanesbridge—Allison looked up to see who had spoken. She had heard some people from out of town were grumbling about the attitude of Georgeville Meeting.

Martha sighed wearily. "That comes up later. Since we now face substantial disagreement on the marriage issue, unlikely to be resolved, are we in accord with referring homosexual marriage to Yearly Meeting?"

"Approved," murmured voices.

"All right. Back to you, Low." She avoided his face.

Lowell said, "If Ministry and Counsel is through, we'll hear next from the Resource Coordinator . . ."

Dave fidgeted in his seat as time passed.

The Coral Vale report came up. Seth was still away, an unusual lapse, but gaunt Letitia Mott brought word that the Splint injured during Casimir's expedition had recovered. A message of apology was approved to send to the Dwelling. A committee was appointed for roads improvement.

"This is all well," said the Coral Vale woman. "Now, I have a query for the off-world blood-sharers: when will the first of you come forward to share blood with the One?"

An awkward pause ensued, since no off-world citizens were present to reply.

Frances rose and said, "It's my understanding that the citizens wish to hold off at this time, for fear of precipitating another incident through inexperience or ignorance. What happened last week was no picnic, you know."

"I understand. There is, however, but one way to gain experience, and, since this matter is of some concern to the One, I suggest that we send my query to the *UNIS-11*." The Meeting approved.

Allison rose then. "I have a pertinent concern. I'm disturbed to see that off-world citizens are getting some distorted notions about what commensals are like. For example, a documentary holoview today compared 'mensals to farm animals such as milk-cows. I think it is our duty to correct these misconceptions."

A man rose far off to the right. "That's not the story I heard on the UNI newscast last night," he said. "What I heard was all about some crazy cult the 'mensals were supposed to run, worshiping auroras or something."

"Well, that's equally absurd."

Lowell raised an eyebrow. "This *is* unfortunate. Perhaps we should prepare our own educational program on the One. Cliff, you'd have time, now that school's out."

Frances added, "That biosphere analyst should help, too. We've helped him enough."

"Perhaps," said Lowell, "before we make any further plans we should take up our next item, the Lanesbridge Motion. I think most of us are aware of the deep concerns which some Friends have raised about our relationship with UNI. Christine Loflin, clerk of Lanesbridge Meeting, has a motion to address these concerns. Christine?"

The Hall completely hushed as the miner rose to speak. "Lanesbridge Meeting," said Christine, "approved this motion last night and sent me to put it before Third Month Meeting." She read from a sheet of paper. " 'We ask Friends of Foxfield to consider whether to secede, or in some manner withdraw ourselves, from the jurisdiction of United Nations Interplanetary.' " She looked up.

No one moved to respond.

Christine added, "We don't see secession as a negative move. Rather, it just might allow a more constructive relationship in the long run. We could cooperate with UNI on an 'international' level, without violating our own principles or our inner Light. There used to be lots of nations, remember?"

Babel revisited, Allison thought.

A man rose far in back and cupped his hands to be heard. "Shouldn't the frog-suit folks be here to comment on this?"

"They chose not to attend this Meeting," Lowell said. "They feel that we should crystallize our own feelings first. Of course, we may reach them at any time. Christine, could you summarize for us the reasons for this recommendation?"

"Certainly," she said, "and we only urge consideration, you understand. First, there's invasion of privacy; the credometers are an invasion, no matter how you slice it. Then, the System 'voting' just doesn't square with our way to truth. Their medical 'miracles' are the same story: what's it all worth, if the price is violation of the self?

"Now I'm no saint, but as I see it, they don't hold any spiritual concern at all, not what I'd call spiritual. They separated church and state long ago—then threw out the church altogether. So where do we fit in?"

Several hands rose at once, keeping Lowell busy. "Clifford Fuller?" he called.

"Christine," said Clifford, wiping his forehead, "I won't touch your theology, but—it's only been four weeks, you know, and some of those concerns might yet work out. Voting, for instance; one idea might be for Friends to reach consensus on each System proposal, and then vote in common."

The Lanesbridge woman shook her head insistently. "That's not my point, at all. The point is that I personally don't want to see my opinion, *or* a Meeting's opinion, win out over that of some other citizen simply because we happen to be part of a majority."

"Even if that is the method they chose?"

"*I* didn't choose it. I doubt whether all of them did, either."

"But your ancestors did—"

"Clifford, please," the clerk interposed, "others are waiting."

"Of course." Clifford sat down.

"Noah Rowntree?"

Noah said, "I think Christine has the right of it.

The question is not what did we agree to on a piece of paper over a century ago, but whether it makes sense now, when everything has changed."

"Noah, what if UNI strongly opposes our, er, secession?" Lowell asked.

"Well . . . we stand on principle, right?" He nodded firmly. "Friends history bears its share of martyrs."

Martyrs—the word fell like a slap on the face. Martyrdom was for old stories you learned in school, not something that happened today.

Edward Crain's beard shook as he rose. "I hope we needn't think of that yet," he urged. "Have any of our visitors from the stars yet made a single threat against us or harmed us in any way? I confess I share grave misgivings about the System mechanism; but if a line must be drawn, let us draw it in a cooperative spirit."

Allison waved her hand and finally was recognized. "Listen, this isn't fair," she said. "You have to give them a chance to respond. Why don't you call them, Lowell; call Silva, or somebody?"

Clifford agreed. "Can't have trial *in absentia*," he observed.

"No," said Noah. "Since when do we conduct Meeting by 'long distance'? Let them show their faces down here; that shuttle takes but a minute."

This thought struck a responsive chord; many heads nodded. Allison fell back on the bench and her brow creased anxiously.

"Bill Daniels?" said Lowell.

"I just think we're getting too jumpy about this," said Bill. "What about all the stuff they have to offer us; they seem pretty generous folks, to me. And think of all the educational opportunities, to say nothing of medical health—like Cliff says, there's plenty of time to work out the bugs."

Martha spoke up quickly. "Frances," she asked, is there any flexibility in the medical requirements?"

"Not on the main points," Frances grimly replied. "Civilized humans bear offspring in vitro, and that's that for UNI—unless you can come up with a valid medical reason otherwise."

155

"What about a psychological reason?" Martha suggested.

"Psychosynchronic, you mean. No; the Catholics tried that."

Allison said, "But they're just a 'Preservation Society.'"

Frances shifted her glasses with a puzzled expression.

"I think," Lowell was saying, "that since our agenda is long, and since we are unlikely to resolve . . . er, Noreen Connaught?"

Noreen was waving her hand desperately. "Listen, folks, I don't know if you realize just how far along we've gone already, into the System. All those credos, and whole shipments of parts made to order—what do we do now, send everything back until we decide?"

"Hey, wait a minute." A woman jumped up across the Hall. "You can't do that. Those wrist-things—one of them saved my husband's life last week. He was up on the roof repairing a solar cell, and he fell and broke a couple things, and—you tell them, Doc."

"That's right," said Frances. "Without the credometer, no one would have found him for hours. Now that the wrinkles are ironing out, my medical opinion would have to be that every man, woman and child should wear one—purely on medical grounds, I emphasize."

"But Frances," called Rennie Fuller indignantly, as she rose with some difficulty. "I *can't* wear one, because I'm expecting and the System won't abide that. What good is it for me? What if a credo-wearer *gets* pregnant?"

"That's one of the wrinkles left, but—"

"Please," said Lowell, "some have waited long to speak. You, Friend—"

"Wilbur Blyden, from Mawrford."

"My apologies, Wilbur; go on."

The man nodded. "I'd just like to know who authorized your Tech Center to bring in all this foreign hardware to begin with."

Lowell considered this. "Georgeville Meeting approved some things; Allison?"

Allison rose with mixed relief and trepidation. "The

156

Georgeville Meeting in special session authorized us to draw up hypothetical plans for System integration, as recommended by the Committee for Extraplanetary Concerns with numerous out-of-towners in attendance. So it seemed only reasonable for the Tech Center to accept credos, transcomms and the model power plant on an experimental basis. It does seem now that we're all getting used to it in a hurry."

"But isn't it true, Allison," said Martha, "that UNI considers credometer acceptance irreversible?"

"So they say," Allison admitted with a sinking feeling.

Lowell pointed out, "In all fairness, the concept of, er, disunity seemed unthinkable to us at that time."

"Beg to differ, clerk," said Wilbur, "but someone did raise the issue that day the citizens first came, over on cousin Anne and Ed's farm. Someone asked that Adjustor, straight out, what would happen if we 'weren't happy' with UNI. Got a bush-beating answer, too, as I recall."

"That's right," called Noah, "they don't tell us a thing till it's too late, except maybe in some language none of us ordinary mortals comprehend. Maybe the tech folks do, and that's why they're all hobnobbing together. Myself I don't need some machine to tell me what's socially useful—"

"Quite right, quite right," the clerk soothed. "Christine?"

"There's one more point to remember," said Christine Loflin.

"What is that?"

"There are plenty of planets now, including Earth. No one has to *stay* here, on Foxfield."

The impact of this statement took some time to make itself felt. Stricken looks appeared throughout the Hall. Allison was stunned; she tried to imagine the scenario of such a choice, of having to turn one's back on Foxfield and all it meant in order to become a citizen. Was that really an answer? How could they, Friends, reject UNI on Foxfield without in some sense rejecting themselves?

No one seemed to have the heart to respond. The silence lengthened; five minutes, ten . . .

At last Celia Blyden rose to speak. "I am very sad," she began, "for I still recall a time when Friends lived within the greater world, with all of its . . . sorrows and contradictions. There were even Fighting Quakers, once, long before my time—Friends who did join in battles for freedom's sake. Perhaps their fraction of the Light was smaller than ours—who can say?—but each one has his share, even those citizens. Who are we to judge their Light; and who are we to reject our duty to bring our own Light back to the world? Can we hide our Light in a chicken coop forever?"

After this sank in, Clifford spoke. "I agree one hundred percent with Celia. United Nations Interplanetary seems to work at least as well as any other nation Friends were ever part of. If it works for two hundred million other folks, I'd say it's only reasonable for us to give it a try."

Lowell nodded. "Wilbur, what do you say?"

The Mawrford man stood once more. "Well, I can hardly contradict my own grandma, can I?"

Laughter rippled through the Meeting, a welcome release of tension.

"The truth is," he said, "I know deep down that Celia's right about the Light. And Clifford's right about how well UNI seems to work—but perhaps it works too well. It's swallowed every other religion, so far, as surely as the whale got Jonah. What will become of us, in the long run?"

Allison grew cold. Judged by past experience alone, their chance of survival as Friends looked infinitesimal.

Martha made a suggestion. "Perhaps we may speak to that concern by resolving that we, Friends of Foxfield, shall fulfill our commitments as citizens of UNI, insofar as our own Light is not violated—since we are capable of so much, but not more."

"That sounds fine," said Wilbur, "if they'll take it."

Christine said, "I think that's exactly what everyone has sought all along. But how far will it take us, Martha?"

Seconds passed.

Lowell's credometer beeped. "Questor Silva Maio."

"Do we accept the call?" Lowell asked.

No one refused.

"We accept your call," he said.

"Friends of Foxfield," Silva announced, "UNI considers your statement an excellent first step in the reintegration of Foxfield, and we sincerely hope that it receives approval of the Meeting."

Some individuals stirred and commented over this, but raised no overt objection. Allison let out her breath in relief, though she still felt a twinge of unease; she generally did, when the Adjustor sounded pleased.

"Are Friends in accord?" Lowell asked. "Noah?"

Noah sat, arms crossed, in frozen silence. "I will not block the resolution," he said at last.

"But do you approve?"

"Approved."

Lowell surveyed the room and said, "I believe we are in accord on this resolution . . ."

Martha repeated the wording for Clifford to record.

Dave tugged Allison's sleeve and demanded, "Can we go home yet?"

"No, business isn't done yet."

"Nothing's done yet," muttered Frances. "Of course they accepted our resolution; what do they have to lose? Time is on their side. And what in fact did we decide, after all?" Slowly she shook her head. "In medical parlance, we labored long to bear a mouse."

XIII. The Lamps of Science

Allison sat as still as possible while Dave sculpted her portrait. She watched critically as her son traced a life-size figure in three dimensions above the transcomm floor. His arm swung at a measured pace, and a line of light grew from the tip of his forefinger like thread on a needle. The luminous form took on details; now it appeared human, at least (definitely not commensal, for instance).

"Hm. Do I really look like that?" she asked.

"Actually," Dave said, "you're shorter and squatter. I'm used to practicing on Terran figures."

"Thanks a lot. Rodin wasn't made in a day, I guess. You'd better finish up soon, because I have to go and—"

"Okay, just another minute."

"Remember to bring the chairs back when you're done in here."

"I will, Mom. Keep *still*, for your nose."

The chair left there since yesterday had half dissolved into the floor by the time she'd found it this antimorn. The cleaning mechanism seemed to lack discrimination. It was a wonder they had any shoes left, she thought.

When she got up at last, pain shot through her neck and shoulders. The Meeting had lasted well into antinight, and she'd forgotten proper covering for the walk back. She was lucky to have escaped with a bad sunburn, this time of year. As she stepped outside, she gingerly turned her head to the sky. Black clouds hid the sun now; where had they been when she could have used them?

The storm was gathering fast, and she half hoped that Kyoko might cancel, but the shuttle descended with customary insouciance. No putting this off, then, Allison thought. She nervously fingered her wristband, hoping that her chosen privacy level would suffice.

Kyoko appeared in the shuttle entrance, her figure neatly sheathed in the standard sea green suit. She came forward and said, "Friend Allison, I sincerely regret what took place; it won't happen again."

Allison nodded briskly.

"I know," Kyoko added, "I mean to respect your preferences. About women, that is."

"What?" Allison frowned. "No, it's not that. Though I—it *was* unexpected . . ." She shifted her hair, feeling acute discomfort. "But I do feel . . . attached, sort of."

"Attached? You did say you were not 'married,' no?"

"Well yes, but—you can be loyal to someone without being married."

"I see. Well, I'm sorry, anyway."

"Well, that's all right. Just took me by surprise, that's all. Is homosexuality common in Japan?"

"Less so than in the West, where the Eradication movement grew strongest. But even today, our overall sex ratio is three to two."

"I see." Allison felt like kicking herself; she should have known, it was plain as day.

Kyoko smiled. "You know," she said, "we're finding it just as hard to figure you people out as you are us."

"So I gather, from the calls we get. They think we're stranger than 'mensals."

Kyoko laughed and waved a delicate hand. "Shall we move on to check out construction at the power plant? We have more mundane problems to cope with on the ship, by the way. A System satellite collapsed a couple days ago, and we've yet to determine the cause."

"Really? I suppose you think I shot it down."

They both laughed and headed downhill toward the silvery towers of the model plant, the 'Babel towers,' as Allison called them. Thunder rolled in the distance. As heavy raindrops began to fall, her rainscreen switched on with a slight hum.

"Kyoko—something still bugs me. Suppose we had opted for 'secession,' at the Meeting last night. What would have happened?"

"That's hard to say." Kyoko's face was impassive. "We counted on your decision."

"That much?"

"Oh, well." The suit creased as she shrugged. "Silva gave you about forty to one."

The Foxfielder paused. "I see," she began, sucking her lips in. "You knew our better side would surface in any case, so why not leave folks alone to let off steam?"

"That was it, more or less. You people take this 'religion' very seriously, don't you?"

Allison stopped then and faced her. "You really don't understand us—at all."

161

"That's unfair. One has to start somewhere."

"Then start out by telling me how *you* get on, *without* religion."

"Well . . . that's loading the question."

. "How do you define values?" Allison asked.

"Scientifically, of course."

"But . . ." She searched for words. *In vain I send my soul into the dark, where never burn the lamps of science . . .* "Even human values? The meaning of existence?"

"Oh, all that. That should take care of itself, in a perfectly synchronized individual; first principle of psychosynchrony. In practice, everyone needs adjustment now and then."

"Faith drugs, you mean?"

"That's an archaic way to put it. Psychormones are available to balance the psyche on several levels. Some are accessible for self-adjustment on the outer level; Adjustors take care of the deeper levels. Silva could tell you more; it's been a while since I studied such things."

"You studied it?"

"For several years. My parentcorp wanted me to become an Adjustor. But I . . . declined to qualify."

"You dropped out."

Kyoko shivered. "One has to change, you see. After all, who can adjust an Adjustor?"

Allison reflected on this. "So everyone depends on, er, adjustment, for mental health?"

"Mental alignment. Don't you ever go through times when you feel like killing yourself?"

"Sure I do. Usually I'm too busy to carry it out."

Kyoko nodded. "It's quite individual. I myself check in for realignment once a month or so; more often when under stress."

Allison said nothing. She watched the streams of rain course down, tracing a cone of dryness about the pair of them.

"What is morally wrong with that?" Kyoko asked. "Your commensal friends seem to regulate their own body chemistry completely."

"But they're not human," said Allison. "Their worldview works on the small end of physics, not the large. We think of levers, of gravity, of Newtonian planets around suns; we grasp that intuitively, more or less. But they think, *She* thinks, of electron clouds around nuclei. Quantum interactions on a molecular scale; that's reality, for a 'mensal."

"You mean that because they deal with the world in terms of chemistry, their conceptual framework relates to quantum mechanics rather than classical physics?"

"Closer to quantum than ours, at least," said Allison. "This was Rachel's most important insight. Humans see objects as 'particles'; commensals see 'probability waves,' or distributions of 'particleness.' We think intuitively that things at rest stay at rest; they think in terms of zero-point energy, and of the finite chance that an electron might jump from its atom, or a planet from its stellar orbit."

"They think of planets as electron clouds?"

"Well, they 'know' intellectually that it's not the same, just as we do. But intuitively, they see no reason why a sun or a planet can't just take off one day. In that sense, every day is a miracle for Fractions of the One."

"Is that why Ghareshl was so frightened in the shuttle craft, when the planet seemed to disappear?"

"That was part of it. The Dwelling has of course developed more sophisticated notions."

"As human scientists developed quantum theory. Most intriguing," Kyoko observed.

"A commensal expects change," Allison went on, "and is surprised by temporal continuity; so instead of greeting or leave-taking, one 'affirms existence' during the course of communication."

"But in another sense, quantum theory also implies a greater continuity."

"That's right," said Allison, "the continuity of the whole. An ensemble of electrons, say, are indistinguishable from one another and may be described by a single all-encompassing wave function. That is how the One sees Herself, and that is why the Dwelling developed."

"As opposed to a collection of individuals with independent wills." Kyoko paused, lost in thought. "The commensals must find us very strange."

"I think," said Allison, "that they may see us as a rather unstable 'compound,' a high-energy state likely to disintegrate as suddenly as we appeared on Foxfield."

The storm blew over by Wednesday antimorn, when Allison rose from bed at four west, as usual. She sat alone in the stuffy kitchen with the blinds tightly shut and sipped her tea. If only Seth were here, she thought; she missed his taciturn gaze across the table. He had been gone nearly two weeks now, ever since Casimir's expedition. Still, it was unlike him to miss a Monthly Meeting.

She had met Seth fourteen Foxfield years ago, when she and Josh had gone to Coral Vale to check out the hematite ore samples found just inside the jungle by Seth's father, Gabriel Connaught. Those had been heady days for Josh and herself, full of excitement and discovery. An auroral glow yet lingered over those memories, though shot through with the pain which had followed.

Years later, when she was entrenched at the Tech Center, Seth had stopped by. After a while, his visits had lengthened. When the Meeting had made known its need for a regular liaison with Coral Vale, he had volunteered without comment. Her relationship with him had developed likewise, almost, without comment. Perhaps, she reflected, the time had come for that to change.

At any rate, other cares crowded her mind now. The System plans were taking too much of her time, and Kyoko was chafing over yet another satellite malfunction. So Allison put her cup in the sink and headed off to the Center to see how much she could get done today without interruption.

Some hours later, the programmer took a break to step outside for fresh air. She let out an exclamation; for there by the door stood Lherin, basking patiently in the sun—after a week's worth of unanswered scent pods.

"Lherin! Where have you been?" Allison signaled.

The Fraction's compound eye stared like a silvery sunflower embedded in green velvet. Her corollar tendrils came to life. *"Dwelling. One visits place of possible blood-sharers."*

Allison was taken aback. *"You mean sky-ship?"* she asked, unsure of her interpretation; Lherin's jungle mannerisms were more pronounced than usual.

"Yes. Now."

Allison rubbed her hands in agitation. *"How certain?"*

"Less certain than sun-flight; more certain than a copterfly."

"How will you get there?"

The Fraction said nothing.

Allison's thoughts raced. "Call Casimir Stroem," she told her credometer.

"Request holding . . ."

"Request urgent," Allison added.

Casimir's voice came in. "Hello, Allison; I'm right at the crucial point in my analysis, so—"

"Sorry, I just thought this might interest you."

"What?"

"Lherin's back; the Fraction, remember?"

"The one that nearly gassed me, right?"

"Right. She wants to visit the ship."

"Really?" Now his voice did sound excited.

"I think," added Allison, "that she expects me to take her there."

"Allison, that's just incredible. You have no idea how hard I've tried to convince one to come back up here. All they've said is something like 'low chance occurrence.' I figured Ghareshl must have talked them all out of it."

"Well, Lherin shares some of Ghareshl, including the ship experience, but she wants to go."

"But what about the magnetic field?" Casimir asked. "I thought that was the main problem."

"I don't know."

"Well, let's not miss a chance. I'll be down in half an hour."

"Well . . ." Allison sighed and turned to the commensal. *"Still want to go?"*

Lherin's corona folded like an inside-out umbrella. " *'One exists, you exist, world exists,'* " she declared.

They approached the shuttle craft on the hill; Casimir waited at the entrance.

"You're not afraid?" Allison anxiously signaled.

"No, Plant-spike," Lherin replied. *"Gateway to another field. Energy waves stink, but tolerable."*

Casimir scratched his golden curls. "I think I missed a phrase before 'tolerable.' "

"Well," said Allison, "it doesn't translate exactly. It refers to the shuttle's electromagnetic radiation, and it's not very polite."

"I see." He looked puzzled.

The craft rose, without any sign of discomfort from Lherin.

"Frankly, Allison," said the biosphere analyst, "I'm floored."

"What's the problem?"

"I was sure I'd figured out just how commensals work, and now all of a sudden it doesn't fit. It occurred to me that those ion storms could produce enough radiowaves to stimulate electron spin resonance transitions in the molecules of the organism; they might be one source, at any rate. I've even devised a model of a biological organ which could pick up the transition signals."

"That's right, just like some folks pick up signals in their teeth. The Fractions love auroras, even though they occur at night when the sun is down. Perhaps the Dwelling is in the south to avoid auroral distractions—"

"But now," said Casimir, "Lherin doesn't seem to need a magnetic field."

Allison shrugged. "Maybe she can do without it for a little while."

"But if they like auroras, why can't they stand *our* radiowaves?"

She grinned. "Now *you* should know that, Casimir."

Casimir groaned. "A matter of taste."

The shuttle control panel came to life and caught his attention. Casimir fiddled with it, then called someone on the ship and spoke in Japanese. *"Wakarima-*

sen, don't understand . . . unsteady . . . malfunction . . . check into . . ."

"What's wrong, Cas?" Allison asked.

"I'm not sure. Don't worry, we'll have the repair squad look into it. We're almost there."

"It seems to me," she observed, "that you folks have run into a lot of entropy lately."

The shuttle hooked up and deposited them in the ship corridor. Casimir led a brief tour for Lherin's sake, including, of course, the garden. The place fascinated the commensal so much that she refused to signal for some time as they wandered up and down the paths of greenery.

"Will she never give up?" Casimir asked. "You'd think she was greeting all her long lost relatives."

"Sh, watch what you say."

"Like humans, enchanted with chimpanzees and dolphins."

Allison's credometer spoke up. "Questor Rissa Nduni."

She winced, tempted to refuse. "Accept."

"Friend Allison," called the doctor's voice. "It's been so long since I've seen you. How have you been?"

"Very well indeed. Especially physically."

"That's good to hear; your credo confirms that. But credos can't tell the whole story, you know."

"Really? I thought that was the whole idea." Allison ducked a branch as Lherin made a sudden turn, and she nearly tripped over Casimir in the process.

"Someday, perhaps," Rissa went on, "but not quite yet. As we noted before, it's good to be sure. A physical checkup will add to your credit level, and it won't take much time; I just have one slot at the end of my appointment schedule."

"All right," she said, "I'll come—if we can ever get this commensal out of the garden."

Casimir finally coaxed Lherin away by promising her some exotic things to smell in his laboratory.

In the lab Allison recognized some of the instruments which she had seen in a holoview from the Center transcomm. Casimir led the commensal to a small stage. A screen nearby beeped and filled with letters.

"What's this?" The biosphere analyst stared at the screen, and adjusted another instrument. "I can't believe this."

"Another malfunction?" Allison asked.

"Not serious—just a magnetic effect which the sensitive equipment picks up. It must come from Lherin; the field could reach as high as a hundred gauss inside of her. How the mind's eye does she manage that?"

Allison's scalp prickled. "I've never heard of such a thing. I don't know—unless the Dwelling did something. She came from there, just before she came back to Georgeville today."

Lherin insistently signaled, *"Where smell?"*

"All right, all right, you magnetic mushroom." Casimir pulled a fine nozzle from a console nearby. *"What chemisense here?"*

Seconds passed. Lherin's tendrils danced. *"Four-hydroxy-three-methoxybenzaldehyde. Also three-hydroxy-four-methoxybenzaldehyde."*

Allison said, "It smells like vanilla."

"Vanillin it is," said Casimir, "with traces of impurity. How about this?" His fingers touched the control board. *"Seventeen-beta-hydroxy . . . four-enthree-one, seventeen-enanthate. Also . . ."*

"I lost track," Allison admitted.

"A testosterone derivative, and she got it. Plus impurities . . . Allison, those impurities are in parts per trillion."

She noddeed, proud of her nonhuman friend. "Why don't you ask *her* to make something for you?"

"That's right, it's like 'speech,' for her." He rubbed his chin. "Does she have anything like an ABC?"

"Yes, but it's rather complex. Multidimensional, actually. You wouldn't want to recite a Japanese 'alphabet,' would you?"

"Numbers, then. Can she count?"

"Sure. The middle tendrils, here, would exude most chemicals."

"All right." He extended a different nozzle. *"Lherin, machine can chemisense. Count by chemisense?"*

"Count? What species? Branches? Order?"

Casimir blinked.

Allison suggested, *"Count aliphatic alcohols. One branch; first order."*

Lherin remained still.

Compound formulae flashed on the instrument screen. They seemed to be a random set of long-chain alcohols: $C_{12}H_{25}OH$; C_4H_9OH; $C_{18}H_{37}OH$ . . .

"I don't get it," said Allison. "Are you sure your machine's okay?"

"Everything's in order."

"Machine low intelligence," Lherin helpfully signaled.

Allison snapped her fingers. "My mistake. *Count second order, Lherin."*

This time a set of smaller chains appeared, carbon numbers two, two, three, five, four, six, nine . . .

"There," said Allison, "that's getting better. *Count hundredth order, Lherin?"*

The machine now showed a series of chemicals in brief bursts at regular intervals of about four seconds. The numerical sequence was perfect up to twenty-five, where she stopped.

"A Gaussian error function," Casimir observed. " 'Second order' meant an even chance of giving a wrong answer; 'hundredth order,' one chance in a hundred."

"I told you, the One thinks in probabilities."

"Is that why they have trouble counting straight?"

Lherin signaled, *"One try branch count?"*

"Yes," signaled Casimir.

Again the alcohol "numbers" flashed on the screen, but this time the entire set of isomers appeared for each one. Hundreds, then thousands of formulae sputtered by. Casimir whistled. "Now that's what I call 'sponential."

"Well," said Allison, "do you think she's smarter than humans yet?"

"I couldn't begin to say. I'll beg off by saying I leave human observation to others."

"Like Rissa, you mean."

"The physical, yes. Mental observation is the province of the Adjustor."

"I see. So I've nothing to fear from Rissa, then."

"You've nothing to fear from either the doctor or the Adjustor, Allison."

"Good afternoon," said Rissa Nduni as she clasped Allison's hand in her huge palm. "So pleased to see you again, and your 'friend,' too."

An outer frond extended from Lherin to attract Allison's attention. *"World here, Plant-spike; big World."*

"Yes," she agreed. *"World is bigger than it seemed."*

The doctor said, "Why don't you step over here, Allison?"

Lherin settled watchfully in a corner as Allison sat in a dark contoured seat and let the instruments surround her.

"Now, relax," said Rissa. "Be sure to tell me if you feel uncomfortable or have to make a sudden move, all right? Watch the holo stage, now. Have you ever seen your own heart beating?"

"Can't say that I have." She stared open-mouthed as a gray fist-shaped organ appeared, suspended above the platform, beating regularly. The beat quickened.

"It isn't really that large, is it?" Allison asked.

"No; the image is enlarged about tenfold. I see a slight anomaly at this valve," she pointed out, "as your credo suggested—what you might call a 'heart murmur'—"

"Doctor Poyser told me not to worry about it."

"It's not serious," Rissa agreed, "though I could correct it for you in a couple of hours."

"What about your appointment schedule?"

"That's very thoughtful of you; let me know when you'd like an appointment. Now let's add the lungs to the picture. There, you have good, strong lungs. You must do a lot of walking."

"A couple kilometers a day, that's all."

"Very good. You Foxfielders do keep in shape, I must say. I'm surprised more citizens don't, since it adds quite a bit to one's credit level."

"It's 'socially useful' to keep fit, then?"

"Very," said Rissa. "It enormously reduces medi-

170

cal costs. Oh, by the way, place your finger in the blood probe; you won't feel a thing."

She tensed, but felt nothing other than the probe's smooth interior.

"Nuclear magnetic resonance," Rissa explained, "is a noninvasive technique. Now let's take a look at your liver . . ."

As they progressed through her body, Allison relaxed, intrigued despite herself. A thought came to her mind. "Doctor, is it true that women have better endurance than men do?"

Rissa nodded. "They also perform better overall in stressful situations. The statistics are irrefutable. That is why women make better leaders than men."

"Is that 'Ultrafeminism'?"

"No, Ultrafeminism is politics, not medicine. Casimir calls me Ultrafeminist, but that's an overstatement. I certainly would not condone a return to Eradication of men. People didn't know any better, back then; that was before the Age of Psychosynchrony."

"Does psychosynchrony show basic mental differences between the sexes?"

Rissa paused to issue commands to her equipment. "Psychosynchrony has barely scratched the surface. I look at history. Men ruled for millennia, and social destruction knew no limits. Now, we've lived a century without war. It is clear that women should dominate advanced civilization."

Allison recalled the 'games,' and wondered uneasily what other forms of violence might replace warfare. But the doctor was watching the blood probe screen. "What curious antibodies," she observed. "Some are specific to Foxfield antigens; many of those chemicals must give your liver a hard time. These other antibodies must be from your pregnancy. I haven't seen them in years."

With interest, Allison surveyed the Y-shaped molecular structures. "Aren't there still noncitizens who become pregnant?" she asked.

"I can't treat noncitizens."

"What?" She looked sharply into the doctor's dark face.

"It's not permitted," Rissa explained. "Not for a registered doctor. That's why I couldn't send a shuttle down to help your worker who was injured during the storm."

Allison felt a flood of anger and disbelief. "You mean there are people out there who go untreated, just because they don't wear credos?"

Rissa's eyes widened. "What are you saying? People don't go untreated; what a crude thing to suggest." Her forehead puckered, and she stared off abstractedly as if experiencing inner conflict. "There aren't many of them left," she said at last. "It's just a technicality; any one can get a credo, if they really need help. Allison, would you tell me about your pregnancy; professional interest, you know. It causes an immense strain on the body, doesn't it? No wonder women evolved such endurance."

Reluctantly Allison let the issue lapse, for now, since she felt at a disadvantage there, immobilized in the examination seat. She thought back to her pregnancy, thirteen years past. "Let's see. I guess I felt sick a lot at first. Then I started to get hungry all the time, and tired. I couldn't really feel him inside until the fifth month."

"What did it feel like, then?"

"Just a fluttering at first, like a copterfly inside. Then Josh used to put his head to my belly, and said he could hear the heart beating. Later, the baby started to kick occasionally, inside . . ."

"Did it disturb you?"

"It was kind of neat, actually. I played music to soothe him." Allison smiled sheepishly. "Maybe it worked, since Dave turned out to be a good singer."

"Mm. The final stage must have been quite a strain."

"You might say that. I was in labor for, oh, about six hours, as I recall. I can still remember the first time I got a good look at him, in the bath while Frances washed him down."

"Yes, it's a beautiful thing to make a child. And if you ever have another one, you won't have to go through the hard part."

Allison looked up. "What do you mean?"

"Well, we're just going to seal your Fallopian tubes now, so you don't have to worry about them, and you're all set to use the incubator at any time."

"You'll *what?* Hey, wait a minute."

"It only takes a minute; every citizen has it done. I already stored your full genotype."

"But I don't *want* it done, not now at any rate. I think I'd like to get up now."

"Allison." The doctor looked puzzled. "You know, all of you will have it done sooner or later. Why not have it over with? I thought that you had—"

"No. I'm getting up, now." She tried to stand up, but found herself immobilized in a strange way; not numb, exactly, but not about to move, either.

"Friend Allison, please be calm—"

"Let me *out* of here." She strained desperately at her neck.

Rissa said, "Yes, but you'll hurt yourself if you don't calm down."

Suddenly she felt very calm indeed. Of course, everything was all right, everything was just fine. The doctor was just standing there, perfectly rational, and she, Allison, was perfectly rational.

An alarm sounded. "Mind's eye," Rissa exclaimed, "something's burning. This is impossible—"

In an instant Allison was free. She rose slowly and flexed her arms. A peculiar pungent odor filled the room; she recognized it from the lightning fire at the Tech Center, the year before, when electrical components had burned. The commensal Yshrin, a predecessor of Lherin, had been present at the time.

The doctor was pressing controls frantically. *"Wakarimasen;* everything checks out. But the alarm— I was sure I saw smoke, too."

"I see no smoke," Allison calmly observed. "Perhaps Lherin made the odor. She's had a long day, you know."

"Of course." Rissa shut off the alarm. There was no further sign of malfunction. "Perhaps your, er, 'friend' would like to return to Foxfield."

Allison nodded judiciously. "Sounds reasonable. Good day, doctor. *Come along, Lherin.*"

A group of very grave-looking Friends awaited them as the shuttle craft landed. Seth was back, and he embraced Allison before she could catch her breath.

"The bastards," he said. "They won't get away with this."

"With what?"

He stared at her. "You're *drugged,* Sonnie."

"Sh," said Martha, "we've registered a firm protest. It won't happen again."

"Everything's all right," Allison insisted. "How did you all know?"

"The System told us," said Clifford. "Someone must have figured it would be good public relations for folks to tune in on your modern medical exam. Set us an example, and all." He shook his head. "They really blew it, this time."

"Mommy, Mommy," cried Dave as he tugged her arm, "what did they do to you? Did they hurt you? If I were there, I wouldn't have let them—"

"Yes, dear, but Lherin was there and she managed quite well. *Lherin*—"

But the commensal Fraction was already moving off down the spongy hill, on business of her own.

XIV. Crisis in Babel

Sunbeams stole in through the shades and played across Allison's desk and shelves. The desk top was even more jumbled than usual; a haphazard pile of printouts mounted indiscriminately over the coral paperweight, the *Thinker,* and assorted defunct Bloch units.

"Questor Clifford Fuller," her credometer announced.

Allison looked up. "Accept." She tossed her latest

printout onto the pile. This last straw precipitated an avalanche, and half the contents of her desk slid gracefully to the floor.

"Damn. I mean, darn. Don't you laugh, either," she warned her brother as she bent down to scoop up the papers.

"I'm not laughing," he said.

She listened. He wasn't.

"So what's on your mind?" she asked. " 'Stuffing kids' minds and chickens' gullets?"

"Education, all right. Reeducation, if necessary."

She tilted her head quizzically.

"Some of us," said Clifford, "felt moved to call a special Meeting tonight."

"Not because of me, I hope? I thought we straightened that out last week. It was all a mistake, Rissa said."

"Some Friends remain, shall we say, unclear on that. Besides, that's not the only thing."

"No? What have they done now?"

"Not UNI; the One Organism." Clifford sighed. "Seems She's gotten upset about something. We've taken Her outlook for granted for too long."

Allison and Dave sat with Frances again. Allison looked up and glanced over the solemn faces. She saw Seth across the room with several visitors whom she recognized from Coral Vale, including Meeting clerk Letitia Mott.

After silence, Lowell took up the matter of Allison's latest misadventure, and called upon Frances to summarize.

"The doctor," Frances pointed out, "intended to perform a simple sterilization procedure—routine practice, I emphasize, for UNI citizens, of whom Allison is one."

"We all are," Clifford added.

Rennie called out, "not without credos, we aren't. I don't see how—"

"Friends," Lowell smoothly interposed, "let us hear Frances out."

Frances's lips hardened. "In any event, Allison objected strongly and the procedure was not per-

175

formed. Rissa and I have discussed the whole mis-understanding, which better communication should prevent. But," she added acidly, "the incident does highlight the dilemma unresolved by our nondecision two Sundays ago: are we or are we not to take on the full trappings of citizenship?" She sat down decisively.

"Allison," Lowell asked, "have you anything to add?"

She shook her head. "That's about it," she said in a low voice.

"They drugged her," said Seth. "Only Lherin stopped them."

People stirred and muttered about this. Allison bit her lip. "Rissa said I could have gotten hurt, with the equipment and all . . ."

"Doctor Rissa Nduni," Lowell asked, "would you have sterilized Allison against her will?"

Rissa's figure towered above the room. "I have given my sincere apology for this misunderstanding. No medical procedure may be performed without knowledge and consent, ever. That is why I explained as I went along—it's all on record.

"It is hard for me to get you to understand a century's worth of medical progress. Remember that before your twenty-first century, many women were unable to bear children at all, for one physiological reason or another—as well as all men, of course. With in vitro incubation anyone can create a child with his or her own genes, or with any assortment from the gene bank, and avoid all the physical hardship of child-bearing.

"The 'natural' method is unsafe, compared to the in vitro process, for both mother and child. Also, sterilization eliminates all occasion for contraception and for pregnancy termination—procedures which citizens have opposed for centuries on moral grounds." She sat down.

Anne observed, "The question of choice remains. We ourselves practice family planning, but—"

"What choice?" demanded Noah. "Allison wanted to back out, but they would have forced her, except that the 'mensal stopped it. Maybe she doesn't care, but won't they force us all some day?"

"I resent that," said Allison hotly. "I was mad as . . . as anything about what happened, but I happen to believe in learning to live with your neighbors. Who is this 'they,' anyway? You call the doctor a liar?"

Allison returned to her seat, shaking. A shocked silence fell.

Martha spoke at last, her grey eyes hard. "I for one see no reason to doubt Friend Rissa's statement. I move that the recorder so note."

"How do Friends feel on that?" ventured Lowell. "Noah?"

"Well . . ." He rubbed his chin. "I just don't know, Low. I don't aim to impeach anyone, but—I'm worried, that's all. I just want to know what's going on, and not have a bombshell land on us every week."

Edward said, "I think we all feel unsettled. Still, how shall we proceed unless we build on trust? Let the minutes show we accept Rissa's statement."

"That's fine," said Noah. "About 'neighbors,' though: what kind of neighbors are these 'citizens,' to come here and try to force all their rules on us? We get along fine with the commensals, without imposing things, and they're not even human."

Silva Maio rose. "Friends, I'd like to speak to that. Humans and commensals are in fact different species, with differing sets of goals and needs. Quakers and other UNI citizens are one species—and all profess belief in the equality of all humans. UNI could not accept a permanent relationship which entails political disunity, and by implication, inequality on a personal level. Where would such a concept lead, when UNI encompasses so many disparate races and cultures, as many as did the old Earth you knew? It would lead us back to the age of war and holocaust —on a galactic scale."

Silva paused. "I do not mean to frighten you; we clearly are far from that era now. But you are part of us as we are of you. Do you feel truly unready for us now? We could depart and dismantle the SLIT station, and leave you alone for several generations more."

Dave's eyes opened wide. "Mom," he whispered hoarsely, "They can't do that, can they? I mean—"

"Sh, Dave."

Frances looked sideways. "Clerk, please?" she called. "David Thorne wants to say something. Come on, Dave, don't hide your Light."

The boy stood with reluctance. "Well, the thing is I want to be an artist, like one of those mobilists who make all kinds of things in the transcomm. I can't do anything like that without the System, 'cause Foxfield can't afford artists. I mean, sure, I do my job here and all—even work nights, sometimes. But on Terra—why, Michiko says it's even 'socially productive' to be an artist on Terra."

He sat down, and Allison rubbed his shoulder encouragingly.

"Thank you, Dave," said Lowell. "Anne?"

"I certainly would like Dave and others to become artists as they choose, and to benefit from modern medicine and other services, without giving up membership in the community of Foxfield. But to renounce control of our own community—that is something which no individual may do. I confess I see no clear way in this, Lowell."

Lowell nodded slowly. "I think you've hit the root of it, Anne, and I also see no way to proceed at this time."

Silva rose again. "Friends," said the Adjustor, "there is time to work out these matters—years, if need be. The Board has patience. If the medical incident is closed, I respectfully suggest we take up the urgent commensal problem."

"The problem is urgent," Lowell agreed. "If Friends are in accord . . . Seth, will you explain?"

Seth said, "The One Organism has discovered a disturbing object in orbit around Foxfield. The source of disturbance seems to coincide with this so-called SLIT station. The One has revealed Her intention to eliminate this irritant."

While this news sank in, Lowell signaled to Rashernu, who squatted in the aisle as usual beside the attenders from Coral Vale. *"What disturbance?"*

Rashernu raised some tendrils, and people craned

their necks to see. *"Sky-object emits wave-forms. Interfere with One's scientific observation."*

The clerk's eyebrow lifted. "Radiowave interference from that far out in space?"

Letitia Mott rose to speak. "We should explain to our off-world attenders that the One has long monitored signals from the stars, at the Dwelling. This stellar observation is taken very seriously, and the SLIT station seems to interfere. The One will not say more; it was only by chance that we happened to glimpse Her intent during a recent interview."

"At the Dwelling?"

"Yes."

Lowell signaled again to Rashernu. *"One knows human significance of sky-object?"*

"Small significance," the Fraction repsonded. *"No blood-sharing wave-forms; not part of you. Extraneous distraction."*

Excited voices mingled, a chorus of confusion. Lowell added, *"The One is surely mistaken."* But he could get no further response from the creature.

A thought struck Allison; she grew very cold. "Clerk, please," she called, "may I try to check something?"

"Yes, Allison. Attention, Friends, please."

She turned to Rashernu. *"How will the One eliminate sky-object?"*

The creature kept still.

Letitia said, "This Fraction can't tell you; the matter lies beyond her grasp. You must ask at the Dwelling."

"Well . . . Can she even show that it's possible?"

That was the wrong question; anything was "possible." But Letitia signaled for some minutes, and finally got an answer.

"One knows. Practice, on lesser sky-objects."

"When?" demanded Allison.

"Five sun-tours past; four sun-tours past."

"That's it," said Allison. "Today is Tuesday; Kyoko's System satellites gave out last week, on Saturday and Monday. That's what She 'practiced' on . . . so as usual, She means what She says."

Allison realized that the One might not even have

connected the satellites with humans. The ship was another matter, of course; it now appeared that She had sent Lherin to the ship for one last look at the "possible blood-sharers" who depended upon the SLIT station.

The room was full of voices now, as everyone seemed to offer advice at once.

"We must keep calm," Lowell insisted. "Silva?"

The Adjustor rose. "Are we to understand that these creatures seriously threaten the SLIT station?"

"Right," said Seth, "She'll jam your space-door for good."

"Seth Connaught," said Lowell, "such an attitude serves the Meeting poorly. Silva, I'm afraid we still have much to learn about the One . . ."

Allison signaled Rashernu once more. *"Let us adjust sky-object. Then we can protect—"*

"Unnecessary. One will inactivate."

"When?"

"One-third per sun-tour."

"Chance," explained the Coral Vale woman. "One chance in six, each half-day from now on. The One rarely plans discrete events, especially events of this magnitude."

"In that case," said Lowell, "we'll send a delegation at once to try to change Her mind. Off-world citizens should come, too, to show—"

"The One is no longer interested in non-blood-sharers," Seth put in.

"Then it's up to us to instill that interest," said Martha. "I suggest," she added bluntly, "that Coral Vale Meeting consider its responsibility for this deplorable lapse in communication."

"But we're all responsible," said Anne Crain. "All of us, who have closed our eyes and left blood-sharing in the hands of a few for too long."

Silva discussed options with those who stayed afterward. "We could remove the SLIT station," she said, "send it to another planet or to one of the moons. Inconvenient, of course—longer time lags—but that's not the point."

"What is it, then?" Clifford asked. "Do you still question the danger?"

"Let me tell you this," she went on. "The Board of Adjustors keeps a close watch on Foxfield, and finds itself . . . increasingly dissatisfied with certain aspects. Frankly, some find it difficult even to credit the existence of this Dwelling."

Lowell's brow shot up. "The Dwelling? Hundreds of us have been there."

"But where? Is it a physical place? Our scanners find no sign of civilization within the jungles."

Allison said, "I can't understand that. There *is* a structure, if not a square building; at least, that's what Seth says. At Coral Vale, they have mapped its location, roughly. You can't bring electronic directional finders which would disturb the Dwelling. The magnetic anomalies would mess up your instruments in any case."

"So you've no records, either," Silva said. "Furthermore, the SLIT station has orbited Foxfield for the past twenty years . . ."

Twenty years? This was news. Someone had told Allison four or five years; had it been Casimir?

". . . and in this space, it is detectable only by gravity waves. How does it disturb your creatures, and why only now?"

Allison's scalp prickled. No one had an answer.

"Just what are you trying to say?" Clifford demanded at last. "Do you think we're all putting on a farce?"

Silva's eyelids fluttered beneath her long forehead, betraying the first hint of fatigue. "Some Board members so conclude. I myself don't see it, not here. I've studied your culture. Besides, you don't have the technology."

"Thanks," said Clifford ironically.

"But the alternative," Silva pointed out, "is worse yet: that these creatures appear to threaten UNI . . . with no known technology at all . . ."

Allison was annoyed. Surely Casimir had enlightened them, by now.

Martha's brow creased thoughtfully. "Friend Silva, you spoke before of breaking contact with us, of leaving us for some generations until we were ready to accept you. Is it possible that your people, too, are unready to accept Foxfield?"

Shadows deepened in the Adjustor's face. "That may be true," she said. "But now, I'm afraid, to break contact would be impossible. To be perceived as backing down before some nonhuman power—the Board cannot accept that."

"Well what *can* you accept?" Clifford asked. "Thermolyze the planet?"

A pause lengthened in the room.

"We still hope to avoid that."

"Lord save us," whispered Lowell.

Allison hurried up the hill at a dangerous pace for the darkness.

"Mom," Dave panted, "I can only walk so fast. Why don't we get an antigrav car?"

"Listen to you. Foxfield could burn in hell, and you tell me about antigravs? Off to bed with you, now."

"I'm a mature citizen, now. I don't have to go to bed."

"You'll be a citizen with a sore seat if I catch you awake past seventeen west."

Lighted windows at the Tech Center—that would be Bill, on night shift. The aurora tonight was a faint bluish white, like the ship corridors. The moon Providence cast a frail gleam on the transcomm, whose once-smooth surface now bore stains and scratches.

Allison cupped her hands and faced the transcomm. "Open, 'Belshazzar'!"

Inside, she called for Casimir. He appeared at last in his study, seated on a mat before a low desk. On one side of the desk top stood an oblong vase with three lines of wisteria, *Ikebana* style. Over the other side hung a globe of Mars.

Allison crossed her arms. "All right, Cas, what's going on? Since when are commensals cows, and Friends covert anarchists? *You* know better."

"Allison, we're doing the best we can." The biosphere analyst wearily pulled a hand through his ruffled hair. "What do you expect of us?"

"Better than thermolysis, that's what. What's wrong with you folks? The minute things go sour you have to blow up a planet?"

"That's enough," he replied sharply. "Don't you know I've worked my head off for the past two weeks trying to figure out what in space is going on?"

"Then do it right; go to the Dwelling and see."

Casimir threw up his hands. "How can I do that when you all turn it into some kind of 'forbidden city'? No electronics—blood-sharing—it sounds like a horror story. What is this place, Angkor Wat? No, it's Stonehenge, and we've interrupted their star-gazing."

"We can't help it if we don't know any more than you do." But she winced, recalling Anne's last words.

"Look," said Casimir with sudden decision. "Let me show you something. I know this is a level-ten credit-loss news item, and I've played it and replayed it to death already, but—I want to show you just what we're up against. How's your credit?"

"Around eighty thousand, as if you didn't know."

Then Allison screamed. Blue-tinted sunlight beat down as she hung tens of meters above a sea of faces which stretched interminably over the stark plain. When she collected herself, she realized that the faces were shouting something, roaring, actually; it sounded like *"roar, roar."* As she stared at the upraised faces and listened more closely, she realized that the word was "aurora, aurora, aurora . . ."

"This," said an urbane voice-over, "is the Pennsylvania Desert. The people are calling on the so-called goddess Aurora to come to Terra. The sign of arrival of this entity is supposed to be an increase in geomagnetic field strength up to the level of planet Foxfield, Tau Ceti-nine. Eight hours ago, one of the cultists claimed to pick up an increase on a magnetic detector. The report has not been confirmed, but since then the crowd's numbers have swelled to over a hundred thousand."

The scene faded out. Two people appeared in chairs. One was a man in a deep blue Terran robe. The other, a woman, wore a full ship suit, with hood and goggles open. Her expression reminded Allison of Silva Maio.

The man spoke. "Bob Watrobski, here, speaking with Board Adjustor Jan Fiorella, North-Am sector. Adjustor, North-Am seems to be a perennial source of trouble, doesn't it?"

"Still full of floaters," she agreed. "Floaters use any excuse to start a riot."

"But many of those cultists are citizens. The cultists say that since expert planetologists have studied the Aurora planet for twenty years and have yet to explain the unprecedented planetary magnetism, the only alternative is a 'magical' explanation of some kind. How do you respond to that?"

"True, the mystery is embarrassing, and the planetologists involved have received reprimands from the Board. I remind you however that the need to keep UNI's presence hidden from Foxfielders during sociological study has also hampered physical study of the planet Foxfield."

"But the cultists say that this was just an excuse to hide the fact that both the native creatures and the human settlers worship this electromagnetic 'goddess.' The natives even have a temple of some sort out in the jungle. And the miraculous survival of the humans in an alien biosphere is seen as further evidence that—"

"The humans," said the Adjustor, "in their beliefs, hark back to the dark Age of Uncertainty. They domesticated the native creatures in order to survive—"

The pair vanished; Casimir returned. "That should give you the idea," he said.

"They're crazy," Allison whispered.

"No, just badly adjusted, that's all."

"They don't know what we are . . . any more than you do." She thought for a moment. "How many 'floaters' are there?"

He winced and rubbed his forehead. "Too many. They infest the cities like rats—"

"But how many?" she insisted. "Hundreds of millions?"

"Space no, not yet. Ten million, perhaps; impossible to count exactly. On parts of Terra, remember, people were uncountable even *before* the Last War. And afterward—" He shrugged his tired shoulders. "Inevitably, some were left behind. And the farther the System developed, the wider the gulf became."

Ten million desperate people—the thought staggered her. "Still," she pointed out, "you outnumber them."

"But they multiply unchecked. Like bacteria in a flask."

"And citizens *don't*, of course." She eyed him severely, recalling his earlier evasion. "So it's floaters you want to get rid of on other planets."

"Well, Terra can't feed them forever. But it's more complex than that. Floaters . . . infect us, Allison."

"But *why*, Casimir? If UNI is so wonderful, then why don't they all get credometers and join in?"

He sighed and leaned over the desk, resting his head in his hands. "I wish I knew. Tradition, I suppose; they live on as they have for centuries. Some are fearful. Some are even 'religious,' like you folks."

"Really? Genuine religion?"

"You can't get rid of such things overnight. Those cultists in the desert, even the citizens, *want* to believe Foxfield has magic, because it wasn't so long ago that the supernatural held the answers to all mysteries. That's why we keep preservation societies: 'cultural museums,' to innoculate citizens against irrational belief by exposing them to the quaint traditions."

"So you're afraid of us," Allison exclaimed. "That's why you stayed away for twenty years."

"Could be. I signed on four years ago, myself, when your existence was acknowledged officially. Who knows how long the Adjustors monitored you before that."

"We're dangerous," she mused. "More dangerous than Titan; more dangerous to you than you are to us. Foxfield is a virus, and you're not immune."

"Those were Terrans," he pointed out. "We Martians are more sensible on the whole; that's a fact, the System will tell you. Comes from strict upbringing; we were pioneers, like you folks."

Allison watched the globe above his desk. It had

been turning steadily all the while, and she recognized some of its contours from that holoview of the Mars Classic.

"Silva knew," he went on. "She didn't wish to make contact now. She sensed the public needed time, another generation at least. But UNI needs good farmland, and the Board insisted. Your famous missive was a good catalyst. 'Let's help out the Lost Colonists,' and so forth. Sorry to run on—"

"Not at all, do go on. That documentary; were you responsible for that?"

"The *Social Newsview?*" He shrugged. "I provided some data."

"So you did try to convince people the 'mensals were cows."

"I only drew an analogy, which is quite correct in a narrow sense. Better cows than priests of some mystical cult. How can I *prove* that's not so?" His voice held a desperate appeal.

"Well, they happen to be neither," said Allison, her voice rising, "so why don't you go to the Dwelling and get the truth?"

Casimir wiped his forehead. "Allison—I can't do that. You heard Seth: the One's not interested in non-blood-sharers."

"Well, come share blood, then. You're human, aren't you? Once She sees that—"

"The commensals are good chemists. Our blood composition differs significantly from yours, and they'll detect it."

"Somebody has to risk that."

His expression grew pained. "Allison, I . . . after the last time—"

Allison held out her left arm and tapped her credometer. "Listen, citizen, I've worn *this* since the first day; I've faced *your* witch doctors and *your* psychoshrinks. Why don't you meet *us* halfway for a change? With a whole biosphere at stake? Well?"

He stared uncertainly.

"Why don't you all go back and leave us alone? You can take *that* and shove it up your *SLIT.*"

The wristband thudded on the floor. Casimir vanished; the chamber dimmed to a reddish glow. The portal slid open and stars winked in. Allison stepped down and skipped off across the wide mattress of ground moss.

"Allison." A faint voice called from behind.

"Who's there?" She turned and saw someone in Foxfield clothes, back near the transcomm. They walked toward each other.

"Allison—I want to help you." It was Kyoko; her tense features stood out in the moon's light.

"What for?" Allison bitterly rejoined. "Convenient farmland? Avoid thermolysis and reculturing?"

"You know that's not so. I don't want to see it happen . . . here. I believe in you people."

"You do? You don't even know who we are." Her eyes narrowed. "Silva put you up to this."

"No."

"But she knew you would, though. High percentage, at least, *no?*"

Kyoko said nothing.

Allison laughed then, soundlessly. "Of course they knew," she mused. "All the Adjustors. They monitored us long enough. Then they chose you, right? A lonely systemist-physicist with a lost love in the background; just the type to synchronize with my psyche."

"You don't know what you're saying. I made sacrifices, my studies suffered; I *chose* to come here."

"You all used me to drive a wedge into Foxfield, right? A sort of sociological SLIT? You can't fool me, I know Earth history; my mother stuffed minds and gullets long before Cliff did. Technology, the carrot; weapons, the stick. It's called *cultural imperialism.* Seduce us with a technological orgasm."

Kyoko sucked in her breath. "Mind's eye, but you people are just—impossible," she breathed. "Allison, I'll tell you something about 'imperialism,' but let me tell you about *honor,* first. People of my heritage believe in honor, life with honor and death with honor, because *death is a part of life* which we don't run away from. That's right, run away; your people ran away from Earth because you couldn't face life, because society didn't quite fit your own ideals. Doesn't everyone have ideals?"

"Run away?" Allison repeated. "A star voyage—because we were *scared?*"

"The Japanese people were not scared," Kyoko said. "We had the courage to stay and preserve our heritage. More than that—we had the guts *not* to build nuclear weapons, for seventy years after Hiroshima. Talk about cultural imperialism; did Japan cry 'imperialism' three centuries ago, when Commodore Perry sailed his cannons into Edo Bay? No; we took those occidental gifts which suited us, and kept our own cultural identity.

"Allison, you decry 'suicide.' Civilizations suicide, too, you know. That's what happened to your Westerran civilization. At least Japan was there afterward to pick up the pieces."

"And did you learn nothing from them, or from us?" Allison whispered.

Kyoko paused. "Do you really believe that this *'Light'* is the whole answer, the whole purpose to life? That it's just the Lord's will whether you live or die in the end?"

Allison said nothing.

"Then what makes you so self-righteous, so sure that your way on Foxfield is the one true way of the universe? So sure you need no help from anyone else? What would you have done when all the old modules finally broke down? Do you realize how slim your chances are alone out here—a mere eight hundred of you? A single epidemic could wipe you out."

"Eight hundred thirty-six. Your logic needs no comment, in light of recent events."

"What if there had been no Rachel Coffin," Kyoko went on. "No lone voice to stand up for the 'killer commensals'? What good would your consensus have been, then? You would have tried to eliminate the creatures, and eliminated yourselves in the process. You're no better than we are."

"Maybe so. The point is that Rachel *was* there, and that with the Friends' way, the lone voice was heard. In UNI, what's an individual? One vote out of millions."

"But I'm an individual, Allison. I want to help you."

"How?"

"I'll go to the Dwelling. I'll 'share blood' with Her."

In the kitchen Allison yawned and sipped her tea. Rufus Jones slept on in the corner, fat and lazy, all eyefeet tucked in. The dial on her ring finger read seventeen-forty-two west. "How many folks do you suppose are watching us, right now?" she mused.

"Zero, point zero zero," said the System.

"What? Where are the impassioned millions?"

"Blackout on long distance," Kyoko explained from across the table. "Effected this afternoon by Special Status mandate."

Allison sighed. "Should've known. Adjustors always keep a card up their sleeve." She looked up. "So you're determined to go, are you?"

Kyoko nodded. "It can't be that dangerous. The Coral Vale people go there all the time, no?"

"They know what they're doing—I think. Still, I never heard of a Foxfielder that died of it. The Dwelling knows a lot; it's much bigger than any one Fraction."

"I see. When do we start?"

"Tomorrow, I guess. If we're not too late already." One chance in six per half-day, if Rashernu had been accurate.

Kyoko nodded. "Will Seth guide us? He did a good job for Casimir."

Allison winced. "You would have to bring that up. I don't even know where Seth is; he didn't want to face me, I guess. Can't say I blame him."

"Well, let's find him. Use the System."

"He doesn't wear a credo."

Kyoko glanced at her wrist. "Locate Foxfield noncitizen Seth Connaught," she ordered.

The voice said, "Last record sixteen-twenty-six local. Proceed?"

"Proceed," said Kyoko.

Seth's voice played back against the crowded aftermath of the emergency Meeting. "Jem—a word with you?"

"Sure thing. Bad break, isn't this?"

". . . need someplace to stay the night."

"Come on over. What's wrong, your woman kick you out?"

Allison reddened. The voices dissolved and broke off; but someone had worn a credometer there, and that was enough.

"That was Jeremiah Crain," said Allison, "Seth's cousin in Georgeville. Mine, too, I think, twice removed or something."

"The Friend who outfitted us? My, it's a small world."

A few good replies to that came to Allison's mind, none of them fit for the ears of young Friends. "I'll go see him," she said.

"Shall I come, too?" said Kyoko.

"No . . . I think I'd better see him alone."

Seth stared at her in the unfamiliar sitting room. His shoulders drooped but his gaze was fierce as ever. "So you want me to take you and your woman-friend to the Dwelling?"

"It's the only way. Once She sees that an offworlder can share blood, She'll have to—"

"You ask *me*," Seth added, "after selling me out, and Foxfield, too?"

"What the—" Allison tried to keep her voice down, and shifted in her seat.

"You think I'm blind when my back is turned?"

"Seth, whatever you've gotten into your head, it just isn't so. And suppose it were; do you think you own me?" She paused for breath. "I've loved you for years and years, and what do I get? Trouble comes, and off you go to Lord knows where."

He shook his head. "You don't understand; never did."

"Did you ever try? What about *me*, don't I know anything?"

"You couldn't face it. Not the Dwelling. You never could face Foxfield; all you ever dreamed of was old Earth, with all those machines to take care of you. To prevent *accidents*—like Joshua, who's still alive in your head. Finally Earth came back, and that was it; you sold out."

"Seth, it's not true. I don't want Josh's ghost; I want

190

you. I want Foxfield, too; I'm trying to save Foxfield, don't you understand?"

"Foxfield doesn't need you. The One will take care of that; I told you She would."

"What? Did you actually tell Her to—"

"So what if I had? After what the frog-suits did to you? I care, if you don't."

"Seth, no," she whispered faintly.

"I only agreed with Her decision, whatever Her reason. We can't change Her mind, even at Coral Vale."

"Then they're all cooked, now, literally," said Allison. "All the 'mensals.'"

He stared, uncomprehending.

"You should've stayed to hear Silva," she added. "Thermolysis; they'll boil the planet like a soup pot, then refertilize with tame things."

"They can't."

"They can, like Vinlandia. Evacuate us; send in stellar energy through a SLIT—"

"They won't."

"They will."

"*No.*" Seth spun around and held his head in his hands. His back shook with sobbing. Allison put her arm around him and kneaded his shoulder.

"Seth," she said, "don't you see? It's you that have forgotten the Light, what Friends are all about. You can't force people. Force only invites counterforce—worse."

"It's no use, Sonnie. I never could reach anyone, not even you. At least the One was always . . . there."

"And haven't I been here, always?" She pulled him back again, and looked into his eyes, at his cheeks, his cleft chin. "What if She *can* change Her mind? Kyoko's got the guts to find out. Isn't it worth a try? What about us, Seth; can't *we* try, for once?"

They kissed, and held each other for a long time.

At last Seth looked up once more, his face still in shadows. "A wheel runs downhill, Sonnie," he whispered. "I thought you knew different, once; do you? Sometimes I wonder what in heaven really is worth trying for."

XV. Silence Multiplied

Noreen looked on anxiously as her Uncle Seth and Allison awaited the shuttle. Their hair blew with the cold morning gusts as the sun poked a finger above the horizon. "Are you sure it's okay, Allison?" Noreen asked. "What will Meeting say?"

Allison's jaw tensed. "No time for that. This is a technical problem, and my job for Meeting is to solve technical problems." She felt ill at ease, nonetheless.

"What exactly would happen to the SLIT station?"

"That's hard to say. Analysis of the satellite failures is not yet complete."

"Would it hurt the ship, too?"

"Well, they'd be cut off from the System core, so . . ."

"Fate worse than death," Noreen observed. "Why don't they move the station out to Wheelwright-ten?"

Allison shrugged. "Too long a time lag, they say. The fact is, they're scared of starting riots all over Terra."

The shuttle craft broke through the billowing cumulus clouds. Seth stoically watched it descend.

"Take Bill along, just in case," urged Noreen.

"Is he here?" Allison asked.

"Any minute, now."

"Can't waste any time; we don't want to spend antinight in the jungle." She frowned. "Noreen—you've been here all night?"

"So what?" Noreen spoke brightly enough, but her cheeks sagged under her eyes.

"It was Bill's turn."

"Well . . . I guess we got carried away," she admitted. "Ruth and I are trying to fix up the old Multi-

192

form, and around midnight we made a breakthrough on one of the circuits."

"That old fossil? Such dedication," Allison wryly observed. "You think we can't depend upon System provisions?"

"The System might not be here tomorrow," Noreen replied bleakly. "It could vanish as fast as it appeared on Foxfield."

The atmosphere was heavy and reeked with dizzying odors. Beyond the clearing lay Coral Vale, a cluster of houses in a valley between hills suffocated by burnt maroon brush.

"Is that the jungle?" Kyoko asked. Like the Foxfielders, she wore thick trousers and heavy boots.

Allison shook her head. "Beyond the town." She pointed toward the horizon, where the hills spilled out into the jungle like a gray sea.

Seth led them down a dirt road among the houses. Kyoko tripped once; she caught herself and picked up a bleached object under her boot. It was faintly orange and convoluted like Allison's old paperweight. "That's coral," said Allison. "The stuff the 'mensals secrete, an organic 'cement.' We'll be seeing lots more of it, I imagine."

Seth swung open the door to a weathered cottage. "Father?" he called. The floorboards creaked as they entered.

"That you, Seth?" A man appeared in the hallway, his features creased and weathered as the cottage. "Welcome, Friends. Good to see you again, Allison, and—"

"Kyoko Aseda," Allison finished.

"Welcome to Coral Vale," he said as he shook Kyoko's hand. "Gabe Connaught's the name. And where is the off-worlder?"

"*She* is, Father," said Seth.

Gabe clapped his head. "No frog-skin, like the others, who brought us these?" He indicated his credometer. "I took you for a Foxfielder."

"The suit's underneath." Kyoko pulled back the flap of her jacket.

He laughed, and Allison thought that he had aged little within, despite the deepened creases.

"We've seen very few of you space-folk here so far," he added. "Not that I blame you. It's a treacherous place here among the hills, and when the rains come from both sides they'll wash you clean out to the swamp lands. But you're from Earth . . ." He touched Kyoko's sleeve as though not quite sure she was real.

Seth said, "We have to get started."

"Your gear's all set in the jeep," Gabe assured him.

"That suit will have to come off," Allison told Kyoko.

"Really?" Kyoko's face wrinkled briefly. "I suppose you're right. Is there a room to change?"

"Thought you citizens didn't care for privacy," Seth observed.

Kyoko looked at him. "Perhaps I've spent too much time among primitives."

"I'm sure Gabe will show you a room," said Allison quickly. They would get nowhere at this rate.

"No problem," said Gabe. "But first, Friends, I ask for a brief silence. I think we may spare a quarter-hour to insure that you embark on your purpose in the proper spirit of the Light."

Seth reddened. Kyoko looked puzzled.

"A Meeting," Allison whispered. "Two people and five minutes, anywhere, are enough."

The four of them clasped hands in a circle.

As Allison stood between Seth and Kyoko, she stared at her toes and tried to "center down." She thought over all the years since she'd last visited this spot, and how they inexorably had led her back here, today. It was a twisted path of years . . . More than once the thought had come to her that she ought to experience the Dwelling, if only in order to understand Seth better. But she had always been busy, too busy with daily needs. She had always gone to Meeting twice a week; yet surely, if there were a Presence beyond humanity, then commensals held as high a place as humans in the scheme of things. How easy it was for some concerns to slip through the cracks until it might be too late.

"The Lord be with you, Friends," called a small voice, from Gabe's credometer.

Allison looked up. "What—who—"

"This is Martha, here with Clifford and Lowell and Anne and Christine . . ."

Her knees turned to water.

". . . all of us, all over Foxfield. We all wait with you now, and we pray for your success with the One."

The ancient electrojeep plodded through a narrow passage carved into the tangled undergrowth. The headlights shone into the gloom, for little light penetrated the foliage even at midmorning. Branches and hanging creepers loomed forward as the vehicle passed. Occasionally a commensal appeared ahead, and then Seth had to halt until the creature had passed or moved aside. Allison wiped her damp face, for the heat and humidity were oppressive. Kyoko took it well, although she must have felt uncomfortable without her suit's thermostat.

The ground grew steadily softer and wetter. Wheels whined and splashed mud up to the windows. At length the trail ended before a murky stream.

Seth switched off the engine. "Leave the wristthings here," he said as he stepped out.

Allison put her credometer on the dashboard.

"Very well," said Kyoko, "but how shall we see our way?"

Seth reached under the seat for the gaslight, fueled by a small pressure tank. He lit it with a flint striker and took it down to the bank of the stream. There was a small rowboat on the bank, and Allison helped him shove it into the water. They all piled into it and with a swish of the oars the boat set off, gliding into the swamp.

Kyoko let out a cry. Allison turned to see the citizen push aside a crawler as long as her arm with a thousand legs.

"Ugh." With an oar handle, Allison flipped it over the edge.

Kyoko said, "It fell down from nowhere—"

"Don't worry," Seth reassured her. "You're as toxic to it as it is to you."

The boat moved on. The oars splashed now and then.

Kyoko asked, "Won't we get lost, without a directional finder?"

Seth said nothing.

Allison recalled lines from "The Cry of the Lost Soul," in her grandmother's old volume of Whittier.

> Dim burns the boat lamp; shadows deepen round,
> From giant trees with snake-like creepers wound,
> And the black water glides without a sound.

A pale shape bobbed up before the boat, where the stream narrowed. It was a commensal, floating calmly as her corona phosphoresced. Seth pulled up his oars and contemplated the creature for some minutes.

"What's up?" whispered Allison.

"Something's not right." He shot her an accusing look. "You tell me what's wrong."

She frowned. "We left everything electronic behind—" She half turned to Kyoko, then caught sight of her own finger. Eleven thirty-three, the dial read.

"Oh, my goodness." With a twinge of guilt at the waste, she pulled off the watch and flung it back as far as she could into the swamp.

The creature slowly moved aside.

"A Guardian," Allison whispered. "Are we close, Seth?"

More Fractions glimmered from the water and the banks, passing back and forth on unknown errands. At times they signaled, but their style was difficult for Allison to read.

Hints of light began to poke through the foliage. Leaves parted and coral surfaces flickered on the banks. The boat rounded a final bend, and full sunlight hit Allison's eyes. She squinted and waited for her eyes to readjust.

A coral mountain rose above the clearing. Allison craned her neck upward at the twisted mass, pitted with clefts and caverns.

Kyoko said, *"Sora—"*

" 'Ra, ra,' " her voice echoed back. Otherworldly silence remained; it, too, seemed to echo back.

Seth's features took on the look of the times when he recounted commensal stories to Dave. "It grows over centuries," he said. "Generations of Fractions, one by one."

Carefully the humans picked their way among coral boulders and staring Fractions.

"Is it their 'city'?" Kyoko asked.

"No," said Allison, "those are just the Guardians."

Seth led them to a tunnel entrance at the foot of the mountain. They stepped into the passage, which glowed orange as the outer light disappeared. The only sound was the muffled tread of their boots as their way wound farther and deeper into the rugged mass of coral.

The tunnel's end broadened into a round cavern. Seth led them down to the center of the cavern, where he stopped.

Eyes. Allison stifled a cry. All about the coral surface, from every crevice, stared eyes; compound eyes, but eyes nonetheless, thousands of them. They were eyes of countless Fractions over the years who had come here, not to die, but to "conjoin" for the last time.

A stalk of coral extended upright in the middle of the cavern. It was pitted with fist-sized depressions.

"Now," Seth whispered, "do exactly as I do." He approached and placed his hand in one depression.

Allison felt her feet glued to the coral floor. She forced herself to remember that the SLIT station could still collapse at any time, unless it was already too late. She stepped down to the stalk and fit her hand into a stony niche. It felt warm at first, then numb.

The cavern seemed to expand into a giant hall, larger than the Meeting House, larger even than Shimuri's Hall of a Thousand Cranes. Then odd memories came alive and crowded her senses; impressions of many times jumbled together, as though an electrode were probing her brain. One moment she was a child in Georgeville, setting off for school with her mother, the schoolteacher, whose face mirrored Allison's own. The next, she was in a Meeting, or in the Tech Center, or talking to her infant son . . .

Then Joshua came back, as real as a holoview; his face just as she remembered, his hair flowing to the shoulders, like George Fox.

"Josh, I finished the assays on Gabe's ferrite samples."

"And?"

"It's good ore, as good as Mawrford's."

"Too bad it's so inaccessible."

"But, Josh, we'll start our own town."

"A sixth settlement? Right at the jungle's edge?"

"My folks will come, and the Braithwaites from Lanesbridge."

"What'll we call it?"

"Thorneville, of course."

Allison felt a strange sense of relief. It hadn't been as bad as she expected. Kyoko was right; you had to live with the dead, as well as the living.

The sight of a *hand* hit her, in almost microscopic detail. The wrinkled knuckles, the rigid veins stood out like carved granite. It was her own hand, she realized; the hand that had grasped the green flesh of a Fractional predecessor to Ghareshl, Thiranne and now Lherin; the hand that had pulled the creature from the river which churned wild.

"I know you now, Plant-spike."

The thought was not Allison's own. It spoke directly in her head, not in words, but in distilled concepts: knowing—plant-spike (label). She could almost feel the tip of a thorn of witch-vine, the commonest of thorny plants on the Tech Center hill. And yet, the thought seemed clearer and infinitely more subtle than any Transac exchange she had experienced with a Fraction.

She came to feel Seth's presence, somewhere, as well, warm and familiar, caring but tense, and—something else? She wanted to lean on his presence, but hesitated, not sure why.

Was Kyoko here, too? Allison searched her consciousness, but fell back into swirling thoughts.

"Puzzlement. Uncertainty. What substance is this?"

The One's thought came through again, but not directed toward Allison.

"*What . . .*" Kyoko's mind called as though from beyond the edge of the world. A feeling of unease grew into a wave of panic—a profound sense of the absurd, a draught of despair which Allison herself had sipped but never swallowed so deeply before, the despair of a man who devours his children because there is no more food left in all the universe. Allison pulled at her hand to break contact, but found that her physical body was somewhere else.

Kyoko called, "*You took away . . . give it back . . .*"

"*Only impediments removed,*" thought the One.

"*Why . . .*" Kyoko asked, a descending, echoing call.

"*To examine your substance: human (blood-sharing) wave-form, first-approximation indistinguishable from these two.*"

"*Put it back, then,*" she pleaded faintly.

No reply. Allison felt Kyoko's despair subside to a muted frenzy.

"*Who?*" Kyoko asked now. "*Who are you?*"

"*I am the One Organism, the Eye of Many Faces, the Seeker of All Things.*"

More than ever, Allison was impressed by the sophistication of this contact, dimensions beyond Transac. She thought, "*What things do you seek?*"

"*I seek the stars. I drink their energy waves to seek the source of their long lives.*"

"*Does our sky-object interfere with that search?*"

No reply was forthcoming.

"*We can readjust the sky-object,*" came Kyoko's faint thought.

The One's presence withdrew, as though in a quandary. Allison wondered whether She might break off contact, then. With a sense of reluctance, the presence did return.

"*Interference with My star-watch is negligible. The sky-object does emit human-seeming wave-forms which perturb My study of (blood-sharing) humankind.*"

Allison was stung. How could they have missed this? The SLIT had been around for five years, but the human "wave-forms" had just arrived on Foxfield. Had the One deliberately led them astray?

Perhaps in answer, the One replied, *"Human substance exhibits exceptional instability. I try both to avoid and to prevent destabilization of the subject."*

"Instability . . . why?" thought Kyoko.

"Source unknown. I theorize that human fragments evolved like 'resonances,' particles which materialize in space as matter-antimatter pairs. The half-particles forever seek to rejoin, but to join is to destroy one another."

"But humans," thought Allison, "also know a greater unity, a one-ness, as you do. In fact, we sense a Presence greater even than You which encompasses all beings . . . "

But Seth warned her, *"Be silent."*

The One thought, *"A Presence greater than the universe?"*

No human responded.

"I perceive," continued the One, *"that human fragments envision such an entity which is in fact an inverted image of your own potential wholeness. This conception, however imperfect, makes communication possible between us."*

"Then why do you destroy the sky-object?" Allison asked. *"You will sunder human unity."*

The thought-storms swirled again, endlessly. Panic swept over Allison as she wondered again whether it was too late, whether the station was gone already. But the thoughts of the One took form once more.

"All things have finite probability over time. It is possible that I will collapse your sky-object. It is also possible that you humankind will destroy Me with stellar energy. Far greater than these is the possibility that you will destroy yourselves."

The thought-storms began to recede.

"Wait," called Kyoko, *"come back; you have to give back the . . . "*

Allison found herself staring at the stalk of coral in the dim orange cavern. She withdrew her hand; it prickled but showed no obvious puncture marks. She cast a furtive look upward. All about the coral dome the eyes were closed. She turned to Kyoko.

The citizen's face was pale as marble. Her eyes stared, unseeing.

Allison touched her arm. "Kyoko? It's all over; do you hear me?"

Kyoko absently rubbed her wrist and muttered unintelligible words.

"Kyoko, I can't understand . . . *wakarimasen*."

"Gone," she whispered, "my inner balance. Ever since I was a child I—how can I go on?"

"The System will fix you—"

"Come on," said Seth. "We can't stay here; it's late."

"Oh, all right," snapped Allison. "There's plenty of shade in the jungle."

"The bigger crawlers awaken by antinight," he said. *"They* can't tell you're toxic without a taste, first."

Allison bit her lip. "Come, Kyo," she whispered, and she took the citizen's hand to lead her back down the winding passage.

Wheelwright's brilliance hit her as they emerged. With her free arm she covered her face as she pulled Kyoko down to the shade of the swamp.

"Allison," Kyoko stated, more clearly than before.

"Yes, Kyo?" Allison paused at the stream bank.

"You know, Allison," she went on conversationally, "there's an object in my jacket pocket; it doesn't look dangerous, but, things being as they are, it might be dangerous to myself."

"What the—" Allison frowned. She fished into Kyoko's pockets until she felt some thing hard. She drew out a flat, polished object the size of her palm. The dark oblong bore inlaid characters. As her fingers pressed the sides, a blade slid out, glittering. She blinked and turned it over curiously. A simple tool, but why . . . *"Christ."* As the reason dawned on her she shuddered, and the knife slipped from her grasp. With a splash it vanished in the black water.

"Dōmo arigatō, yujin Allison." Kyoko took one step more; then she fell, unconscious.

Seth helped Allison lift her into the boat. As Allison lit the gaslight, he looked down at the still figure with a curious mixture of surprise and pity. "She was so weak," he mused. "The One took away her chemicals, and she fell apart."

"No, she's strong," said Allison, as she felt the citizen's pulse. "She managed to do without them for hours." Though those hours had seemed but minutes to Allison.

"You managed. I manage all the time."

"You've done it all your life. She'll be okay, if we just get her back to the ship . . ." Allison averted her eyes. There was nothing more she could do, now, for her friend. She watched Seth shove the boat off from the shore. "Seth," she asked, "why did the One take out her psychormones?"

"To see if she was really a blood-sharer, like us." He pulled the oars with long strokes.

"It's not easy for you, either, is it? To visit the Dwelling, so often."

"Going to Meeting," he said, "is harder still."

Allison blinked at him. "Seth, wait a minute." She grabbed the oar handles to make him stop and look into her face. "You believe what the One 'said,' don't you? That all of our faith in the Light means nothing more than a mirror in the sky, turned down at us?"

He looked away.

"You think *that*? And yet all this time you've kept on going to Meeting as though it mattered, when inside—no wonder you never talk about it; no wonder you're all half crazy at Coral Vale. You're just like the off-world citizens, don't you see? Were you afraid they'd find you out?"

She paused for breath. "Maybe the commensals can make it on their star-gazing. But we're humans, and we need something more than that. If the One is right, if there really is no Presence beyond us, then there's nothing *for* us, either; we might as well curl up and die. But suppose there just might be something beyond, even though we could never know for sure. Isn't that what makes it worth living on?"

"The One knows better, Sonnie. She is eons older than we are."

"Seth, love, what difference does that make? Is She infallible, just because She's not human? When did you last think for yourself?"

XVI. Still Forms on Foxfield

The days which followed bore an air of unreality. Most off-planet citizens kept to their ship, still on emergency alert, while Foxfielders tried to keep up their daily tasks despite the invisible sword which hung above their world. But the days turned to weeks with no change except for the usual progression of summer crops and harvests. People relaxed and took up other pressing concerns, following the ancient instinct that what had not happened yet was not about to happen. Even Allison knew that, WEATHERCAST notwithstanding, the best way to predict rain was to put one's hand outside the window.

The UNI-Foxfield dialogue was renewed with greater activity than ever, but its focus distinctly shifted. Citizens talked less about "reintegration," and more about sending field teams to figure out the Dwelling, a process in which both Allison and Seth became increasingly involved.

Clifford watched the shift with bemused interest. "It's a textbook case," he would say. "Now that they've run up against the real power center, they'll lose interest in us, thank goodness."

But Allison noticed that his wrist was always bare when he said such things. She also sensed the hidden strain which remained among UNI officials, who now sought to settle the Foxfield problem as soon as possible in order to quench the flames of fascination which had spread abroad.

On one occasion she saw the tension break the surface. It was a conference session which included Lowell, the Fullers and herself as well as Silva and two senior Adjustors who rarely spoke. Their oriental features reminded Allison painfully of Kyoko; she still

203

wondered what had really become of her friend since the shuttle last carried her away. The conferees sat in an alcove of the ship garden, amidst pine trees and shiny grasses which yielded pleasingly to the feet, unlike the rugged turf of Foxfield. Allison suspected the setting was meant to lull Friends with remembrances of their lost Pennsylvanian homeland.

Martha was speaking to the immigration question. "The Meeting feels," she concluded, "that we can sponsor as many as five immigrants or immigrant families within the coming year. One household in Mawrford already has volunteered to take in such a family."

"Five?" Silva's voice rose slightly, as if she thought she had misheard. "Did you say five hundred per year?"

"Five, period—this year." Clifford leaned forward above the translucent table covered with UNI figures and projections. "We'll appoint overseers to supervise and inform Yearly Meeting of their adjustment to our community. Then we'll see."

Silva's fingers clenched the table edge. "We need solid numbers, a plan for the future. If the Board finds that Foxfield is unready for immigration at this time, we'll keep Special Status another year."

"But we want to accept them," Lowell objected. "We can't just turn people away."

Martha's brow creased. "In good conscience, we can only take them so fast. They will find us strange, at first; they will need time to learn our ways and to become one with us."

A senior Adjustor spoke up. "Question dismissed."

Silva's face turned to stone, and she spoke in terse phrases for the duration of the conference.

Allison mentioned the incident to Rissa the next time she visited the ship for preventive cancer therapy.

"Of course she was upset," the doctor exclaimed as she fine-tuned the magnetic resonance device. "You all made a joke of it, that's why. Five immigrants, indeed—Mars alone takes in twelve thousand a year, and that place is desolate compared to Foxfield, no matter what Casimir tells you."

"But what's that got to do with us?" Allison settled herself into the examination chair.

"You?" Rissa sighed in exasperation. "Why don't you *negotiate,* like any normal civilized people? For a few hundred immigrants, you could have had trade discounts, free stratogeysers, full-scale planetary development. Now, we're scared to let anyone near this place."

"Scared of us?" Allison considered this while her limbs grew numb before the treatment. "We can only absorb five, and five is what we said. Will you let no citizens come at all?"

"That's nothing; *citizens* can always work around the System, if they're sharp."

That was not the real problem, Allison knew. UNI feared the expansion of floaters as much as Foxfielders feared UNI.

Rissa smiled sardonically. "Barbarians you are; bush people, actually. But we'll tame you yet."

Allison tensed momentarily, then reminded herself to stay calm as she watched the multicolored image of her organs revolve in space. She did not believe Rissa's last remark; she herself would be too sharp for that. Besides, there were still enough folks like Seth whom the System had barely touched as yet.

The night sky was as clear as a glass bowl. Allison was pointing out the stars and constellations. "Seth, do you see that reddish star, Arcturus, and the ones around it? That's the Charioteer, and Terra's sun is at his foot. From Terra, our own sun would sit in the Whale . . ."

He was silent. Allison turned and asked on impulse, "Have you never wanted something from the stars?"

Seth regarded her levelly. "I've wanted you. And I've wanted a child."

She stared at him. "You . . . what?" she whispered faintly.

"I want a child, our child. A daughter, since you have a son."

"How long have you felt this?"

"Too long."

"But why didn't you say something?"

"I tried, that day the frog-suits came. You're always too busy to listen. You don't need me any more."

"Seth, what are you saying?" She put her arms around him and looked into his pale face. "I always need you; I can't bear it when you're gone. But you never stay long enough to give me a chance."

"I'm always afraid you'll say no. Then I would have to face the end. I need a commitment, a family of my own, of *us*. Nothing else matters to people who must grow old."

She tried to keep her voice steady. "Seth, I want to be with you always, more than anything; do you understand?"

"Do you really mean that, Sonnie?" His face brightened as if the sun had dawned.

"Of course I do. And I want a daughter, too, but . . . that part's hard, at my age."

"I know." He sighed. "And there's the Center, and now the System to watch out for—if *you* don't keep an eye on it, no one else will."

"There is another way," she began carefully. "If we use the incubator, as citizens do—"

"The what?"

"Then she could have your genes, too," Allison went on. "UNI doesn't worry about genetic drift."

A soft look came into his eyes. "She will really be part of us then, just like the One."

They embraced tightly, and Allison fought back tears as she felt that the two of them would never be alone again. And she realized, with mingled sadness and relief, that now even Seth had joined the new age.

"Lanesbridge Meeting is pleased to report that the mine quintupled its cobaltite output over the last four months, thanks to the modern laser rig installations. Further increases projected . . ."

Allison yawned as Christine droned on in the packed Meeting House. Friends from all over Foxfield, plus a sprinkling of offworld citizens and commensals, were gathered for three days of Yearly Meeting, held as always after the close of Month Fifteen.

The first two days' business sessions had already covered guidelines for development of natural resources and the establishment of a Yearly Meeting Committee for Extraplanetary Concerns. Social issues had received varying dispositions. For example, the UNI statute on organ donation was accepted after someone had pointed out that Foxfielders recycled all of their bodily nutrients in any case. Homosexual marriage, on the other hand, had been referred to the Yearly Meeting Committee for Ministry and Counsel, for further study.

Today was the final session. The room was stuffy despite the autumn breeze which wafted in through open windows. Allison shifted her legs and loosened the jacket of her beige suit. She glanced sideways at Seth, who was busy interpreting Christine's report to Rashernu in the aisle. Discreetly she rested her head on her hand, and the credometer squeaked in her ear.

". . . present commentary on this unprecedented anthropological spectacle, a genuine human ritual as it unfolds before our very eyes. It still amazes us that these people can't seem to make any decision, no matter how elementary, without a 'sponential crowd of bodies in physical proximity.

"Well, not much action now; let's turn to our studio guest Hiroko Shimuri, genius of our day, for comment on this immense alien Foxfield creature known as the One. Hiroko, how do you explain the behavior of this extraordinary creature?"

"I would say that this 'One' behaves just like a good scientist. She has been studying her isolated population of humans, and has sought to remove possible contaminants."

"Why then, Hiroko, has this creature apparently withdrawn its threat to the UNI SLIT station at Foxfield?"

"I can only speculate. One: the threat was only a bluff. Two: She decided that UNI citizens make more interesting subjects than do Foxfielders. Three: She's just an eccentric old professor, like people say I am, so She doesn't give reasons for changing Her mind."

207

"Ha, ha, that's very clever. Tell us, Hiroko, is it your professional opinion that this creature contains a gigantic biological magnet—"

Allison sat up straight as Seth stood to begin his report on human/commensal relations. Silva Maio pointed out that a special UNI agency was being set up for communication with the commensal race.

"You've reinvented the 'embassy' concept," observed Clifford.

"In a sense, yes," said Silva. "For nonhumans, the concept seems entirely appropriate at this stage."

That line, thought Allison, was directed at the System audience.

Anne Crain, clerk for Yearly Meeting this year, recognized a Friend from Mawrford.

"I'm still not clear yet," said the woman, "on the One's intent toward the SLIT station. Is She satisfied or not?"

Anne said, "I don't think that can be determined with absolute certainty. Martha?"

"We've tried to find out," Martha replied, "but the One has refused all further comment since the visit of the first off-world citizen to the Dwelling, last Month Ten. The probability of action must be low, since nothing has happened to the SLIT station. In any case, backup stations have now been brought to other planets."

Anne nodded. "We are all grateful to Friend Kyoko Aseda for her courageous action, and I move that the Meeting approve a minute to that effect."

"Approved," murmured voices in a low rumble which filled the room.

"Bill Daniels?" said Anne.

"Well," said Bill, "it seems to me that we can take the One's last statement at face value. I mean, what She said was there's more chance of us destroying ourselves than of a destructive act on Her part, right? And *that* chance is pretty small, isn't it? So I think we have little to worry about."

This observation fell rather flat, to say the least. Frances clucked her tongue and leaned back over the bench in front of Allison. "My dear, *someone* really

208

must take that boy in hand, don't you think?" Her face was startlingly free of eyeglasses.

Allison glanced at Dave, who was trying to contain the squirming wurraburra which he had insisted on bringing along. "Not me," she said. "One son is enough."

"Now, now. I've raised four daughters, and they're no easier, as you'll see."

Later, Silva read out the proposal of the Board of Adjustors for a twenty-year transition to Standard Status on Foxfield. Allison was well aware of the hours of consultation behind it; nevertheless, she now wondered uneasily whether they expected to "tame" the Friends within that interim period.

Noah had a question. "This agreement mentions 'provision of emergency services' on our part. Could that include armed conscription?"

"Certainly not." The Adjustor permitted herself a slightly scandalized tone. "UNI forbids warfare and maintainance of armies and armaments of any sort."

"What about SLIT thermolyzers? Aren't they weapons, of a sort?"

"Thermolysis of inhabited planets is not allowed. The chance of such an accident is infinitesimal; all SLIT stations are operated by highly qualified, psychosynchronically registered personnel."

Anne added, "We will always offer whatever human aid we can to other Sectors. Rennie Fuller?"

Rennie rose with the child she had been nursing. "Are you sure we can still wear credos when we are pregnant?"

"Yes, that is clear. Rissa Nduni, would you like to speak to this?"

The ship doctor's voice carried well across the room. "We have determined that in vivo pregnancy fills a psychosynchronic need for some Foxfielders which cannot be met by alternative therapy at this time. Therefore, the in vivo procedure will be permitted, where justified, although we expect that within a few generations . . ."

Frances sniffed. "Pregnancy as 'therapy'? And they call *me* a witch doctor."

Allison chuckled. She couldn't imagine anyone getting away with calling Frances a witch doctor, except Frances herself.

Lowell rose to ask, "Is it also clear that Friends may exercise their individual consciences with respect to System voting?"

Heads nodded in approval; this issue, too, had received thorough scrutiny over the past two days, but for consensus, it never hurt to check once more.

"Are we clear on our freedom of religious expression as well?"

Silva pointed out, as she had on the first day the citizens had arrived, that freedom of communication was the first principle of UNI.

"Does that mean," he persisted, "that Friends may spread their beliefs without hindrance wherever they travel?"

"Yes," said Silva, "so long as the rights of others are respected."

"Friends, I'd like to speak to that." A strong, throaty voice called out from Allison's right. There stood Celia Blyden, firm as iron; she almost seemed to have grown a few centimeters over the past six months. "Ever since that day when our long-lost brethren first stepped down from the stars and broke bread with us at Anne's farm, I've been thinking of my dear granddaughter's words on that occasion. 'Ours is to follow where the Lord draws on . . . for wherever His work is wrought shall be your Holy Land.' Now there's a whole universe out there, full of sufferers in need of Friends' service. I feel called upon to go out to minister to them and to witness their measure of the Light; and I ask leave of Meeting to do so."

The room buzzed with voices. Allison was not caught entirely unawares—word spread about such things—but a few folks from out of town clearly were. Wilbur Blyden rose to ask, "Grandma Celia, are you sure your health's up to this?"

"Yes, indeed," Celia assured him, "thanks to the medical miracles of our new friends."

The UNI doctor qualified this. "We don't promise miracles," Rissa said, "although I can't deny feeling proud of our success in this case, considering Friend Celia's already advanced age. With booster treat-

210

ments, I expect her to last another fifty years at least."

Fifty years? Allison wondered whether she'd heard correctly.

"That sounds mighty fine," said Wilbur. "But I personally would like to hear doctor Poyser's opinion, as well. What do you say, Doc?"

"Well, Wilbur," said Frances, "I wouldn't have believed it possible, but after full examination I support Rissa's prognosis. As for Celia, now, my opinion is she's always done what she wanted to do and probably always will."

The room resounded with laughter and applause.

Allison thought that if she herself would have another century or so, she could even leave the Tech Center and . . . *she* wouldn't be one to opt for 'senior suicide,' that was certain.

Martha was saying, "I understand, Celia, that you've planned your mission with care."

"That I have. I'll stop first at my birthplace, wasteland though it is today. Then I'll go on to serve the folks who need me most: the sick, the floaters, the faint of heart. And I won't be alone in this effort."

Allison stretched her neck to get a look at the dark-clad woman who rose next to Celia.

"I am Aelfrida Tillyard," the woman said. "My fellow Friends and I enjoyed your warm hospitality some months past. We of the Quaker Preservation Society now extend Celia our welcome, and we offer her aid in all her travels. Although we on Terra have preserved the outward forms, we believe that she will do more than any of us to keep alive the authentic spirit of Quakerism."

This was a new twist. Was the Preservation Society intended to legitimize Celia's mission in the eyes of UNI? Allison frowned at herself; she had grown distressingly cynical of late. It was part of the price she paid to live in a wider world.

Anne said, "The Meeting thanks you, Aelfrida. Do Friends agree to release Celia for her calling?"

"Approved," stated many voices.

"Thank you, Friends," Celia responded with a mischievous glint in her eye. "I hope to see many of you

211

called to join me during my remaining half-century in this world."

When all the year's proceedings were complete, the final silence fell on nine hundred-odd still forms in the Meeting House. Then everyone was talking and shaking hands; the doors opened wide as people streamed out into the fresh air. Allison met Seth's gaze and they shared a look of tranquil joy.

"Allison?"

She turned and jumped up with an exclamation. "Casimir—that *is* you, isn't it?"

The sanguine citizen glittered in red and gold; medallions and tassels bedecked his chest.

"Don't look so shocked," he said, with a flourish of the flat-topped cap in his gloved hand. "This is what Martians wear for special occasions, usually 'parades,' the national pastime. I'm even a 'major general' back in my home town."

"A modern major general?" said Allison.

"Hey, Friend Casimir," called Dave. "I've got something for you." He pulled the four-eyed wurraburra from his bag and held it out squealing.

"Mind's eye, Rufus," Casimir exclaimed. "You've lost weight, I see, and eyes."

"Not Rufus—Jones," said Dave. "We keep Rufus; you get Jones."

"Ah, I see," The citizen smiled gamely as he accepted the lively creature. "Perhaps I'll unload him on my grandson. If he'll survive Mars, that is."

"No problem," said Allison. "World's most omnivorous garbage recycler."

He nodded. "I look forward to seeing lots more of you folks, once the embassy's set up. We still have to figure out what makes those 'mensals tick, and why they need your minerals when they can do all these other high-powered things—and don't tell me it's just taste, either."

"At least they're not cows, eh?" needled Allison.

"Nor priests; just good scientists. They study us like I'd study this little fellow; what do you think of that, Jones?"

"Eek—eek—eek," said the wurraburra.

"But why *do* they study us?" Allison asked. "She, I mean; what makes us so interesting to Her?"

"Don't ask me, I've barely scratched the surface. At this point I couldn't even swear the Dwelling doesn't hide some sort of particle accelerator in that—now, Jones, watch it there . . ." The creature had tangled an eyefoot in his tassels.

"Let's get outside," said Allison as people pressed by. With Seth and Dave, she headed for the door. Outside, she blinked and squinted as her eyes adjusted to the sun, now well overhead; she would soon have to return to the shade. At least it was autumn, now, when the sun's hours were more critical for commensals than for humans. Already she saw shiny young Splints here and there, recently uprooted with the waning daylight. There were human children, too, of course, dozens of them racing up and down Georgeville Road.

Seth tried to contact one of the Splints. *"Enjoy warm sunlight,"* he signaled, while the credometer glistened on his wrist.

"Warm-sun-warm," the creature mimicked, shaping awkward Transac symbols with her damp tendrils.

"Noreen!" called Allison. "Listen, I've got a proposition for you . . ." Her voice trailed off as she stared at the citizen who conversed with Noreen resplendent in a silken kimono. A multitude of white cranes were embroidered throughout the material.

"Kyoko," said Allison, "I'm so glad to see you. You're all better now, aren't you?"

Kyoko's dark coif inclined slightly. "A few months back in Hokkaidō restored my equilibrium. But I couldn't miss this, now, could I?"

Her daughters stood by her, in kimonos of geometric design. Dave and Michiko began to make faces at one another.

"You're all cured, then?" Seth demanded. "Did they wipe your brain clean?"

"Whatever for?" she countered. "I am a 'human wave-form, to a first approximation indistinguishable' from yourself."

A faint smile played on his lips. "You remember."

Dave tagged Michiko and called out, "Got you

213

last." He ran off, and she chased after him, her kimono flapping like a fluorescent copterfly.

Laughing, Allison hugged Seth. "Did you hear we are getting married?" she asked Kyoko. "I hope you will come; that's another 'genuine religious ritual' for you," she teased.

"Yes," she smiled, "I'll look forward to it."

"Don't you have any sort of rituals in UNI?"

"Ritual murder?" Seth suggested.

"Seth, be civil now." Allison shuddered as the sea of fear swept back to her. *The whale got Jonah,* someone had said, *and what will become of us?* But the tide ebbed for now.

Noreen was shifting her feet impatiently. "Allison, I'm waiting to hear your proposition."

"All right, here goes. You can take over the Tech Center, Babel towers and all, while I go off to study at the Shimuri Institute."

"Go on, now. Why can't you do both? Commute to Japan."

Allison groaned. "We'll have enough commuting as it is, between here and the Dwelling, what with the 'embassy' and all."

But Kyoko had a suggestion. "You can always use the transcomm. I myself will use it to conduct my lectures from now on."

"Does that mean . . . you're staying here?"

Keiko bounced up and down, and announced in Japanese, "Mama says we'll stay here forever and ever, and catch all the stickworts we want!"

"Well, now," her mother replied in the same tongue, "forever is a long time."

But Allison was delighted. *"Hai,* you are staying! You're a Foxfielder now, you can't deny it."

"I wouldn't try, dear citizen."

JOAN SLONCZEWSKI was born in New York, studied biology and chemistry at Bryn Mawr and Haverford colleges, and earned her P.h.D in molecular biophysics from Yale. She is now a professor of biology at Kenyon College in Gambier, Ohio, where she lives with her husband and their two children.

STILL FORMS ON FOXFIELD, Ms. Slonczewski's first novel, was written after she graduated from Bryn Mawr in 1977. Her second novel, *A Door into Ocean*, available from Avon Books, won the 1987 John W. Campbell Memorial Award, the first book by a woman ever to receive that honor.

UNICORN & DRAGON
BY LYNN ABBEY

illustrated by
Robert Gould

A BYRON PREISS BOOK

An epic tale of two very different sisters caught in a fantastic web of intrigue and magic—equally beautiful, equally talented—charged with quests to challenge their power!

UNICORN & DRAGON *(volume I)*

75567-X/$3.50US/$4.50Can

"Lynn Abbey's finest novel to date"—*Janet Morris*
author of *Earth Dream*

AND IN TRADE PAPERBACK—

CONQUEST
Unicorn & Dragon, (volume II)

75354-5/$6.95US/$8.85Can

Their peaceful world shattered forever, the two sisters become pawns in the dangerous game of who shall rule next.